PRA

MW01075301

Letters from Strangers

"A propulsive and poignant story about family, secret lives, and sacrifice. Walter knows the complexities of the human heart, and her emotionally rich characters ring true. Thoughtful, empathetic, and replete with deep meaning."

—Paulette Kennedy, author of *The Devil and Mrs. Davenport*

"With brilliant prose and secrets that upend everything you thought you knew, Walter shows us she's at the top of her game with this well-crafted novel full of tender moments—and gut-wrenching situations. *Letters from Strangers* will invoke every emotion inside and leave you begging for more. Poignant, smart, and utterly unputdownable, this one-sit read is sure to be a standout hit of 2025."

—Jaime Lynn Hendricks, bestselling author of *A Lovely Lie*

"A delicate, emotional deep dive about good people trying, against the odds, to solve the complex puzzle of their lives. But in its tender examination of such major life issues as adoption, sexual orientation, self-image, love, and loss, it reminds us that sometimes the understanding and redemption we seek are there for the taking—if you're willing to face the truth."

—Gary Goldstein, award-winning author of *Please Come to Boston*

"I loved reading *Letters from Strangers*, even when it was twisting my heart. Thoughtful and ultimately hopeful, this family saga is as good as it gets."

—Wendy Walker, bestselling author of *All Is Not Forgotten* and *American Girl*

"Strap in for this emotional and suspense-filled roller-coaster ride . . . With relatable characters and well-executed arcs, this novel is a truly moving and heartfelt exploration of self-discovery and acceptance."
—Marcy McCreary, award-winning author of
The Disappearance of Trudy Solomon

"Wow! What a story! Mesmerizing and gut wrenching, Walter is a captivating storyteller, weaving narratives that draw you in and leave you wanting more."
—Patricia Sands, author of *The Secrets We Hide* and *The Bridge Club*

Running Cold

"Set in a stunning but unforgiving landscape, *Running Cold* is chilling—both literally and figuratively. This twisty tale of murder, secrets, and exceptional human grit had me flying through the pages!"
—Robyn Harding, bestselling author of *The Drowning Woman*

"When Julie's life is ripped apart by her husband's untimely death, it's just the beginning of the journey that will lead her into her dark past and the secrets that swirled around her, sight unseen. A taut page-turner that draws you in and never lets go."
—Catherine McKenzie, *USA Today* bestselling author of *I'll Never Tell*

"Like an avalanche roaring down a mountain, *Running Cold* will ensnare you and not let go until the nail-biting finish. Walter masterfully explores the triumph of grit, the bonds of friendship, and the majesty of nature."
—Lori Brand, author of *Bodies to Die For*

"*Running Cold* starts with a memorable protagonist: a former Olympian put to the ultimate test in the wake of her husband's death. What begins as a fight for answers turns into a fight for survival—but through it all, she's tough as nails, easy to believe in, and fun to cheer for. Susan Walter delivers a satisfying race to the finish."

—Jessica Strawser, *USA Today* bestselling author of
The Last Caretaker and *Catch You Later*

"With top-grade plotting, breakneck pacing, complex female friendships, and a setting that's as ruthless as a hard-hearted killer, *Running Cold* is the murder mystery/thriller mashup of my dreams."

—Tessa Wegert, author of *The Coldest Case*

"Heart-racing, action-packed suspense, *Running Cold* takes you from the sunny splendor of California to the frigid Rocky Mountains . . . I could feel the snow chilling my skin and the adrenaline rushing through my veins as I turned every page of this cunning, spellbinding read."

—Samantha M. Bailey, *USA Today*, Amazon Charts, and
#1 international bestselling author of *A Friend in the Dark*

"*Running Cold* is an atmospheric thriller packed with sharply drawn characters and breakneck twists, but it's the rich details that really set it apart. They make you feel like you've been air-dropped into the story, racing for your life right alongside the protagonist."

—Jess Lourey, Edgar-nominated author of *The Taken Ones*

"With *Running Cold*, Susan Walter solidifies her place as an expert teller of twisty, surprise-packed, enormously entertaining mystery-thrillers. Set mainly in wintry Banff, Canada, this one moves like a shot as it snowballs into an involving tale of murder, crossed allegiances, double-dealings, and startling revelations."

—Gary Goldstein, author
The Last Birthday Party and *Please Come to Boston*

Lie by the Pool

"The most fun I've had reading a thriller in a long time! *Lie by the Pool* is a delicious page-turner you will finish in one sitting. Full of juicy twists, a wildly original plot, and nerve-shredding tension, *Lie by the Pool* catapults Susan Walter into the top echelon of thriller writers."
—David Ellis, *New York Times* bestselling author of *Look Closer*

"A thriller that thrills; crime fiction that is criminally good and feels like the real thing. A rich ensemble of characters, and protagonists that you hope don't wind up dead . . . because danger lurks around every twisty corner."
—Ken Pisani, *Los Angeles Times* bestselling author of *AMP'D*

"Susan Walter has a knack for writing thoroughly entertaining stories that keep you flipping pages. Fun and fast and full of surprising revelations. What a pleasure to read!"
—W. Bruce Cameron, #1 *New York Times* bestselling author of *A Dog's Purpose* and *Love, Clancy*

"Susan Walter, in her signature shifty thriller style, weaves a story of blind ambition and intersecting lies as four people and their secrets collide in Beverly Hills. Sit by the pool with her, and turn the pages. But keep an eye on who's in the cabana."
—Judy Melinek and T.J. Mitchell, *New York Times* bestselling authors of the Dr. Jessie Teska Mysteries and *Working Stiff*

"Get ready for a sleepless night! *Lie by the Pool* is a blistering, fast-paced thriller, confidently plotted and executed. Fiendishly clever!"
—Paulette Kennedy, bestselling author of *The Witch of Tin Mountain*

"This book is better than any on-screen thriller. A seamless, exhilarating plot that draws you in so immediately and completely, you feel like you're living Bree's nightmare instead of just reading it. In a genre that can seem glutted by stale ideas and stock characters, Walter brings us something fresh, fast paced, and utterly fantastic."
—Lindsay Moran, bestselling author of *Blowing My Cover*

"A page-turning Beverly Hills tale with characters to root for and suspect all at once. Susan Walter is simply the master at luring readers in with breezy prose and then walloping with a killer twist. Dive in and enjoy the ride!"
—Wendy Walker, bestselling author of *What Remains*

"With [*Lie by the Pool's*] alternating perspectives told by compelling characters, you'll find yourselves turning the pages to get to the bottom of this skillfully rendered mystery. The perfect summer read!"
—Katie Sise, Amazon Charts bestselling author of *Open House* and *The Break*

Over Her Dead Body

"Susan Walter is a master storyteller with an insider's view of the film business, and her novel glints with danger and brilliant insight into the hopes and dreams of an aspiring actress. I read it in one sitting, guessing the whole way through, stunned by the conclusion."
—Luanne Rice, *New York Times* bestselling author of *The Shadow Box* and *Last Day*

"A devilishly fun romp, full of eccentric characters and unexpected twists, *Over Her Dead Body* will keep you turning pages as it pulls back the curtains on Hollywood from the point of view of a struggling actress caught up in a mystery laced with darkly comedic beats. Thoroughly enjoyable!"

—Ben Mezrich, *New York Times* bestselling author of *Bringing Down the House, The Accidental Billionaires*, and *The Midnight Ride*

"Susan Walter swerves the reader back and forth and around blind corners in a page-turning domestic psychodrama that will twist your sympathies and drop your jaw. An A-list Hollywood thrill ride, right through to the breathtaking end!"

—Judy Melinek and T.J. Mitchell, *New York Times* bestselling authors of the Dr. Jessie Teska Mysteries and *Working Stiff*

"With its eccentric ensemble cast and all the family drama of *Knives Out, Over Her Dead Body* is darkly funny and highly entertaining, with more twists than a bus tour through the Hollywood Hills. Fans of Janet Evanovich and Elle Cosimano will be delighted."

—Tessa Wegert, author of *Death in the Family*

"*Over Her Dead Body* is a whodunit with more twists and turns than a boardwalk roller coaster, where secrets abound and nothing is what it seems. If you're looking for a book that will keep you turning pages deep into the night, Susan Walter has absolutely written one."

—Barbara Davis, bestselling author of *The Keeper of Happy Endings*

Good as Dead

"Susan Walter's debut novel is so full of surprises it should come with a warning label. From the daringly original premise to the shocking climax, you'll never see the plot twists coming until you turn the page. I cannot wait for her next book!"

—W. Bruce Cameron, #1 *New York Times* bestselling author of *A Dog's Purpose* and *A Dog's Courage*

"Susan Walter's *Good as Dead* had me holding my breath through every thrilling twist and turn until the downright explosive ending. Fearlessly tackling themes of love, wealth, personal responsibility, and life and death, it was pure pleasure to read and a brilliant debut."

—Alethea Black, author of *You've Been So Lucky Already* and *I Knew You'd Be Lovely*

"Susan Walter delivers a thrilling puzzle of a story that she feeds you piece by twisty piece. A wonderfully unique premise, a deep cast of flawed but relatable characters, and a mind-blowing ending. I could not put down this book. Five stars!"

—Sawyer Bennett, *New York Times* bestselling author

"A mystery set in Los Angeles written by a filmmaker? Yes, please! Susan Walter's *Good as Dead* is a fun, fast ride through Hollywood's suburbia. As they say, sometimes the cover-up is worse than the crime. Couldn't put it down!"

—Judy Melinek and T.J. Mitchell, *New York Times* bestselling authors of the Dr. Jessie Teska Mysteries and *Working Stiff*

LETTERS
FROM
STRANGERS

OTHER TITLES BY SUSAN WALTER

LETTERS FROM STRANGERS

A NOVEL

SUSAN WALTER

Text copyright © 2025 by Susan Walter
All rights reserved.

No part of this book may be reproduced, or stored in a retrieval system, or transmitted in any form or by any means, electronic, mechanical, photocopying, recording, or otherwise, without express written permission of the publisher.

Published by Lake Union Publishing, Seattle

www.apub.com

Amazon, the Amazon logo, and Lake Union Publishing are trademarks of Amazon.com, Inc., or its affiliates.

EU product safety contact:
Amazon Media EU S. à r.l.
38, avenue John F. Kennedy, L-1855 Luxembourg
amazonpublishing-gpsr@amazon.com

ISBN-13: 9781662523496 (paperback)
ISBN-13: 9781662523502 (digital)

Cover design by Faceout Studio, Spencer Fuller
Cover image: © Cavan Images, © Nadia Audigie, © Douglas Sacha / Getty; © Volha Kratkouskaya / Shutterstock

Printed in the United States of America

For my Gen X sisters, who helped build the bridge.

Inspired by true events.

May 10, 1977

Dear Richie,
Last night was unforgettable. I don't know how you have the energy. I got to sleep on the plane, but you can't do that when you're flying it!

After I drove home, I put on the dress you bought me and drank a glass of wine on my balcony. You missed a beautiful sunset. As the sky turned from golden yellow to burgundy-violet, I closed my eyes and imagined your arms around my waist, pulling me into you.

I hate that you have to go back to her. But I'm grateful for the time we have together, even though it always leaves me wanting more.

I can't wait for our next adventure. Write back if you can. And don't let her get you down. You are an amazing person. She may not see it, but I do.

Love, me

PART 1

SPRING 2001

CHAPTER 1
JANE

I had no idea how many people would come, so I just kept cooking.

I made all his favorites—fried chicken brined in yogurt whey, morels stuffed with ground lamb, orzo with hot Italian sausage, blackened rib eye. Dad was a big meat eater. That's probably what killed him.

My father's death was as startling as it was unremarkable. He went for a swim, took a shower, then parked in front of the TV to watch the Red Sox hammer the Yankees. Mom found him snoozing on the couch. She thought he looked pale, so she went over and shook him. Then she called me.

"Dad won't wake up," she said.

My dog was barking—he goes crazy when the phone rings—so I didn't hear the panic in her voice.

"Sorry, Tarzan's flipping out." People think it's hilarious when I tell them our dog's name is Tarzan, since my name is Jane. But he came with that name. We hadn't planned to adopt when we wandered into the pop-up pet fair, but some might say we had no choice.

"I'm calling Sal," Mom said, then hung up. Sal was her neighbor and a retired radiologist. Whenever Mom had an ailment—a stubborn rash, an ingrown toenail, a burning sensation when she peed—Sal got a call. I wondered if he was the kind of guy who resented being asked for help or appreciated the opportunity to feel useful in retirement. I thought it best not to ask.

I hung up the phone, then looked down at the puddle by my dog's feet.

"Tarzan!" I scolded, but only gently. He peed when he was nervous. He came with that too. I rummaged under the sink for some paper towels. A minute later, the phone rang again.

"Hi, Mom," I said as I clipped the leash on Tarzan's collar. I don't know why I was taking him outside, he'd already emptied the contents of his bladder on my kitchen floor.

"It's Sal," my mom's neighbor replied. "I'm really sorry to tell you this, but your dad has passed."

In the movies, when a person is told a loved one is dead, they often fight back ("That's impossible!" "There must be some mistake!"), but no such thoughts went through my head. I knew I believed him, because a second before, I was standing, and then I was gasping for air on the floor.

I don't know how long Dr. Sal let me cry like that, but I suddenly felt terribly rude. He was probably sitting down for dinner when my mom called. People like me were the reason he retired.

"I'm sorry," I blurted once I caught my breath. "I'll come right away."

I hung up and called my husband. He doesn't always answer when he's at work, but thank God he did this time, because that would have been a doozy of a message.

"Are you OK to drive?" Greg asked when I told him I was getting in the car.

"I'll be OK," I said, because the only thing scarier than driving to my mom's was being home alone.

"I'll meet you there."

"I'm fine, don't rush." I didn't want him to announce to the whole company that his wife's dad just died, and run for the door like the building was on fire. I had to see those people at the Christmas party—it was awkward enough.

Greg and I rarely fought, but sometimes it felt like our hearts beat to different songs—mine to an eighties hair band, his to smooth jazz. But then a crisis rolled around—a rear-end collision, a sunspot turned malignant—and we found our way back to each other. Maybe that's what crises are for? To remind us that life hurts, and you're damn lucky if you don't have to go through it alone.

My car radio was tuned to KIIS-FM. I left it on, because why cry alone when you can cry with Celine Dion? Tears were waterfalling into my open mouth. *Inhale . . . exhale . . .* I focused on my breathing to keep from breaking to pieces. Dad was my protector, my backstop when life hurled a curveball at me. I still called him for help with things adults were supposed to know, like if I should choose air miles or cash back and what to do when the "check engine" light goes on. He was the only person who ever told me to "get tough," and the only one who was proud of me when I did. *And now he's gone.*

A car cut in front of me, and my foot hit the brakes. Normally, it was a thirty-minute drive to my parents' place—or three hundred breaths, by today's metric—but it was rush hour, and this was LA, so all bets were off. As I slowed, accelerated, slowed with the flow of traffic, the cheery banter of the radio cohosts was a blunt reminder that, for everybody else, my dad dying was just another day.

My parents' condo was in a new development a few blocks from the beach. They bought it when it was still an idea in some builder's head. Dad loved being the first—first in his family to go to college, start a business, own a house. Mom was huddled in her bedroom when I arrived, so I had to walk past Dad's dead body to get to her. Someone had moved him from the couch to the floor, and he was laid out flat and covered with a plain white sheet. I later learned paramedics had come and tried to revive him. It must have been them who moved him, because my dad had a good forty pounds on Dr. Sal, thanks to all that meat.

I knelt down on the floor across from Mom. Her hands were shaking, so I reached for them, careful not to squeeze too hard and drive her rings into the delicate skin between her knuckles. She wore a diamond eternity band on her left hand and rubies on her right—both surprise gifts from Dad during a time when Mom would have preferred not to get any more surprises.

"He was supposed to make lamb chops," Mom said. "They're defrosting on the counter." She looked up at me. Her eyes were marbled like raw meat. Her sudden frailty was jarring. The ground beneath us had shifted, as if between that phone call and my arrival, I'd become the grown-up and she the child.

"I'll cook them for you," I said, stepping into my new role. "They'll be OK in the fridge for a couple of days."

"It doesn't matter."

I let go of her hands and stood up. Mom wasn't a hugger, and I forgave her long ago for not being able to give me what she hadn't gotten herself. "Can I get you something? A glass of water?"

"What are we supposed to do with him?" she asked.

This was my first dead body, and I had no idea. "I don't know," I admitted. "I'll call Kenny."

My brother lived in Phoenix, Arizona, just off the air force base where he trained fighter pilots. I was no psychologist, but it seemed fairly obvious Kenny joined the air force to one-up my dad, who was only rated to fly puddle jumpers and would never know what it was like to feel the throttle of an F-16. "I can't come until Saturday," Kenny apologized after I told him the bad news. It was Tuesday.

"That's fine," I said, even though he wasn't asking my approval.

"Are you going to be OK?"

"Yes. I'm fine. *We're* fine. It's just . . . we don't know, um . . . what to do with him?" It came out as a question, which I guess is how I meant it.

"Hold on," he said, and this was a day of many firsts, because my big brother didn't know either.

He left me holding for two minutes, then came back with a simple solution—call a funeral home to come get him. Dad thought he would live forever so hadn't made any arrangements. We picked the one that was still open. Two muscular, appropriately somber young men arrived within the hour.

"Do you want a moment alone with him?" one of them asked after they'd loaded him onto a gurney. I looked at Mom. I guess she'd had enough time alone with him when he was alive, because she shook her head.

"No," I told them, but as they started rolling him away, I cried out, "Wait!"

I don't know why I stopped them. I didn't have anything to say. I didn't pray or have the courage to roll back the sheet and look at his dead face. But they gave me a moment, so I took it to breathe in the strangeness of it all. My father was dead. Two strangers were about to wheel him away and lock him in a freezer. We were all about to take on new identities: *fatherless*, *widow*, *mourner*, and one I didn't expect—*detective*.

It would be two weeks before I found the letters in an unmarked file folder at the back of Dad's desk. So I still thought I knew him as I pulled the sourdough breadcrumbs out of the oven and set them on the stovetop to cool. We'd decided not to call it a memorial service. Dad didn't even go to his own father's funeral—"too sad," he'd said. No, we wouldn't have a memorial. We would have a party. It was his birthday, after all—we'd been planning to have one anyway. The only thing that had changed was that he wasn't going to be there.

Given that this was definitively Dad's last birthday party, we decided to expand the guest list to "anyone who wanted to drop by." I was happy to have an excuse not to leave my kitchen, doubling or tripling every recipe. Dad had retired, but in addition to the friends we'd already invited, former business associates, aviation buddies, random neighbors he'd chatted up in the hot tub would likely drop in. I had no idea how many characters from his past might show up.

And so I cooked.

CHAPTER 2
JANE

The party favors were my sister-in-law's idea—little model airplanes the size of Matchbox cars. When I walked into the "event room" at Mom's condo complex to light the chafing dishes, Cindy was arranging them on the tables like hostess gifts for wedding guests. I hadn't asked her to bring anything, but my brother's wife was as caring as Kenny was stoic and knew better than to show up without food. Plus we needed decorations. I had planned to get balloons, but that seemed macabre now that the birthday boy was dead.

"Those are great, thank you," I said to her back as she placed a pair of red-nosed warbirds on a plate. It was a buffet, but I'd set the tables to make it look less sad.

"Jane! How *are* you?" she asked when she turned around to greet me, leaning into the word *are* to give me permission to not be fine.

"How are *you?*" I said, gaping at her belly, which was puffed too big and round to be mistaken for monthly bloat.

She cupped her underbelly, like all pregnant women do.

"Kenny didn't tell you."

She said it like an apology, because she knew this was an awkward way to find out you were going to be an auntie. Cindy and Kenny were living proof that opposites attract. She was a bouquet of brightly colored balloons that lifted you off your feet. He was strong arms that brought you back down to earth. Cindy came to the marriage with two kids from a first husband who could barely be counted on to send cards on their birthdays. My brother was punctual, reliable, organized, accountable—the ultimate antidote to the man she'd divorced.

"I don't know why he's so tight lipped about these things," Cindy said. "It's not like I could keep it a secret anymore, even if I wanted to."

I knew why he didn't tell me. It was uncomfortable. Like announcing you're training for the marathon to someone who doesn't have legs.

"Well, you look wonderful," I said, then glanced up toward heaven. "Circle of life." I didn't mean it literally. I just wanted my sister-in-law to think the catch in my voice was about my dad.

"Where do you want these?" my brother asked as he walked in with a bag of ice over each shoulder. I'd asked him to pick up a bag, but he was Kenny, so he got two.

"Just pour it on top of the drinks," I said, pointing under the buffet table where my cooler was waiting to do its job. My brother completed the task with military efficiency, slitting the bags with his handy pocketknife, then letting their contents waterfall onto the cans.

"Anything else?" he asked, rolling the empty bags into tight coils and then tucking them under his arm.

"That's it for now." He nodded, and I almost let him leave, but the elephant in the room was blocking the door. "Congrats, by the way."

Cindy's eyes flicked up with interest.

"Yeah, thanks," he said, like bringing life into the world was no big deal.

"When are you due?"

He looked at Cindy.

"July sixth," she said. "But my other two were late, so I'm not counting on it." I wanted to tell her not to worry, Kenny doesn't tolerate lateness, but surely she knew that by now.

"Well, I'm super happy for you both," I said, because you should be happy for your brother and his wife when the most amazing thing that can happen to a couple happens to them.

"I know you've had your struggles," he offered. Cindy looked at me in that way you look at someone when your team won the championship but you know the other team wanted it more. "Sorry I didn't tell you sooner."

"Are you going to go see Dad?" I asked to remind everyone that this weekend wasn't about me. Dad was scheduled to be cremated, but there was a wait list for the oven, so he was presently still in the freezer and available for viewing "should a family member want to say goodbye."

"Nah. You?"

"I saw him already," I said. "When they came to roll him away." I didn't mean to be passive-aggressive, but I'd been ping-ponging between cooking for Dad and crying with Mom for four days, and I was tired.

Kenny could have dinged me back—he was serving our country, not blowing us off—but he just nodded. He knew every time I told Mom, "It's OK to cry . . . I'm here for you . . . don't worry, you're not alone," she'd responded with, "When's Kenny coming? . . . ask Kenny what he thinks . . . let's not make any decisions until Kenny gets here." Kenny had always been closer to our mom than I was, and it was no secret she preferred his company to mine. And who could blame her? I'd picked my side long ago. Growing up, I watched ball games and washed the car with Dad instead of helping Mom plant tomatoes or make soup. Dad was the one who knew how to ride a motorcycle, fly a plane, charm the supermarket checkout girl into giving me a free pack of gum. An outing with Dad meant singing to the Pointer Sisters with the windows open, then stopping at Baskin-Robbins for hand-packed pints and tunneling out the peanut butter. I chose Dad because he was fun. Kenny chose Mom, I had to assume, because I didn't.

"What time do you want me back to help with the food?" Kenny asked.

"I'm fine. Go be with Mom."

I hadn't seen much of Kenny since he disappeared into military life. I sometimes wondered if he was attracted to its "keep calm and carry on" culture because, after growing up in our home, he'd had his fill of drama. Or maybe he just wanted to wall himself off from the rest of us. If I could have found the words, I would have told him we weren't at war—he didn't have to pick sides. But that would have meant reopening a wound that had long since scarred over, so I kept my mouth shut.

CHAPTER 3
JANE

"My first memory of my dad is from when I was six," I said to Dad's party guests after we'd eaten. The tables were arranged so there was no front and no back, like kindergarten circle time. The room was packed with—among others—neighbors my dad had befriended in the hot tub; Dad's brother, Paul, and his wife, Maureen; Dad's flying buddies; a few cousins I only saw when someone died or got married; my one friend from childhood who had moved from Boston to LA like my parents and I did; and Kenny's friend Rowan from the academy, who flew in from Colorado for the day because he owned a charter airline and could do that, I guess?

"It was my birthday," I continued. "He got me a bike. It was turquoise with a bright-white banana seat, and rainbow tassels on the handlebars." I glanced at my mother. Her face grew dark, like a cloud had passed in front of it. And I realized she was the one who'd picked out that bike. Just like she'd picked out all my birthday presents, then wrote "from Mom and Dad" on the card.

"It was love at first sight," I said, holding my mom's eyes in case it wasn't too late to thank her. "The only problem was, I didn't know how to ride a bike."

The solemn faces gave way to smiles. I knew everyone was looking to me to set the tone, and I wanted to give them permission not to cry, at least for a little while. Over the last five days, I'd indulged every variety of crying—keened on my kitchen floor, sobbed into my pillow, hiccup-cried while driving, ugly-cried in the shower. But today, with the help of a stolen capsule of Valium, I held it together. For my mom. For Dad's friends. For myself.

"Thanks to Richie, that was the day I learned," I said, then proceeded to tell the story of how Dad had taught me how to ride a bike. "He held onto the back of that banana seat as I started pedaling. I remember shouting at him, 'Don't let go, Dad!' and him shouting back, 'I won't!'"

As I looked out at all the people who came to honor my father's memory, I was struck by how many I'd never seen before. Who were all these people? Did they come to give my mom a hug? Or take one last whiff of the charmer who'd always greeted them with a "How are ya?" and a joke? Dad was the Pied Piper, and his charisma was his song. Now that he was gone, the silence was deafening.

"I assumed he was running behind me as I pedaled down the sidewalk," I said to the smiling faces. "But when I glanced back, he wasn't there."

Kenny and Rowan were off to the left, by the fireplace. Seeing them sitting shoulder to shoulder in their matching military haircuts was like being zapped back in time, and for a flickering moment, I was once again that lovestruck little sister embarrassing her big brother, like a wrong note at the Christmas concert. Sometimes I wondered if everyone has a Rowan—that man who shot an arrow through their heart, then every time he's near, he tugs on it just enough to remind you it's still there.

"Of course I fell immediately," I continued, shifting my gaze to keep from falling into the memory of what happened between us. "'You said you wouldn't let go!' I yelled at Dad. To which he replied, 'Why are you mad? You just learned how to ride a bike!'"

My punch line got a polite laugh, except from Kenny, who had a sudden need to adjust his belt buckle. "Dad was always a look-at-the-bright-side kind of guy," I said. "Even when I crashed his car. 'Now we don't need to argue about whether or not you're allowed to drive it!'" I finally got a smile from Kenny, who got a job cutting lawns when he turned sixteen so he could buy his own car and watch me beg for rides while his keys puffed out his pocket.

"There's no agenda for this gathering," I said. "But I want to invite anyone who has a memory they'd like to share to relieve me from embarrassing myself any further." I looked at my uncle Paul, who'd already asked me if he could say a few words, and he stood and cleared his throat.

"My brother was a character," Paul began, blurring his *r*'s like people from Boston do. And then he grimaced, like this was the first time he had spoken about his little brother in the past tense. "Sorry." Aunt Maureen squeezed his hand. He choked back a sob, then inhaled and exhaled like someone about to jump off a cliff. I'd heard the story of how my dad had donned Paul's signature plaid shirt to take his calculus final for him at least a dozen times, and hearing it again was like seeing an old friend.

"Luckily I cut that class so often my teacher didn't know what I looked like," Uncle Paul joked, and I let myself laugh about how effortlessly my dad could deceive people.

We went loosely around the circle. My mom didn't speak, but no one expected her to—she had always been the audience not the performer. Cindy spoke for Kenny, telling the story of the first time she'd met her father-in-law; how he took them out to dinner and ordered everything with extra meat. "'I'd like extra bacon bits on the salad,'" she said, imitating my dad's slight Boston accent. "'If you can do it with more bacon than salad that would be great.'" (Laughter from the crowd.) "'And the steak I want as rare as the health department will allow you to serve it. If it's not bleeding all over my plate, I'm sending it back. And I'll do the side of pasta with meat sauce, but more meat sauce than pasta, if you know what I mean?'" Everybody except the person who grew up with an eating disorder thought this recollection was hilarious, but I did my best to chuckle along.

After the speeches, I put out dessert—homemade lemon bars and chocolate cheesecake, which I'd cut into one-inch squares so people could eat them with their fingers.

"Can I give you a hand?" Rowan asked, appearing beside me as I peeled the Saran wrap off the platters. His navy button-front was tucked into sharply creased khakis pinned to his hips by a shiny black belt.

"Oh. Hi, Rowan." He was looking at me expectantly, so I answered his question. "Thank you, there's not really anything to do." At six foot and then some, he was easily the tallest person in the room, but it was the mistakes that could never be taken back that made me feel small.

He took a step closer, and I got a whiff of his Barbasol-fresh shave. "Are you holding up OK?" he asked.

"It's been a long week. But I'm all right. Thanks." He nodded, and for a second I thought he might hug me.

"I'm sorry for your loss. I know what your dad meant to you." He held out his hand like he was asking me to dance. "Here, I'll throw that away."

"Thanks," I said, placing the balled-up plastic wrap in the curve of his palm.

"Take care, Jane." He smiled, and I felt the tug of that arrow. As he walked away, he tossed the Saran ball into the trash can like Larry Bird making a fallaway jumper.

"What were you talking to Rowan about?" Kenny asked as he caught me staring.

"He was just offering his condolences." I didn't mean to sound defensive, but it was annoying that my big brother thought he still had to run interference between Rowan and me.

"I'm taking Mom home, she's tired." He grabbed a cheesecake square off the tray and popped it in his mouth. "Damn, Jane, you really outdid yourself with the food."

Cindy and Aunt Maureen insisted on cleaning up so Greg and I could join Kenny and my mom back at the condo. "Go," Cindy said, shooing me out the door. "We got this."

"It was a really nice remembrance," Greg said when the four of us were alone in Mom's living room. The place was like a flower shop, every surface covered with bouquets. Lilies from Mom's hairdresser, carnations from the building manager, pastel-colored roses from family members who couldn't make the trip. "Richie would have been pleased."

"You made too much food," Mom said, ignoring Greg. "What am I going to do with all these leftovers?"

"Cindy and I need to leave tonight," Kenny said, looking at me, so I knew not to suggest he would help her eat them.

"That's a long drive," Greg said. It was already dark. I glanced at my watch. Phoenix was a painfully boring six-hour drive from our mom's place in Playa Vista. Even if they left now, they wouldn't get home until two in the morning.

"Rowan will fly us." He muttered something about the kids and not having an overnight babysitter, and I wondered if that's why Rowan had made the trip. I knew from growing up with a pilot for a dad that they will jump on any excuse to take their planes for a spin.

"What about all Dad's stuff?" I asked. I knew he wouldn't want any of Dad's saggy jeans or T-shirts; I was already planning to box those up myself. But Dad's office was full of all sorts of goodies—old aviation maps; bookends made from lava rocks; a Howard Miller desk clock; a vintage leather attaché that had literally traveled the world.

"Can you take care of it?" Kenny asked, as if he didn't want anything to remember his father by.

"Sure," I said, feeling stupid. His wife and our country needed him, he couldn't stick around to sort through old maps. Or maybe he remembered his father well enough.

March 2, 1984

Dear _____,
I can feel you kicking now. It doesn't hurt. More like
tickles, like a tiny bird flapping its wings inside my belly.
It's how I know you're really coming. Until I felt you,
I told myself that maybe it was all just a bad dream.

I'm going to meet with the lawyer tomorrow. She said
she has a really nice family picked out for you, a couple
that's been waiting a long time and can give you a great
life. But I'll make sure before I sign the papers.

You don't have a name yet. Your new mom will give
you one. Given how you came to be, it's probably better
that you don't know mine. So I'll just sign this letter with
an . . .
    X

CHAPTER 4
ADAM

Days until training camp: 108

Every night I dreamed of cheeseburgers. Thick, homemade cheeseburgers; flat, fast-food cheeseburgers; cheeseburgers with pickles, ketchup, mayonnaise; on buns with sesame seeds, pretzel buns, or no bun at all. After three months on a twelve-hundred-calorie-per-day diet, I was hungry every hour of every day, even in my sleep. In my dreams, the tickle of the fan was the juice running down my arm after I bit into the perfectly charred patty and it exploded in my mouth. I wanted so badly for it to be real, when I woke up, I checked my teeth for bits of beef I prayed had gotten stuck there so I could have a taste.

My dietitian gave me a list of approved foods that I could mix and match, because "this shouldn't feel like torture." In the morning I was allowed one of the following appetizing combinations: small bowl of oatmeal, farro, or barley, with one cup of skim milk, kefir, or nonfat yogurt. I got a midmorning snack of a fistful of almonds, a piece of fruit, or a protein bar that resembled cardboard in taste, texture, and smell. Lunch was usually some sort of salad with boiled chicken or flaked tuna on top. I got one piece of fruit in the afternoon, unless I'd had fruit for my morning snack—then I'd get to choose some other decadent treat, like a hard-boiled egg or avocado wedge. And dinner was pureed soup (to fill me up), six ounces of lean meat (baked or grilled because pan-frying was the enemy), and as many vegetables as I could cram into the steamer.

I told my mom I could lose the weight on my own, but she insisted on hiring a dietitian so I didn't go off the rails. She'd heard stories of wrestlers and ballet dancers starving themselves literally to death, and after all the time and money spent to turn me into a sports superstar, she didn't want me following them to their bony graves. She knew how stubborn I could be when I wanted something. Being stubborn is how I got fat in the first place.

My parents wanted me to be a professional tennis player. I'm really tall, with the wingspan of a pterodactyl. I would be deadly at the net, my coach said when I was fourteen and already over six feet. He would make me a serve-and-volley player, like Pete Sampras. Serve deep, rush the net, hit a volley winner, repeat until world domination. At least that was the plan.

Coach was right about one thing—I was good at the net. I wasn't just tall; thanks to the hours of speed drills he made me do, I was also fast. Fast to react. Fast to get in position. Fast to reset. I didn't always make my shots, but I always got to the ball. *Always.*

We didn't bother with the high school team, I was too good for that. Halfway through my sophomore year, my dad announced we were moving to Florida because New England winters were long, and he wanted me to be able to play outside all year. I would train with Michael Chang's coach, Dad said. He'd seen my tape and already agreed to take me.

But we didn't move to Florida. Because something unexpected happened. A few months before my sixteenth birthday, when I was on the verge of becoming a seeded player in junior men's singles, I accidentally discovered there was something I liked more than tennis. *A lot* more.

I didn't normally participate in phys ed, but Mr. Drucker, our regular PE teacher, was out, so we had a sub. I tried to tell the sub that I was excused—I played two hours of tennis before school, and as a nationally ranked junior, I had met the requirement five times over. But he wouldn't have it.

He asked if I wanted to play offense or defense. I chose offense, naturally, because the only thing a serve-and-volley player knows how to do is attack. Plus everyone knows the best defense is a great offense, and if I was going to play, I wanted to be relevant.

He lined me up on the outside as a wide receiver, then pointed to a spot ten yards diagonally in front of me. "Run to that spot, then turn around and look for the ball," he ordered.

I learned later that this was called a slant route, and that the guy trying to stop me from getting to that spot was called a cornerback. I learned that cornerbacks are the fastest players on the field, and that to beat the cornerback on a slant, you had to get a good push off the line, because if he's close to you, he can jump the route and beat you to the ball. I learned you can fool the cornerback by mixing up your footwork, and if you fake to the left but run to the right (or vice versa), that's called a juke. I learned that the guy who runs short slant routes is called a slot receiver, and if you're a slot receiver who wants to earn the affection of the quarterback, you'd better get open, because if his outside receiver gets covered up and he can't find you, he's going to get clocked. And, catastrophically, I learned that I loved playing football.

I loved being part of a team and how we all worked together toward a common goal. I loved the pushing and tackling and wrestling for the ball. I loved standing shoulder to shoulder with my teammates, feeling the heat radiating off their bodies. I don't think it changed me, more like awakened something that was already there, waiting to be discovered, like money inside your birthday card.

Mr. Drucker was only out for a week, but that was enough for me to know I didn't want to be a tennis player anymore. My parents did not take it well.

"We're moving to Florida, Adam!" my mom objected when I told her I wanted to try out for football. At five feet, zero inches tall, my mom looked like a different species than me. People couldn't resist joking that I must be adopted. I loved seeing their ears turn red when I told them yes, I was in fact adopted, that I'd never met my birth mother, and that I presumed she was an Amazonian queen who loved cheeseburgers.

My parents assumed the football thing was a "phase," so they let me try out for the team. I was too tall to be a slot receiver, but Coach Fitz told me if I kept my weight up and learned to tackle, "maybe" I could be a wideout. Those were the guys who lined up on the outside and ran the whole length of the field. He invited me to summer training camp with a noncommittal "We'll see."

Dad was not about to let me quit tennis for a "We'll see." We fought like feral cats. But I had the advantage. I was the one in my body. And I couldn't play tennis if I gained a bunch of weight.

But I could play football.

So, in March of sophomore year, five months before the start of football training camp, I began to eat. Muffins and waffles with syrup for breakfast. Burgers and fries and milkshakes for lunch. A double portion of whatever Mom was cooking for dinner. A whole pizza before bed.

I ate what I wanted, whenever I wanted. It was glorious.

Except I couldn't stop.

I didn't have a target weight, and even if I did, it wouldn't have mattered. I was too afraid to weigh myself. My six-pack abs disappeared like a sea turtle in the sand, but I just kept eating. I couldn't tell you if I was hungry, because I'd forgotten what being hungry felt like. My methodology was simple: if there was food, I would eat it. I could see the concern in my mom's face when she looked at me. Which only made me want to eat more.

I made the football team that August, but not as a skill player, as an offensive lineman. Those are the big, burly guys who protect the quarterback by forming a human wall around him. You don't need to have talent beyond the ability to hold your ground while opposing players try to shove you aside. The bigger you are, the harder you are to shove. And, thanks to all that late-night snacking, I was *big*.

There weren't that many refrigerator-size humans at our high school, so I became a bit of a star. Funny, when I was an actual star in the tennis world, nobody paid attention to me. But now that I was "that tennis player who got really fat," everybody knew my name.

I ate my way through football season junior year as the only starter who played every offensive and special teams snap. Girls never looked at me, but I had zero interest in girls. To my teammates, I was a hero. I had never been anyone's hero before. A win at tennis is a high five from your coach. A win at football is a big, warm team hug.

We didn't make the playoffs—not because we couldn't score points, turns out I was wrong about what makes a great defense—so our season was over the first week in December. Most of the guys went straight into track or basketball. But not me. Because you needed to be able to run and jump for those sports. And running and jumping were no longer in my repertoire.

We never used to go anywhere for Christmas because I always had tennis, but this year my parents surprised me with a trip to the Bahamas. Any normal kid would have been thrilled. But any normal kid could walk around in a bathing suit without feeling like the whole world was judging them.

I told my mom I didn't want to be fat anymore while we were standing in line at the Christmas buffet. My plate was piled high with turkey and stuffing, but the thought of eating it made me want to kill myself. We hired a dietitian as soon as we got back to Boston, and I started my diet the first day of basketball season. I lost ten pounds by Valentine's Day.

I gained it back by spring break.

My goal was to go back to football my senior year, not as a lineman but as a skill-position player. I knew somewhere under all those extra pounds was an athlete. I just had to find him.

I studied the playbook and learned how to tackle. But something in me wouldn't let me lose the weight. I needed more than a diet. And if I wanted to become the team's star wide receiver, I needed it soon.

CHAPTER 5
ADAM

It was my dietitian who suggested talk therapy. Maybe she could tell I had mental problems, or maybe she just didn't want it to be all her fault if I couldn't lose weight. Mom couldn't look at me without tearing up, so when I told her "I think I might like to talk to someone," she got me an appointment for the very next day.

Sandy was Mom's roommate at Wellesley—a nice Jewish lady who looked like Elaine from *Seinfeld*, all the way down to her dopey Italian loafers. Her home office was on a tree-lined street in Cambridge, three blocks from the Porter Square T stop. Mom offered to drive me, but this was something I wanted to do alone, so I took the train.

It was warm for April, the kind of day that makes your hair puff up like bread dough. I didn't wear shorts because of the way my thighs rubbed together when I walked, so I sweated it out in shiny Adidas joggers with "slimming" stripes down the sides that fooled exactly no one. People treat you differently when you're fat. When skinny, tan-from-tennis me got on the T, the other passengers were all smiles: *here, sit next to me, I'll move my groceries.* But fat me wasn't invited to sit down. Instead of looking up and smiling, people suddenly needed to study the subway map or their fingernails or that sticky thing on the bottom of their shoe.

The door to Sandy's waiting area was propped open with a flowerpot (geraniums, I think), so I let myself in. Instead of a receptionist, she had a little switch on the wall by the inner door ("Flip up so I know you're here!"). I flipped the switch, then sank down on a dainty tweed sofa that prickled the backs of my thighs through my pants.

"Hello, Adam," Sandy said when she saw me suffocating her couch. "Come on in."

I imagined, being my mom's former roommate, Sandy knew all about me, but she pretended she didn't. So I told her about switching from tennis to football and doing pretty OK in school.

"How about friends?" she asked.

I told her how I'd never had friends when I played tennis, and how joining the football team changed all that. "They're like brothers but better because you don't have to share your stuff." I didn't tell her about the other feelings I was having. Just because my overeating started right after my discovery didn't mean they were related.

"Do you wish you had a brother?" she asked, and I just shrugged.

"Maybe I do have a brother. Or five. One never knows in my situation."

"Does the not knowing bother you?"

I didn't know how talking about being adopted was going to get me to stop eating every doughnut in the box, but I answered her question. "I'm grateful for my parents, and I know they love me," I said, because while I didn't think she would report back to my mother, it couldn't hurt to be on the record as not being a whiny bitch.

"But?"

"Best-case scenario, I was a mistake. Somebody's 'oh shit!' moment." I paused. I didn't want to speak the worst-case scenario.

"You know that's not your fault."

"I'm still probably the worst thing that ever happened to someone." I didn't know I was crying until a tear plopped onto the fabric above my man boob.

I found out in the worst way that I was adopted. It was the summer before second grade. I had just turned seven. An older boy at the playground wanted the swing I was on. "Hey, adopted kid!" he said. "Get off the swing." I didn't know who he was talking to, so I didn't move. But then he pointed right at me. "Yes, I'm talking to you. Do you see any other adopted kids here?"

I knew being adopted was bad because my "parents" had just taken me to see Newton North High School's production of *Annie*. After watching Annie and her fellow orphans get shoved around, I concluded there must be something wrong with kids who don't have parents, because why else would grown-ups treat them like crap?

I didn't want to tell my mom what that boy had said to me. I was embarrassed that someone would think I was anything like those sad, unwanted kids. But she finally coaxed it out of me with a gentle but stern "What happened at the playground, Adam?" I told her about the swing and the boy and the mean thing he called me. She didn't say anything at first. But then there was a hushed phone call and spaghetti dinner and a conversation that made me never want to eat spaghetti again.

"Have you ever talked to your mom and dad about wanting to meet your birth parents?" Sandy asked, and I shook my head.

"Is meeting your birth parents something you think you might like to do?" And I didn't have to say anything, because the problem that was threatening the seams of my clothes and my life said it for me.

CHAPTER 6
ADAM

"How did you like Sandy?" my mom asked as we sat down to a dinner of poached salmon and vegetables—baked broccoli, curried cauliflower, little wheels of a slimy-looking vegetable I later learned was okra. God bless Mom, she did her best to make vegetables taste like real food. My dad tried to look disinterested in the conversation, but I could tell by the way he was studying his ice cubes that his indifference was an act.

"She asked a lot of questions," I said, both dreading and desperate for Mom to ask, *Like what?*

"Did you learn anything?" This was my opening. Mom wouldn't pry. We both knew the whole point in sending me to Sandy was to give me a chance to talk about what I couldn't talk about with her. But she was fishing. And if I wanted her help, I would have to let myself get swept up in her net.

"Yeah, I think so."

Dad's eyes flicked up. Unlike my mom, who dared to express concern about my weight gain in real time ("What's going on with you? Should we take you to see Dr. Bennett? Are you depressed? Rebelling? Mad at me and your father?"), Dad acted like he barely noticed.

Dad wasn't a dick or anything, he was just from that generation of men who never learned how to talk about their feelings. I knew he felt betrayed. He had invested ten years and thousands of dollars to turn me into a tennis player. He was the one who got up at five a.m. to take me to practice every day, even on Sundays. He spent hours with my coach, strategizing about when to "launch" me, what tournaments were worthy, what to do about my aching wrist, my flat feet, my inconsistent inside-out forehand. He did this for me, to make me into "something extraordinary." Not realizing that the unspoken message—that there was nothing extraordinary about me without tennis—was a cruel thing to say to any kid, even one who wasn't adopted.

"Well, if you want to share, we're here," Mom said, then added, "But only if you want to."

"Thanks, Mom." My palms were sweating, and not just because of that spicy cauliflower. I knew I was one of the lucky ones. My parents were caring and affectionate. We lived in a nice neighborhood, took expensive vacations, ate out on the weekends, had a big house and fancy German cars. *We chose you!* I imagined them saying when I told them I wanted to meet my birth parents. *Shouldn't that be enough?* I had a mom and dad who gave me more than most kids got in their whole lives, and it was embarrassing to want more.

But I did want more. I wanted to know who I was—if I was the only one in my family with freakishly long arms, a cleft in his chin, who hiccuped when he laughed, talked in his sleep, ugly-cried when he listened to Joni Mitchell. I wanted to know that I was actually *born* from someone's womb, not picked up from somewhere where unwanted babies are dumped. I knew my adoptive parents wanted me. But I wanted to know why my birth parents didn't.

"There is one thing," I started, but my dad cut me off.

"I'm sorry if I put too much pressure on you," he blurted. "It's just that you had so much potential, I didn't want it to go to waste." It was an apology, but not really. Because when you follow "I'm sorry" with "it's just that," what you're really saying is "I didn't do anything wrong," which is not an apology at all. "I'm sorry I hurt you / lied / lost your dog

. . . *it's just that* I was upset / confused / hungover." These nonapologies were classic Dad. But I didn't feel like getting into it with him.

"It's OK, Dad," I said. "I know you wanted the best for me."

"I thought maybe that's why . . ." His voice trailed off. *Why what? I got fat?* He didn't want to say the word any more than I wanted to hear it.

"I'm not mad at you, Dad. That's not what this is about."

My mom got super still, like she knew I was about to say something and didn't want to spook me.

"I think I know why I'm flipping out," I said, doing my best to stop my nervous knee from bouncing. "I didn't want to tell you because I didn't want to seem ungrateful." I paused. I thought they would read between the lines, finish my sentence for me. But they just stared at me, lips parted like steamed clams.

"You guys are great parents," I said, just as I'd rehearsed. "And I feel really lucky that you chose me. But I don't know who I am."

Blank stares from my parents. They were going to make me say it.

"I want to know who my birth parents are."

My mother's face went from steamed clam to boiled lobster. For a second I thought she might cry.

"I'm sorry—" I said.

"Don't apologize!" Mom snapped back.

"We're the ones that should apologize," Dad said, then added something that scared the shit out of me. "We should have told you a long time ago."

I felt my face grow hot. "Told me what?"

Mom and Dad exchanged a look, and I was back at that spaghetti dinner, desperate to know the truth and desperate for them not to tell me. Mom's eyebrows ticked up. Dad nodded.

"I'll be right back." Mom got up and went upstairs. I heard the floor creak above my head as she padded down the hall. A minute later she returned with an old cigar box.

"We were going to wait until you were eighteen."

She set the box on the table in front of me. I flipped the lid open. It was full of letters.

"What are these?" I asked.

Mom gripped the back of the chair so she wouldn't fall down.

"They're from your birth mother."

April 20, 1984

Dear _____,

I imagine one day you'll have questions about who I am, and who your father was. You'll probably think you have a right to know. And maybe you do. But you also have the right to make up whatever you want about us. This way you can grow up to be a famous surgeon, or a fighter pilot, or the star pitcher for the Boston Red Sox, because there's nothing in your past to hold you back.

I'm getting too big to hide you now. So I don't really go out. I don't have anybody to talk to these days except for you. I don't know if you'll ever read these letters, I'm not even sure if I'll send them. Maybe I'm just writing them to get my feelings out. Like I said, I don't have anyone else to talk to.

When I can't sleep, I try to imagine you surrounded by so much love you never think about where you came from. Hopefully one day you'll understand I'm giving you up so you never feel as alone as I do.

X

CHAPTER 7
JANE

"How frequently are you having sex?"

I looked at Greg. Not because I didn't know the answer, but because I wanted to give him the opportunity to flex a little. The guy was as dependable as a sunrise, I didn't even have to do my hair.

"Every day? Once a week? A few times a month?" our fertility specialist prompted as her pen hovered over the clipboard. We'd spent the past hour describing our moods, meds, exercise regimens, eating habits, sleep hygiene, and alcohol consumption in glorious detail. Now that we were sufficiently loosened up, it was time for the main attraction: a deep dive into our sex life.

"I mean, the days before and after ovulation, obviously," my husband offered. "But otherwise about twice a week, I guess?" Greg's knee started bouncing. *Is he nervous? Embarrassed? Does he have to pee?*

"For a couple of months we were doing it every night," I added, because if there was ever a time to be thorough, this was it. "In case the ovulation tracker was wrong."

"But I couldn't keep that up," Greg said, then pantomimed wiping his brow with the back of his hand like an overworked farmhand. *Yep, nervous.* I smiled at him in solidarity. Dr. Chen was not amused.

"When was that?"

"We started right after Christmas and continued through Valentine's Day," I said. *It was awful,* I would have added, but it didn't seem relevant.

"So not quite two months," Dr. Chen corrected me. She didn't mean it as an accusation, but I still had to choke back the urge to defend myself.

"No, not quite."

She wrote something on her paper, probably that we weren't trying hard enough. But why should this be so hard? I was only thirty-four. Greg and I had all the necessary parts, and we were doing the thing people do to get pregnant—doing it *a lot*. I had gone off the pill fifteen months ago. I imagined all those unused eggs tumbling out like a pent-up sneeze. We felt like we were playing the lottery with a ticket that couldn't lose. It wasn't a matter of *if* our number would come up but when.

Over the months, doubt crept in, but we didn't give up. We took a few breaks here and there, but always wound up feeling guilty and fighting about stupid things, like who left the lights on (he did) or if the car was making a funny noise (it was). Our Christmas-to-Valentine's Day sex marathon was our final blitzkrieg before we admitted our lottery ticket was a loser and we needed help. My dad's ashes were still in a shoebox waiting for Mom and me to pick them up—I arguably should have postponed this appointment. But it took almost two months to get it, and after my father was taken from me with zero warning, I was desperate to feel in control of at least one prong of my life.

Dr. Chen asked about my medical history, and I was as truthful as I could be without slipping into an ABC Afterschool Special: eating disorder in my teens, intermittent tobacco and marijuana use in my twenties, three surgeries for early-stage skin cancer right before I turned thirty. She took it all down with the matter-of-factness of making a shopping list.

She looked up at Greg. "I recommend you do a semen analysis," she said. "Thirty-five percent of the time, infertility is caused by the sperm's inability to reach its target." I braced myself for the deflection I knew was coming.

"Jane has a history of abnormal periods," Greg said, as if Dr. Chen couldn't extrapolate that I'd had the defining symptoms of anorexia when I was gripped by the disease. "So we're pretty sure it's, y'know . . . on her end?" He said it like a question, like she was meant to confirm it.

"How have your periods been since you recovered?" she asked. The word "recovered" was presumptuous—once an addict, always an addict—but I let it slide. I was part of a whole generation of women held to an impossible standard of skinniness. I still had occasional flare-ups of body insecurity, but nothing a swift stroke of my meat cleaver couldn't handle.

"My periods are fine," I said. "Even before I went on the pill." Birth control pills are sometimes used to force a body to menstruate on a schedule, but I'd never needed them for that.

She turned the interrogation back to Greg. "Is there a reason you don't want to do the semen analysis?" His jaw muscle flexed. He was too polite to say what he was thinking, probably something like, *Jacking off in a cup is gross, no one wants to do that.*

"I'll do anything to move this along."

"Good. My nurse will set it up."

We had planned to go out to lunch after the appointment, but the play-by-play of our failure killed our appetites, so we said goodbye and went our separate ways—Greg back to work and me back to my amorphous existence. I'd quit my job as the head chef at Scratch Kitchen because if we were going to blame my inability to get pregnant on my long hours, then I couldn't work there anymore. "You can start your own business!" Greg had suggested, as if running a business was less stressful. "That way you can take as much time off as you want when the baby comes!"

"When the baby comes" became our daily refrain. "We'll get a new car *when the baby comes*." "We'll turn the garage into a home gym *when the baby comes*." "We'll make new friends, join a book club, learn how to play bridge, get a housekeeper, fall in love all over again *when the baby* comes." Life would begin anew. Our grievances would melt away. We'd be revitalized, reborn, catapulted into domestic bliss. *When the baby comes.*

There was no contingency life if the baby didn't come. Worse, we'd committed the cardinal sin of telling everybody we were trying. We solicited baby names. "What do you think of Logan?" I asked my yoga friends. "For a boy or a girl?" they asked. "Both!" "Love it!" We bought used baby furniture from our friends who were already done—a crib from Suzy and Mike, a high chair from Jeannie and Dave, a light-up mobile of the solar system from the neighborhood garage sale. I took prenatal vitamins and left the bottle out for all to see, let my natural honey-blond hair grow in because I would not be going anywhere near a bottle of bleach when I was pregnant! We'd set the table for a meal that might never arrive as everybody watched and cheered us on.

My phone rang as I pulled out of the parking lot at Dr. Chen's office. It was half past eleven. If I hurried, I could still make it to my lunchtime yoga class. Then maybe I'd try to scare up some work. It might seem strange that someone with an eating disorder would become a chef, but it also makes perfect sense. During those times when I didn't feel safe eating food, chopping, sautéing, deep-frying, and baking scratched the itch I couldn't scratch by putting it in my mouth. Over the last ten years, I'd worked my way up from lowly line cook to creating menus for LA's most finicky clientele. But now, besides the occasional catering gig—a graduation dinner, a fiftieth birthday party, a book launch—my schedule was as barren as my womb. I tried to stay positive (thus, the yoga), but the despair I was swimming in was as thick as pea soup. I'd given up a job I loved to make a baby. A baby that might never come.

"Hello?" I said into the phone as I flipped it open and squinted into the sunny midday sky.

"The Salvation Army is on their way to pick up your father's office furniture," my mom said without a "hello" or "how are you?" as was her custom. "They'll be here between three and six." I was the one who had suggested Mom give Dad's desk to charity when she announced she didn't want it in the house anymore, but I hadn't known she had already arranged for pickup.

"Did you empty it?" I asked, because I couldn't imagine her doing that without telling me what a pain it was.

"No."

"Well, don't you think you should?"

Silence.

"Hello?"

"I don't have the energy," she said, which was unsubtle code for "I need you do it." I pulled into the center lane to make a U-turn.

"Do you have any boxes?"

"Why would I have boxes?" It was a fair question. Dad was dead, not moving out.

"I'll be there in forty-five minutes," I said, factoring in a ten-minute stop at Office Depot. I understood why Mom didn't want to go through Dad's desk drawers. His death was still fresh, seeing his name on all those old bills would be a stinging reminder that he was no longer around to pay them. There would be a bunch of other stuff, too—contracts, property deeds, tax returns. How would she know what to keep, what to shred, and what she could throw away? It was overwhelming for her, I reasoned. Her grief-stricken brain couldn't handle it.

As I turned into the Office Depot parking lot, I dismissed the thought that maybe Mom's reluctance to open those desk drawers had nothing to do with being overwhelmed and everything to do with what she knew was in them.

CHAPTER 8
JANE

I had a key to my mother's front door, but my arms were full of Bankers Boxes, so I rang the bell.

"Thank you for coming," Mom said, like I was some sort of hired hand. Her platinum hair was curled under in a smooth bob, and she wore pink lipstick to match her blouse.

"You look pretty, Mom," I said as I stepped into her foyer and set the boxes on the floor.

"Let's not get carried away."

She turned around before I could hug her. I didn't take it personally. Dad had always been the hugger, I never needed or expected hugs from Mom. "Don't ask her for something she can't give," Greg once wisely said. "And you won't be disappointed."

I had called my mother every day since Dad's posthumous birthday, but she always had an excuse why I shouldn't come over. "The neighbors are here," "I'm too tired for company," "I have a hair appointment," "I want to be alone." I could have insisted on seeing her—she wasn't the only one who'd lost someone—but I'd needed to get my head straight for the appointment with Dr. Chen, and spending time with my mom tended to have the opposite effect, even under the best of circumstances.

Losing a parent is largely inevitable, but when it happens, it's as incongruous as losing a piece of the sky. Something that's always been there suddenly isn't. It's like looking in the mirror to discover there's no one looking back. I'd be doing a mundane task—chopping vegetables, folding laundry—and the thought would hit me like a rock smacking my windshield: *I don't have a dad.* Unlike a car or a home, you never get another one. The finality of it is terrifying. Maybe because it signals you're one step closer to death yourself.

"Did you eat lunch?" I asked, heading for the kitchen. I'd only had coffee and a piece of toast and wanted to eat something before I tackled Dad's office.

"Why would I have eaten lunch? It's not even twelve o'clock yet."

"It's twelve thirty," I corrected her.

She squinted at her watch. "I don't know why I wear this thing, I haven't been able to see it since you were in diapers." That was an exaggeration. She did need glasses, but not until recently. I'd bought her some drugstore readers, but she thought they made her look like "that old bat from *The Golden Girls*," so they sat in a drawer while the small print, and her watch, went unread.

"I'm hungry, mind if I make us something?" I asked.

"Don't do it for me."

I knew from therapy that mother-daughter relationships can be tricky, and I'd stopped beating myself up over my role in souring ours a long time ago. Unlike reliable, responsible Kenny, I was not an easy teenager. I imagined Mom was as upset at me for injecting drama into our family as I was at her for not knowing how to deal with it.

People are surprised when I tell them I was the one who realized I needed help, because it was obvious to anyone who was paying attention. My friends told me I was "so skinny," but all I saw when I looked in the mirror was fat. Then one day I was at a bus stop and caught my reflection in a store window. I remember thinking, *My God, that girl looks like one of those starving kids from* National Geographic. And then I raised my arm to push my hair behind my ear and my repulsion turned to terror as the girl in the reflection did the same. That was the first time during those fraught months that I saw myself for what I'd become. And it scared the shit out of me.

I told my mom "I think I might have a problem" the moment I got home. I think her exact words were "You don't think you need a doctor, do you?" She and my dad saw it as a trivial thing that would blow over, like thumb-sucking or fear of the dark. Kenny once asked me "Why are you doing this to us?" like I could turn it on and off. Everyone understands how being sick can make you depressed but forgets that the reverse is also true.

My therapist was two bus stops from my school, and I went every other Friday for six months. Jennifer had me write letters to my mom and dad to tell them how their "careless" words hurt me. I think it was supposed to embolden me to talk to them about it, but I never did. I don't know if those letters helped me work through my feelings or I just started eating because I was tired of writing them.

"I'll heat up some leftovers," I offered.

"I can't eat any more meat," she said as I scanned her freezer to discover she hadn't touched any of the food I'd made.

"Who brought this lasagna?" I asked, removing a rectangular tin from on top of one of mine. I had made Dad's favorites to honor his memory, momentarily forgetting that someone's memory can't eat your leftovers.

Mom shrugged. Her friends had been bringing food all week—casseroles, coffee cakes, fruit plates, cookies. There was no way she could eat it all, but that wasn't the point. Food is a language. A sheet cake says "Congratulations"; a sandwich says "Enjoy a fun outing"; beef stew says "It's OK to stay home." Food is also currency. Home cooking is worth more than restaurant made; restaurant made is worth more than store bought. Like all currency, food has a dark side. Once we discover its power, it can control us just as we can use it to control others. I know that sounds hyperbolic. I would have thought so, too, if I hadn't once fallen under its spell.

I was thirteen and in love with Klondike bars and Kraft mac and cheese when my dad started calling me "Porky." He said it with a little laugh, like having a pig for a daughter was funny. No one ever told him to stop—he was the dad, and dads got to say whatever they wanted. "If you keep eating like that, you're going to get fat," he'd admonished when he caught me with a spoonful of ice cream in my mouth, even though it was summer, and isn't that what summer is for?

I remember the moment I decided to stop eating. We were on vacation in Cape Cod with another family. The Refsnyders had two daughters who were both dancers. Rachel, the older daughter, was my age, and had bald spots on the sides of her head from pulling her hair into too-tight ballet buns. Her little sister, Sarah, was skinny like a pencil. I was getting into the boat for a ride across the bay when my dad remarked, "Uh-oh! I hope Jane doesn't sink the boat!" Nobody laughed.

Rachel, Sarah, Kenny, and I were all wearing life preservers because that was the rule. Once we left the dock, the other minors took theirs off. It was a sunny day. I was wearing a bikini as all girls my age did. I wanted to work on my tan, but not enough to expose the spongy flesh on my stomach. As I looked over at my dad, with his dark hair curling around his chubby cheeks, an emotion I'd never felt before hit me like a lightning strike. Everybody assumed I'd kept my life preserver on because I was scared. But what I felt was not fear or even embarrassment. It was rage. I didn't know how to be angry at the person I idolized, so I turned all that hatred on myself.

"All she has to do is put food in her mouth!" my father would shout during our doctor-mandated family-therapy sessions. And he was not wrong. To not die of starvation, all I had to do was eat. Mom roasted chickens, grilled steak, sliced fruit, boiled spaghetti, baked bread, stir-fried vegetables. There was plenty of food in our house. But I couldn't bring myself to eat it. I wasn't trying to upset Dad. I was trying to make him love me. Because isn't that what he wanted? For me not to be fat?

The scale told me I was skinny—even skinnier than Rachel Refsnyder—but I couldn't see it. Sometime between that boat ride and the beginning of freshman year, I'd crossed the line between discipline and disease. I played little games with myself: *How long can I go without eating? Can I eat less today than I did yesterday?* I told myself if I didn't eat now, I could eat later. Not that I would, I just felt safer knowing that I *could*. I was on a hamster wheel of delayed gratification, running and running but never getting closer to a full stomach. For some insane reason, that felt safe. Even as it was killing me.

I set the lasagna on the counter and preheated the oven. "It's frozen solid," I warned my mother. "It will probably take an hour."

"That's fine. I have to wait for the Salvation Army pickup anyway."

"How are you doing, Mom?" I asked, noticing her cuticles that she had picked raw.

"It's quiet around here," she said, and my heart broke a little. Dad liked to have the TV on at all times, even if he wasn't watching it. Usually it was baseball. But if there was no baseball on, it was news. He wasn't a political guy; I don't think he listened to what the talking heads were saying. Mom used to quip that if you knew what was rattling around in Dad's head, you'd be terrified of silence too.

"I'll get started while the lasagna cooks," I offered. The oven wasn't hot yet, but it was a frozen brick of noodles, I couldn't really ruin it.

I popped the lasagna in the oven, then started toward the office. But before I took two steps, Mom grabbed my arm.

"I don't need to know what you find," she said, holding my elbow like she did when I was five and needed a talking-to. "Use your best judgment."

I didn't understand the request, but I nodded, then walked out of the kitchen and through Dad's office door.

My dad always had his own room. Besides his big oak desk with twin, built-in filing cabinets, Dad had furnished his "office" with a couch, a TV, and, as I'd accidentally discovered during a childhood game of hide-and-go-seek, a chest of dirty magazines. I thought that's what my mom was worried I'd unearth. Until I opened the bottom-right desk drawer.

My parents had fought as I assumed all parents do. My dad made the money, so naturally he had opinions about how it should be spent. The problem was, he was gone a lot. With Dad out of town, Mom was left to manage the house. She bought the groceries, paid the mortgage, electricity bill, gas, water, car insurance. She paid for haircuts, braces, new sneakers, piano lessons for me, club baseball for Kenny. It cost a lot to run our family, and it stressed Dad out. "You're spending too much money!" he'd yell at her from behind their closed bedroom door. "Raising kids is expensive!" she would clap back. She must have won the argument, because Kenny and I wanted for nothing growing up. Which I always thought was because of my dad, but I should have known better.

Not all "Dad's" money went toward us kids. He had an airplane—a single-engine four-seater, which he kept at the private airport in Bedford, a Boston-area suburb five miles from our home in Lexington. He loved that plane like a moth loves a flame. The walls of his office were covered with pictures of the cockpit. The call sign ("November" 201 "Yankee" "Lima") was his email password. I don't know how much it cost to own a plane, only that it was a lot more than Mom spent on orthodontics. Mom used to joke that that airplane was his other wife. And then one day she stopped making that joke.

The letters were still in their original envelopes, so they made the file folder bulge at the bottom. If they weren't so eye popping, I might have just shoved them in a box to sort through later. But their rainbow-colored envelopes intrigued me—pastels in springtime, green at Christmas, red on Valentine's Day. Some of the postmarks were faded or blurry, but the eighteen- and twenty-cent stamps told me they were all from when I was growing up.

As I counted ten, twenty, thirty, thirty-three—there were thirty-three of them!—my heart thumped in my chest. Not with curiosity. I knew what they were.

CHAPTER 9
JANE

"Who are all those letters from?" Greg asked when he came home and saw them spread out on our dining room table. I couldn't tell my husband that everything I'd told him about my upbringing was a lie—he was already critical of my family—so I just bit my lip.

"Jane, are you OK?"

I don't know when I'd started crying. Maybe I'd been crying all afternoon. The drive home from my mom's was a blur. And some of the envelopes had pruney tearstains on them that must have come from me.

"Jane, talk to me." My heart was beating so hard it made my eardrums throb. The rock I'd been standing on my whole life had just turned to dust. I used to be a normal girl from a normal family. Now I didn't know what I was.

"Jane?"

"I found them in my dad's office."

"So . . . they were your dad's?"

Tears blurred my vision. Greg put a gentle hand on my shoulder but kept a safe distance from the letters, like he was Superman and they were kryptonite.

"Does your mom know?"

"Know what? That my dad had a girlfriend? I have no idea." That last part wasn't true. Mom's cryptic request—"Use your best judgment"—indicated that if she didn't know, she suspected. As to why she would send me into the lion's den without warning me about the lion, I guess it didn't occur to her that discovering Dad had another life on the side would rip my heart open too.

I don't know how I'd sat across from Mom eating that watery lasagna in silence while those letters screamed at me from the other room. If I'd had a shred of good sense, I would have thrown them straight into the fireplace and set them ablaze. But morbid curiosity superseded self-preservation, and I snuck them out of the condo under a pile of old bank statements that I told her I was taking to shred, even though we both knew Dad had a shredder.

"Could they be from before your parents were married?" Greg asked.

"They're not." I held one up and pointed to the postmark: 1982. Mom and Dad got married in 1964 and stayed married until the day he died. There were at least nine years of letters, all from the same Boston-area address, starting in 1974, with the most recent one postmarked September 28, 1983.

"At least he'd had the good sense to get a PO box," I said, pointing to an address that I had never seen before.

"Are you sure they're not from a family member?"

I showed him the back of the envelope I was holding. There was a mouth-shaped stamp of lipstick where it was sealed, flanked by two little hearts drawn in red ink.

"Yikes."

I used to think fidelity was the defining characteristic of marriage. Because why get married if you still want to sleep around? But then my best friend from college told me she had an open marriage, because, unbeknownst to the rest of us, "loving someone means never telling them 'You can't.'" I don't know if giving her husband permission to screw around was a sign of low self-esteem ("I know I'm not enough") or maximum self-esteem ("No matter who he screws, he'll always come back to me"), just that I didn't keep a lover on the side, and I didn't want my husband to either.

I'd never cheated on Greg, not in the way that society defines cheating. Sure, sometimes I fantasized about making out with that hot guy from yoga and what those muscular, tattooed arms might feel like wrapped around my ribs. But I'd never acted on it! I had zero interest in getting physically or emotionally entangled with another man. One relationship was challenging enough.

I don't know if Greg ever cheated on me. I told him if he did, I didn't want to know. "Don't unload your guilt by confessing to me," I told him after we found out good friends of ours were divorcing because of an infidelity. I never bought into the refrain that the disrespected partner "has a right" to know. A confession is for the confessor. Ignorance may not be bliss, but being in the dark is better than stumbling around in the haze of mistrust. People make mistakes, succumb to temptation, do self-destructive things. Every former addict knows that. Could I forgive my husband if he cheated? Probably. But I'd prefer not to have to.

"This doesn't change the fact that your father loved you," Greg said, and I almost laughed.

"It changes everything, Greg." I looked down at the kaleidoscope of communications from my dead father's lover. A sob caught in my throat. It would have been one thing to find this out when my dad was alive and I could demand an explanation. But all I had were my memories—corrupted memories now.

"I can't read them," I blurted through my tears. My father was not a perfect person. He was critical, sometimes bordering on cruel. But I couldn't hate him for holding me to a high standard, because I'd always thought he'd held himself to one too.

"Then don't."

I shook my head. Because we both knew I wouldn't have taken those thirty-three letters if I wasn't going to read every single one.

December 10, 1981

Dear Richie,

I know this is a hard time of year for you, with Thanksgiving and Christmas and all the family stuff you have to do, I just wanted you to know I'm fine, and not to worry. Going to Florida in January will be perfect. Since I'm working through the holidays, my boss said he'll give me a little extra time off, so we don't have to hurry back.

I know how hard it is for you to juggle everything. I don't ever want to be a source of stress. I only want to make your life more fun. Never forget that!

If you can drop a line, it would make my day. And of course if you can sneak out for an evening I'll drop everything. I miss you!

I look forward to the day when we can be together always. You are worth waiting for times a hundred.

Can't wait to hold you in my arms again . . .

Love,

Me

CHAPTER 10
ADAM

Days until training camp: 98

"A bunch of us are getting together after school to study for the AP World History test tomorrow," Matty Carlson said when we saw each other at our lockers. "If you want to come?" I had never been invited to a study group before—leaving after fifth period to go to tennis had made it impossible to do anything after school, and nobody expected football players to study during season.

"Sure, thanks." I tried to sound nonchalant, but yeah, I was pumped. Matty was the quarterback, and contrary to the cliché about QBs being dicks, he was the nicest, most unpretentious guy in our class. I never cared about being popular when I played tennis, but now that I was ordinary, being popular was all I had left.

"Great! Meet us on the quad right after sixth period. It's like a fifteen-minute walk to my house, less than a mile." I knew he'd added the "less than a mile" part so I wouldn't be put off by having to walk, but being around him made me feel lighter than air, I could have walked to the moon.

"Cool. Yeah, I'll be there." As per the other cliché about quarterbacks, Matty was tall and looked like he belonged in a toothpaste add, dimpled with dazzlingly straight white teeth. He was that rare person who made you feel good to be alive, even on your dark days—a squeeze of lemony sunshine on a cloudy day. We'd bonded during football season over our shared obsession with *Edward Scissorhands* and *Buffy the Vampire Slayer*, and spent many a bus ride arguing over who could kick the other's ass. I was team Buffy, even though I arguably had more in common with the guy with weapons for hands.

"I'm going to a study group," I told my mom when she pulled up in front of school to pick me up. "I'll call you later." I didn't wait to see if she was pleased or disappointed that she'd come to get me and I wasn't going with her. I didn't think Matty would leave without me, but I didn't want to keep him waiting.

I looped my thumbs under the straps of my backpack and pulled it to my body as I took off running toward the quad. I knew it wasn't cool to look so eager, but I had no experience looking cool without a racket in my hand. It was maddening to discover how much tennis had stolen from me—hangouts, parties, laughter, flirting . . . basically everything you're supposed to do in high school. Tennis was like this impenetrable bubble—I didn't even know what lit me up until I broke it. I hated seeing the disappointment on my dad's face every time he looked at me these days, but just because he adopted me didn't mean I owed him my whole childhood . . . *did it?*

I pushed the thought away as I jogged across the grassy courtyard. Matty was standing by a big oak tree in the shade. He waved me over with two arms like he was flagging down the coast guard.

"Hey," he said as I joined him under the tree. If he noticed I was winded, he was too kind to say so.

"Sorry to keep you waiting," I huffed, even though I was the first person there. There were eighteen kids in our AP World History class. A third of them didn't need to study, another third needed to but wouldn't. That left half a dozen candidates to join the group.

"Everyone else bailed," Matty said before I could ask how many of those half dozen were coming.

"Oh." I didn't mean to sound incredulous, but I couldn't imagine anyone bailing on Matty. Matty was oxygen, the thing that saved you from being suffocated by the dullness of everyday life.

I was about to head back into school to call my mom to come back, but then he said, "I still need to study. I mean, if you want to?" My pulse quickened. *Is he inviting me over? Just me? By myself?*

"I need to study too," I said with a little shrug, like it was no big deal.

"Great!" His face erupted in a smile, which made me smile too. "My house is just on the other side of the parkway."

As we walked across campus, Matty asked me what I thought of the class, and I told him I liked it but there was way too much reading. "I don't know how they think we can learn the history of the whole freakin' world in one semester," he said. "I mean, it's the world!" He had a good sense of humor, and talking to him was easy. Until the subject turned to football.

"Are you coming to camp this summer?" he asked.

Matty had never seen me play tennis. He didn't know I had the potential to be more than the human caboose that kept him from being tackled.

"I don't know yet," I said, because he'd invited me to study not spill my guts.

"You're good enough, you could miss and you'll still start." He meant it as a compliment, but I heard the quiet part. ("Any dumb lug could be a lineman.") You didn't need training camp to learn to stand there like a dump truck. But you sure as hell needed it if you wanted to be a skill player. As the name implied, that took skill.

"I want to go," I said, the "but" dangling like a loose thread. I wasn't trying to bait him. Telling him I wanted to be a receiver meant telling him I was trying to lose weight. And then I'd actually have to lose the weight or risk wearing my failure across my chest like a flashing neon sign.

"Well, hopefully you can make it then," he said brightly. "Would be fun to have you there."

We walked in silence for a bit. I could feel the armpits of my T-shirt getting droopy with sweat. When I was in tennis shape, walking a mile was as easy as walking from the service line to the net. But now, even in good shoes, my flat feet screamed with pain. *You are not your body,* I told myself, echoing the diet books while trying to ignore the sensation of my loose flesh bouncing against my body. *All you need to lose weight is the will to change.*

If only it were that simple. I had will up the wazoo. There was nothing I wanted more than to not be fat. But there was some invisible force inside me that grabbed my determination by the throat and strangled the life out of it. Sandy told me to focus on "small, makeable goals." "One good day will become two good days will become ten!" she'd said. Thinking small must have been the new thinking big, because Coach Fitz said the same thing about football. "One play at a time," he would preach. "Concentrate, execute, repeat. That's how you win games." But executing one play is easy; making five, ten, a hundred in a row—only champions do that.

"This is my street," Matty said as we reached the intersection of Brattle and Fresh Pond Parkway. "Just two more blocks." It had been a good eating day so far, and I silently begged myself not to blow it. If Matty offered me food, of course I'd say no. I never ate in front of people. The hard part was keeping my mouth shut when no one was watching. "Visualize how good it will feel when you reach your goal," the diet books said. "Not just in your mind, in your whole body."

I knew how to do this from tennis. My coach had me visualize before every match, from the kick of my opening serve to the pop of my winning volley. As I stood next to Matty, waiting for the light to turn, I looked down at his hands. I imagined them fanned out like palm fronds behind the center's rear end. I gripped the insides of my shoes with my toes and imagined my cleats sinking into the earth. A car horn became the shriek of the whistle. Truck tires thumping across asphalt was the crash of bodies at the line. As we stepped off the curb, I visualized my lean body springing forward like a rock from a slingshot.

A bird flying overhead was the ball, sailing toward me. *Fwap!* I reached up and caught it! The end zone was fifteen, ten, five yards away . . . and then—*Touchdown!* I was light as meringue pie as my teammates hoisted me in the air.

"Adam?"

Matty's voice snapped me back to reality.

"This way," he said, beckoning me to follow him.

He waited for me to catch up. As we walked side by side, I wished I could bottle that fake feeling and drink from it until it was real. Those letters from my birth mom were still in the cigar box. I wanted to know she had a good reason for giving me up, but what if she didn't? What if she gave me up the minute she saw me? Or worse, took me home, then once she got to know me a little, decided she didn't like me? What if I ruined her marriage, her chance at college, her career as a prima ballerina? Did I really want to know that? Was there anything in those letters that could make me feel better?

"This is my house," Matty said, opening the gate to a prissy brick colonial. The front path was flanked by spiny white roses that bit my arm as I passed.

"Hi, Mom," Matty said to the athletic, forty-something woman drinking a Diet Coke at their kitchen table. "This is my friend Adam. We're going to study in my room."

"Nice to meet you," his mom said. She stood up, and the resemblance between mother and son hit me like an ice-cold bucket of Gatorade. Same long neck. Same dimpled smile. Same narrow hips and rounded butt. I would never know sameness. My adoption was closed, which meant the identity of my birth parents was sealed. Even if I read those letters, I would still never know who my parents were.

"You boys want a snack?" she asked, looking at me.

"No, thank you," I said as rehearsed.

"Let me at least get you a glass of water, it's hot out there!"

As she padded to the sink on pigeon-toed feet just like her son's, I wondered what it would be like to look at my mother and see bits of me. Would I feel less alone in the world? Or was I just trying to blame my self-sabotage on someone else?

"Here you go," she said, handing each of us a glass.

"Thanks, Mom," Matty said.

"Yes, thank you," I echoed.

I took a big sip of water to show my appreciation and also so it wouldn't spill—she'd filled the glass all the way to the top—then followed Matty up the stairs to his room, which looked a lot like my room (bed, desk, dresser, clothes heap on the floor). The only notable difference was the life-size poster of *Baywatch* star Pamela Anderson on the inside of his open closet door.

He must have seen the horrified expression on my face because he kicked the door closed.

"Don't make fun of me."

"What?" I said dumbly. "She's hot."

He narrowed his eyes. My delivery was unconvincing, I could tell he didn't buy it. Sweat sprung from my pores like sprinklers going off. Pam Anderson, in that tiny red bathing suit that strained to contain her boobs, was every straight man's wet dream. *Did I just give myself away?*

I hadn't hoped he liked me back, not really. Getting my head around all these irresistible new feelings was challenging enough, I didn't want to have to act on them too. I paused to give him a chance to ask me to leave immediately. But he didn't. Just plopped down on his bed and pulled out his notebook.

"We can work from my study guide, I finished it last night," he said.

There was a sweatshirt draped over the back of his desk chair. I tossed it on the clothes heap so I could sit because I didn't dare join him on the bed.

Because what if he knew what I was?

CHAPTER 11
ADAM

The attack started as a tightness in my chest. I was sitting in class waiting for Mr. Greenleaf to hand out the blue books when a boa constrictor snuck up from behind me and coiled itself around my ribs. I couldn't speak. I couldn't breathe. And, even though I'd studied my ass off at Matty's the day before, there was no way I could take my AP World History test.

"Write legibly. If I can't read your writing, I can't give you credit for the answer." I couldn't tell if Mr. Greenleaf's voice was coming from across the room or the far side of the moon. My head was an ember from a campfire floating in droopy circles above my body. My lungs were filling with sand. The harder I tried to breathe, the tighter the boa constrictor squeezed. I didn't realize I was panting until Mr. Greenleaf was standing over me, making a sour-lemon face.

"Adam, are you all right?"

The room started to spin. I imagined a hundred Egg McMuffins lodged in the arteries between my heart and brain. *This is what a heart attack feels like,* I thought. And if the way I was eating these days had something to say about it, I was due.

"Adam?" Greenleaf's annoyance turned to concern.

"I . . . can't . . . breathe . . ."

"Melissa, go get the nurse!" Greenleaf barked. I heard a chair scrape the floor, sneakers on hard tile, the door open and close.

"What's wrong with him?" a girl asked.

"Should we call 9-1-1?" another girl asked.

"He's going to be OK," our teacher said as my vision became two tiny pinholes. Tears were leaking out the sides of my eyes. I was scared. I was embarrassed. I wanted to disappear into a puff of smoke.

"Adam, can you hear me?" Matty said, crouching down beside me. His hand was on my leg. Even in the face of death, I cringed at the sight of his fingers sinking into the spongy flesh above my knee.

"Mmm-hmmm," I managed.

"I'm going to stay with you until your mom gets here, OK?"

"Thanks," I squeaked.

"Everybody take out your books and study. We're still having the test."

There was a chorus of zippers unzipping. My eyes were glued to the wall clock. I calculated my breathing at one inhale per second. I felt like the Little Engine That Could huffing up the hill: *I think I can, I think I can* . . . I was grateful Mr. Greenleaf had given my classmates something to do besides sit there and stare at me, but wondered how they could concentrate over the sound of me gasping like a dying fish. As the second hand on the wall clock finished its third full circle, the classroom door opened, and Nurse Hennessey entered in a white coat as wrinkly as her forehead. She walked straight up to me, grabbed my wrist, and took my pulse.

"Hm," she grunted, unimpressed. "Do you think you can walk?"

I felt bad that I was cutting into my classmates' test-taking time, so I said, "Yes," and willed myself to make it be true.

Someone moved my desk—I think it was Matty? And then there were two sets of hands on me, easing me out of my chair.

"Are you OK to stand?" the nurse asked.

I didn't want to open my mouth and risk losing any of the oxygen I'd fought so hard to suck in, so I just sort of groaned. "Mmm-hmmm."

"I'm going with him," Matty announced without asking for permission, like the star quarterback he was.

Nurse Hennessey steered me toward the door, and I put one foot in front of the other in my best imitation of a normal person. Matty escorted me soldier-style toward the door, with one shoulder tucked under my armpit and an arm around my waist.

"I got ya," he soothed. Under different circumstances, I might have been pumped to be in the clutches of my crush, but all I could think about in that moment was how to stay upright without squashing him.

I made it to the door, which someone opened for me. Classes were in session, so the hallways were empty. Thankfully AP World History was on the first floor, so it was a straight shot to the main entrance with no stairs to navigate. Nurse Hennessey pushed opened the double doors to outside, and sunshine blasted my cold, clammy skin.

"Adam!"

My mom was waiting in the circular drive, her car still running, her eyes as wide as her luxury car tires.

"OK, easy does it," Matty said as he eased me into the front seat. I could hear Mom exchanging hushed words with the nurse: "hospital . . . just to be safe . . . going through a hard time . . ."

"Thank you, Matty," Mom said, half smiling at him, because the other half of that smile had been swallowed by embarrassment.

"Of course," he said, then to me, "Hang tough, I'll check on you later."

We drove straight to the hospital. My chest still felt like my ribs were cinched too tight, but I'd been able to slow my breathing a bit and keep my head attached to my body.

"Any history of heart disease in the family?" the admitting nurse asked when she checked me into the ER, and Mom's answer was the most dramatic part of this whole ordeal.

"We have no way of knowing."

They wheeled me into a little room and had me take off my shirt and lie down on a rickety gurney that I was sure would buckle under my weight.

"I'm going to put some stickers on you," a guy in scrubs said, then proceeded to adorn my chest, arms, and legs with little squares with wires coming out of them so they could do an ECG. When the test came back negative for any blockages, Mom nodded knowingly, as if the nurse had already told her this was a panic attack likely brought on by having to take a big, important test.

Hearing that there was nothing medically wrong with me was the best medicine, and the pain in my chest faded away like the ending of a seventies love song.

"Why don't you go upstairs and rest," Mom said when we got home.

"It wasn't because of the test, Mom," I said. And to my surprise she nodded.

"I know."

"There's stuff you don't know about me," I said, then bit my tongue, because nobody wishes for a gay child, and I didn't want to pile on.

"You can tell me anything, Adam. It wouldn't change how much I love you."

But I was already on shaky ground. So I didn't dare.

CHAPTER 12
ADAM

It was weird being home while everyone else was in school. Especially since there was nothing wrong with me . . . except everything.

I wasn't sick, but I still went to bed. Mom made me noodle soup, but I told her I wasn't hungry, and I couldn't tell if she was worried or relieved. Being hungry had not been a prerequisite for eating for many months. Was I depressed? Or making progress? If it helped me lose weight, I was fine either way.

That box of letters from my not-mom was sitting on my bookshelf between a gumball machine I made in woodshop and a potted plant my mom must have been watering, because I never did. I didn't know if having a panic attack in front of the whole class was rock bottom, but if it wasn't, I didn't want to know what came next.

As I lay there in a fetal position, staring at the wall, contemplating what a bad job our painter had done, Mom knocked on the door.

"Adam?"

I flopped onto my back to look at her.

"You have a visitor."

She opened the door wider, and Matty gave me a goofy Miss America wave.

I sat up in bed. "Matty! What are you doing here?"

"I came to check on you."

And I felt equal parts thrilled and mortified.

"Can I come in?"

"Yeah, of course," I said, pulling my shirt down to cover my belly. Mom hadn't bought me new clothes since my weight gain because that would have signaled she'd accepted it was here to stay. So I mostly just wore track pants that bisected my waist like string around a ham.

"The test was impossible," Matty said, tossing his backpack on the floor by my desk and then sinking into my chair. "I wrote down everything you need to know for the makeup."

He unzipped his backpack and pulled out a sheet of notebook paper with questions on it. "Explain how the transfer of crops and/ or domesticated animals during the Columbian exchange affected the environment, and one way it benefited the populations involved," he read. "I couldn't even remember what the Columbian exchange was, so I'm sure I got that one wrong."

He offered me the paper.

"The other three questions weren't as bad. I didn't write them down exactly, just what they're about, so you'll know what to study."

As I took the offering from his outstretched hand, shame rose up from the pit of my stomach. Matty deserved good-looking, popular friends who went to parties not the hospital.

"Why are you so nice to me?" I wasn't fishing for a compliment. Or hoping for a proclamation I knew he would never make. I asked because I couldn't think of a single reason why someone as amazing as Matty would be nice to someone as repulsive as me, and I genuinely wanted to know.

"What do you mean?" he asked as if he didn't know how kids, parents, teachers, even strangers, tsk-tsked when they heard the tub of marshmallow fluff walking among them used to be a somebody in the tennis world and now could barely make it up a flight of stairs.

"I'm adopted," I said to explain it all away—the weight gain, the panic attack, the epic fall from grace.

"OK," he said, low and uncertain, like he'd just stepped on thin ice.

"Those are letters from my birth mother." I pointed to the cigar box with the name "Romeo y Julieta" printed across the front in big block letters.

"What do they say?"

"I don't know. I'm afraid to read them." And before I knew I was asking for help, he walked over to the box and picked it up.

"Can I look?" he asked. I must have nodded because he flipped up the lid and peered inside.

"How many are there?" I asked.

His lips moved as he counted. "Eight."

"Are they open?"

"Yeah." He took one out and flexed it open. "Someone used a letter opener."

"My mom," I guessed, then clarified. "The one you met."

"Makes sense that she would want to read them first. Y'know, before she gave them to you."

I nodded slowly, processing the thought. She hadn't said how long ago she'd read them or how old they were. But also I hadn't asked.

"They can't say anything bad," Matty reasoned. "Otherwise she wouldn't have given them to you."

"She kept them hidden for sixteen years," I said, assuming they came with me from the hospital or arrived soon after.

"She could have kept them hidden forever," Matty countered.

"Is there a return address?" I asked.

"Nope."

"Who are they addressed to?"

"Banks and Murdoch LLP."

"A law firm?"

He shrugged. "It's on Boylston Street in Boston."

"So probably a law firm."

"Probably."

"And you said there's eight of them?"

He counted again.

"Yep." He flipped through the pile. "Looks like they're sorted in chronological order, first to last."

"Why do you think she wrote to me?"

"Because she cared about you."

"If she cared about me she wouldn't have given me to a law firm."

"You want me to read them first?"

"What, you mean right now?"

He nodded. I shook my head no.

"Then why don't we read them together?" he asked. I did not want to read these letters, from the woman who'd abandoned me, in front of Matty. But more than that, I did not want to read them alone.

"You want me to start at the beginning or the end?" he said, interpreting my nonanswer as consent.

My chest got tight. I reminded myself it was all in my head.

"Beginning."

September 28, 1983

Dear Richie,
I called your house today. Your daughter answered. I almost hung up, but I didn't want to spook her. She said you weren't home and didn't know when you were coming back. I didn't leave a message, don't worry!

I didn't want to put this in a letter, but there is something I need to tell you. Something happened since we last saw each other. Well, actually it happened during our time together, but I only just found out about it this week.

I have to see a doctor. I was hoping you'd come with me. This is not something I want to do by myself. I might not want to do it at all. I love you. And I can't help but think maybe it's a sign? That it's time to be together out in the open, like we talked about.

You deserve to be happy. You only get one chance at life, you should spend it with the person who brings you joy. Even if it's not the person you married.

If I don't hear back from you by the weekend I'm going to make the decision without you. Honestly, I can't see myself ending the life of a child conceived in love. What if he has your eyes? I'm not twenty anymore. This may be my only chance. I wouldn't be the first woman to do this on my own. But I'd rather do it with you.

I love you with all my heart, now and always.

Love,

Me

CHAPTER 13
JANE

When I was in high school, I had a crush on a boy named Jesse McBride. He was two years older than me, with spiky blond hair and a runner's body—long legs and a weightless stride. He played on the basketball team. So naturally I went to all the games. I made sure to cheer for all the players so he wouldn't know I liked him. One time, after he hit a three-pointer and I woo-hoo'ed extra loud, he looked up and smiled at me. I was so happy I nearly floated out of the bleachers.

That look spawned a journal full of fantasies. From our meet-cute at the water fountain: *"You go first." "No, you go first!"* (cue lips bumping as we both lean over) . . . to our first date at Baskin-Robbins: *"I tunnel out all the peanut butter too!"* . . . to me surprising him with (my dad's) tickets to the Celtics: *"We're season ticket holders, I'll take you whenever you want!"* . . . to being the only freshman at junior prom. I even picked out a dress. That's how far gone I was.

I've disassociated from my body to escape pain twice in my life. The first time was three weeks after that smile, when I walked into school to find out Jesse McBride had been killed in a car accident. I don't remember being taken to the nurse's office or what I did once I got there, only that my mom showed up in a leotard because she'd had

Jazzercize that morning. Just as I had no memory of what I did in the hours after I discovered I might have a half brother.

"How long have you been sitting here?" Greg asked when he got up and saw me at the dining room table in my clothes from the night before.

I didn't know, so I shrugged. Greg and I rarely went to bed at the same time anymore. Even when we were doing nightly conjugal visits, one of us would often get up to read or watch TV after. Sometime between deciding we were going to try for a baby and not making one, we'd gotten out of sync.

"Maybe you should go lie down." The letters were spread out on the table. After Greg had gone to bed, I'd read them in chronological order, tucking each one back in its corresponding envelope before moving on to the next. I read them all twice. Or maybe three times. Or more.

"My dad had another family," I said like I was informing him that I'd fed the dog or picked up the dry cleaning. Greg looked uncertain how he should react.

"Like, kids and everything?"

"Here," I said, picking up the last letter and then handing it to him. I watched his face as he read the words. *I called your house today. Your daughter answered. . . . I can't see myself ending the life of a child conceived in love . . .* I knew the whole thing by heart, like a poem you memorize for school.

"She spoke to you?"

"So she says."

"Do you remember? The date on the letter says . . ." He looked down. But I had already done the math.

"I was seventeen."

"So . . . a senior in high school?"

I nodded. 1983 was a deluge of catastrophes. It was the year I started eating again and my weight doubled; the year I got my period back and Mom made me go to Stop & Shop to buy my own sanitary products because "it's nothing to be embarrassed about"; the year our dog, Brutus, was diagnosed with lymphoma and we had to put him down. And apparently, it was the year I spoke to the woman who was pregnant with my dad's baby.

"I don't remember talking to her. People called the house for my dad all the time. He had a lot of friends."

"More than just friends," Greg remarked. And I had a sickening thought.

"You think there were others?"

"No! That's not what I meant. I was just . . . sorry, it was an insensitive remark. There's no evidence there were others."

"There was no evidence of this one until twelve hours ago," I pointed out. Was my dad a serial cheater? Or did he just have one serious girlfriend? And which was worse?

"Let's just focus on the one."

"The woman he was madly in love with, you mean?" I asked.

"Just because she was in love with him doesn't mean he loved her back."

The "which was worse" question reared its ugly head again. Devoted to another woman? Or just using her for sex? I wanted to believe my father stayed in a loveless marriage for the sake of the children—as in, for *my* sake. That he was a long-suffering character who met his true love after it was too late. Unhappy people say mean things. If he wasn't unhappy, then all those mean things he'd said really were about me.

"If he didn't love her, why would he carry on with her for so many years?" I asked, still fighting for my memory of him as a tragic figure.

"She obviously gave him something your mother couldn't."

"Yeah," I said. "An illegitimate child."

"We don't know she had the baby. He could have, y'know . . . talked her out of it."

Exhaustion descended on me like a curtain falling. I put my elbows on the table and pressed my forehead into my palms.

"Why don't you go upstairs to bed, try to sleep a little," Greg urged.

"There's a return address," I said, not getting up.

"Jane, these letters are from twenty years ago."

"Seventeen years. The last one was dated September 1983."

Greg exhaled. Something between a sigh and a huff. "So, what? You want to write to her?" he asked. I shook my head.

"No more letters."

His annoyance turned to alarm. "Jane, you can't just show up on her doorstep. What if she's angry? Or wants money? If your dad left her broke and pregnant, she may have an axe to grind."

"So I'm just supposed to pretend this child doesn't exist?" I asked.

"Or just let it go," he replied, and I almost laughed.

"That's easy for you to say, you have two brothers who love you. I have one who didn't even tell me he's having a baby." I knew why Kenny didn't want to tell me Cindy was pregnant, and also that having a third kid would make the chasm between us grow wider, because it's unkind to feast in front of someone who's famished.

"I know you're hurt," Greg offered, "but meeting this woman is not going to make that go away."

I shook my head. Yes, I was hurt that my father had stepped out on our family, but I could get over being hurt. What I couldn't get over was having the story of my life smashed to smithereens. Up until a few hours ago, I'd had a vivid picture of my family. It was sharp and full, imperfect but complete. But now it was as if someone had taken a hammer to it, and some of the pieces had fallen away. I needed those missing pieces. Not just to understand my father, but also to understand myself.

Frustration percolated through my veins. This woman was not part of my family, but what happened between her and my dad was still part of my story. Where was he during all those "business" trips? Who put the spring in his step? Who did he love? Why weren't we enough?

"I deserve to know the truth about my family," I said. "And so does that child."

Greg crouched down and spoke to me like I was a five-year-old who just fell and skinned her knee. "Jane, just because you're related by blood doesn't mean you're family."

"That's exactly what it means!" I shot back, like he was the bully who'd pushed me. "Two people who share a parent are siblings. By definition."

"Half siblings," he corrected me, like that didn't count.

"Half siblings are still siblings."

When Kenny got engaged to a divorcée with two kids, our mother was aghast. "Raising another man's kids is going to be so complicated," she'd warned. He just shrugged and said, "All families are complicated." And I just now understood why that shut my mother up.

Like my brother, I wasn't afraid of complicated. Quite the opposite. I was afraid of *un*complicated. Of my life forever being only about me. In my younger days, I enjoyed my untethered lifestyle—Sunday double features, barhopping on Abbot Kinney, jetting off to Catalina for a day or a week. But I wanted something three dimensional now, roots not scattered leaves.

"Kenny doesn't want me in his life," I reminded him. "If we never have a baby, that's the only family I'll ever have!" I was getting hysterical now. Greg was right. I needed sleep.

"Kenny loves you. I'm sure if you wanted to visit him and his kids he'd be thrilled to have you," Greg said, tacitly acknowledging that Kenny wouldn't come to me. And who could blame him? The stress I'd injected into his life when we were young was more than any teen should have to bear. If our situations had been reversed, I probably would have run away too.

"This is all really fresh," he continued. "Why don't you get some rest, give yourself time to process?"

I shook my head. This wasn't just about me. My father's duplicity cast a shadow over my life, but his illegitimate child—if he existed—lived in complete darkness. He deserved to know where he came from and that he mattered, at least to me.

"I don't need to process," I said, because I already knew my next move. "I need to find that child."

CHAPTER 14
JANE

"Janie!"

No one had called me Janie since I was in high school, but I still turned to look.

"Over here!"

The sidewalk outside Logan airport was swarming with people—it was spring break, and Boston was a college town. I could tell who was coming and who was going by the hue of their sunburns. Spring had sprung in New England, and the locals had shed their pasty winter sheens, but the ones coming back from Fort Lauderdale were red like a spanking.

"Jane!"

I scanned the crowd—frat boys from Northeastern, prepsters from Harvard, cheerleaders from BU. Same as it ever was.

"Jaaaaa-nie!"

I finally saw her. Samara was my best friend from high school. She was standing beside a kelly green Ford Explorer, one arm over her head like she was hailing a cab.

I waved back, then walked over to her, dragging my aging carry-on behind me.

"Ahhhh! It's really you!" Samara bellowed, opening her arms to smash me in a hug. She smelled like coconut and baby powder, and her thick black mane tickled my nose as I hugged her back.

"Sorry, I would have walked over to you, but I didn't want to risk jail," she said, then pointed toward the back seat, where an infant was snugged in a baby carrier.

"Oh!"

"Cal can only handle two, and just barely."

Of course I knew Samara had recently had a third, I had the birth announcement on my refrigerator. But seeing baby Emma up close like that still hurt like a bee sting. It was not jealousy, I didn't have those kinds of feelings toward Samara. No, it was sharper and deeper, more like failure.

"Sorry I couldn't come for your dad's memorial," Samara said, taking my hand and squeezing it.

"Don't apologize. I know you have your hands full." I hadn't told my mother why I was going to Boston, and she didn't ask. A good daughter would have felt bad for sneaking off so soon after her father's funeral, but my mother didn't look to me for comfort, and now that Dad's things had been cleared out, there was nothing more to do. The one thing I did feel guilty about was not telling Kenny. This half sibling, if we had one, was as much his as he was mine. If I was going to drop a match in our shared powder keg, I probably should have warned him.

"Here, I'll take that." Samara took my suitcase and tossed it into the back. Looking at her, it was hard to believe she'd had a baby a few short weeks ago. Her stomach was as flat as the "No Parking" sign over my shoulder, and her cheekbones were so chiseled they could slice cheese.

"It's open, get in!"

I stepped up on the running board and slid onto the camel-colored leather, where I was greeted by the smell of new car. With three kids, black would have been a more practical choice, but Samara was never one to put practicality over style.

"How was your flight?" my oldest friend asked as she got behind the wheel.

"It was fine. Uneventful." I spoke softly so I wouldn't wake the baby.

"Oh, you don't have to whisper. Once Emma is sleeping, you'd need a bullhorn to wake her. All babies are like that."

I felt my cheeks warm with embarrassment. "Right. Well, you would know," leaving the "and I wouldn't" unspoken.

She started the car and flicked on her turn signal. "How's that all going?" she asked without a trace of pity in her voice. "Move, you putz!" she shouted at a Nissan Maxima with out-of-state plates. Cars were coming from all directions, but she maneuvered around them like the Boston driver she was.

"So?" she asked again.

"Nothing to report, except we're working with a specialist now."

"Do they know what's wrong?"

"Not yet. We only just met with her. Greg's going to jack off into a cup."

"A third of the time it's the man," she said. And before I had a chance to ask how she knew that, she added, "You remember Missy Morgenstern? She was having problems too. Turns out Nick had a low sperm count."

"What did they do?"

"He had to have a whole bunch of tests—urinalysis, scrotal ultrasound, rectal probe."

"Fun times."

"He whined about it like a big baby. Turns out his sperm was swimming the wrong way. They did a surgery to reroute it."

"Nice to hear about the man having to do some heavy lifting for a change."

"Ha! Right?" Samara smiled, revealing her perfect, straight white teeth. "So unfair how we do all the work. Did I tell you? Cal fell asleep while I was pushing Emma out."

"Seriously?"

"Baby number three," she quipped. "The thrill was gone."

I felt that bee sting again. Everything came easily to Samara. She got all As in school. Was a state champion in track. Got into every college she applied to, including Harvard, so that's where she went. When I teased her about being a golden child, she got all serious and said it was karma for how her immigrant parents had suffered. I didn't believe in karma. If I did, I'd have no hope.

The road dipped down as we approached the Ted Williams Tunnel. Logan airport was surrounded by water on three sides, so unless you wanted to go to Revere (you didn't), the only way in or out was to go under it. I had mild claustrophobia, so it wasn't ideal. We didn't have tunnels in Southern California—we had earthquakes instead. Pick your poison, I guess?

Traffic was stop and go, but Samara was as happy to have a break from her kids as I was to have a break from trying to conceive one. Greg wasn't upset that I'd left but didn't like the reason. He thought I was confusing my desire for a baby with the need to find my dad's. I had no idea what my subconscious mind was doing, only that I couldn't ignore it.

As we descended into the inky darkness of the Ted, Samara and I chatted about her home renovation, my recent catering gigs, current events—nothing too weighty. She told me a former classmate of ours had become the mayor, while another one was in jail, and we laughed at how they canceled each other out in our alumni hall of fame. The conversation helped keep my claustrophobia at bay, but I breathed easier when we popped out of the tunnel in sunny Southie. We stayed on the expressway through downtown, then merged onto Storrow Drive. Bikers and joggers in spandex and Ray-Bans zoomed along the Charles River, which was peppered with sailboats and the occasional skiff.

We crossed the river at Harvard Street and continued through the square, past Cambridge Common and through another short tunnel. Three turns later, we were in a neighborhood flecked with stately single-family homes that looked straight out of last century. Samara's house was in the middle of a block inhabited by Harvard professors, a former ambassador, a Rockefeller. Samara's husband came from old money, and he made sure their choice of real estate reflected his aristocratic roots.

"The house looks great," I said as we pulled into the driveway of her boxy brick colonial. Samara's yard was in full bloom—pink camellias, tangerine-colored roses, fragrant rosemary bursting with tiny purple flowers. Every time I came back to Massachusetts, I was struck by how green the landscape was compared to the balding, brown hills of California.

"We had an early thaw this year," Samara said. "The garden is going nuts!"

She pulled into the detached garage, then popped open the trunk.

"I gotta grab Emma, can you take your suitcase?"

"Of course."

I extracted my bag and closed the hatch. Samara emerged with Emma, holding the baby carrier by the handle like an Easter basket.

"See? Still sleeping," she said with a told-you-so smile.

The back door led to a mudroom. There was a basket of shoes, so I took the hint and slipped mine off.

"Cal! We're home!" she shouted. Then to me, "Come into the kitchen. I'll make you some tea, and you can tell us why you're here."

CHAPTER 15
JANE

"You remember Auntie Jane," Samara said to her two school-age boys. It was more of a command than a question, and they both nodded. Samara's mudroom opened up to a giant cook's kitchen with two sinks—one on the island, one overlooking the backyard—a six-burner Viking range, and enough counter space to skin a pig. I knew Samara didn't cook, it was the one area where I might be able to earn my keep.

"Say hello," Samara instructed her sons as she set her daughter's car seat down on the gleaming, knotty pine floor.

"Hi, Auntie Jane," the older one said. He looked about eight. The younger one was a head shorter and missing his two front teeth, so maybe five or six? He didn't speak, but he did flash a forced, gummy smile.

"Hi, Brandon, hi, Henry," I said with a little wave. I hadn't seen them since they were toddlers; they were completely different children now, whereas I was painfully the same.

"Can we go back to our game now?" the eight-year-old asked.

"Go ahead," Samara said as she put the kettle on. The boys sprinted off, nearly knocking over an incoming Cal.

"Whoa, watch it!" Cal said, raising his hands in the air like a bank teller at a stickup. Samara's husband was blond and freckly with a dancer's good posture and a singsongy British accent. They were opposite in every way.

He came to the marriage with a pedigree and a trust fund. She came with immigrant grit and a chip on her shoulder. Yin to his yang. Together they were invincible. If I didn't love them so much, I would be terrified of them.

"Hi, Jane," Cal said in his non-dad voice. "You look wonderful."

"Thanks, Cal."

He took my hands in his and kissed me on both cheeks. "Sorry Greg couldn't make the trip. I would have liked to see him."

"Greg wasn't invited," Samara informed her husband. And Cal raised an eyebrow.

"Oh?"

"He had to work," I said to fend off any suspicion of marriage trouble.

"But that's not why he didn't come," Samara said. "Jane's here because she has a mystery to solve."

"What kind of mystery, pray tell?" Cal asked. Their curiosity was as palpable as their eyes were wide.

"You have anything stronger than tea?" I asked.

"I'm British," Cal reminded me. "If it can get you drunk, we have it."

"Wine?"

"Well, that's French, but we can accommodate," he said. "Red or white?"

"Red, please." He dipped into the pantry and extracted a bottle of pinot noir, then held it up for me to approve. "Perfect." As he twisted out the cork, I took the letters out of my suitcase—all thirty-three of them—and plopped them on the table.

Cal's eyebrows ticked up.

"I'll take a splash," Samara said as Cal poured the wine. She was breastfeeding, so joining in was only for show.

"To solving mysteries," Cal said, raising his glass, and we all clinked.

"What is all this, Jane?" Samara asked without taking a drink.

"Behold the evidence of forbidden love," I said, sweeping my hand across the letters.

"May I?" Samara asked, setting down her glass.

"Go for it."

Samara plucked a pastel pink envelope from the middle of the spread. Her eyebrows merged as she examined it. "Wait. Are all these addressed to your father?"

"Yep."

"And I'm guessing they're not from your mother?" Cal said.

"That is correct."

Emma stirred in her bucket, but Samara didn't take her eyes off me. "Jane, what's going on?"

"Turns out my father had a lover for nine years," I said. "Possibly longer. These are from her."

"She lived in Malden?" Samara asked, eyeing the return address.

"So it appears."

"Where's Malden?" Cal asked.

"Don't be a snob," his wife replied.

"I'm serious, where is it?"

"East of Medford."

"Where's Medford?"

"OK. Now you're being a jerk."

"I didn't know where Malden was either," I said. "But I'm going there tomorrow."

"You've spoken to her?"

"Not yet."

"But she knows you're coming."

"Not exactly."

"Jane?" I could hear the disapproval in her voice. But I hadn't flown all the way across the country to be talked out of it.

"I would have called," I explained, as if I didn't understand her objection, "but I couldn't get a phone number. She only ever put her initials, never her first or last name." I picked up an envelope. "They all just say GM."

Baby Emma let out a little cry. Samara handed the pink envelope to Cal, then bent over and unbuckled her daughter.

"Let me make sure I understand," Cal said. "You intend to drive to Malden and knock on the door of a woman you think was having an affair with your father—"

"I have nine years' worth of letters," I said, because I didn't *think*, I knew.

"How old are these letters?" Samara asked as she picked up Emma and hugged her to her chest.

"The last one is from September 1983." I offered her the most recent one. The one that spurred this trip. But she didn't take it from my outstretched hand.

"That's two decades ago, Jane."

"Not quite."

"What exactly are you hoping to accomplish?" Cal asked. I could tell by the looks on their faces that they thought I was nuts. So I figured I'd seal the deal.

"I think she had a child with my father," I said. "And I want to meet him."

All the air went out of the room. Even baby Emma went silent.

"Jane," Samara said, like she was telling her kids that they just did something very dangerous. "That child, if your father's lover had one, has a life now. A life that he, or she, may not want disrupted."

Cal was pressing his lips together so tightly they'd turned white.

"Are you saying I should just pretend he doesn't exist?"

"No. I'm saying you can't assume that, just because you want to meet this person, they are going to want to meet you." I knew she was trying to protect me from getting hurt—and perhaps the kid too. She was a mother, after all.

"What was your impetus for wanting to make a connection?" Cal asked. Cal was short for Calvin, which was also his father's name. I tried not to take offense that Cal Jr. would question why someone would want to know who their father was, but I didn't answer right away either.

"Do you think the grief you're feeling might be a factor?" Samara prompted, in a not-so-subtle suggestion that I might not be thinking straight.

"My *impetus* was learning this child existed after my father—excuse me, I mean, *our* father—tried to pretend that he didn't." I knew in their hearts they were on my side, but I could feel myself getting defensive.

"I don't mean to be insensitive to what you're feeling," Cal said, "but he—or she—may have a new father now."

"He," I clarified. "The letters imply that it was a boy."

"The point is, you don't know what you'll be walking into."

"What if he doesn't know his biological father rejected him," Samara asked. "You don't know what he was told."

I'd thought about that. It was also possible that my father's illegitimate son knew all about us and was deliberately staying away. In which case our meeting would be over quick.

"I'm not going to force myself into this boy's life," I said. "But now that I know about him, I can't pretend he doesn't exist. He's part of my family."

"We're not saying you don't have the right to try to connect with him," Samara said. "We're just asking you to consider if it's in everyone's best interest."

Greg had raised the same concern. Would I be a life preserver in a storm? Or a grenade?

All I had to go on were my instincts, and my instincts told me there was a boy out there who needed to meet me as much as I needed to meet him. What I was doing, I was doing for love—a love so pure and deep it overpowered all doubt.

"I understand the risks," I assured my friends. "I'll tread carefully."

CHAPTER 16
JANE

I woke at seven a.m. (four a.m. California time) to the sound of kids getting ready for school. My room—originally a maid's quarters, now a plush guest suite—was right above the kitchen. Plates clapped on counters, backpack zippers zinged, parents sang songs of "let's go," "eat your breakfast," "hurry up." You might think the sounds of a happy family would have made me sad for the one I didn't have, but the opposite was true. It gave me hope, because if it happened for other people, it could happen for me.

I didn't want to interrupt the intricate morning dance, so I stayed in bed until the commotion passed. The sound of the back door slamming and a car engine turning over told me the coast was clear, so I slipped out of bed, made a quick pit stop in my en suite bathroom, then padded down the narrow, twisting staircase to the kitchen. There was a grand staircase in the front of the house, but this one was the most direct route to the coffee, which I could smell and sorely needed.

"Morning," Cal said when I appeared in his kitchen in my sweats and bedhead. For some reason I thought he would have been the one to take the kids to school. I must have gasped, because his next words were "Sorry, I didn't mean to startle you."

"Sorry, no, it's early for me. I think I'm still half asleep."

"You need coffee?"

"Desperately."

He put down his *New York Times* and pushed back his chair.

"Cups are here," he said, opening the cabinet above the coffee machine. "Do you take cream and sugar?"

"Just cream."

He retrieved the cream while I chose a mug. No two were the same. Some had silly slogans on them ("I hate Mondays," "Hang in there," "But first, coffee"). Some were gigantic. Some were dainty and meant for tea. I chose a turquoise one with a kangaroo on it that said "G'day, mate!" because it had a big handle you could slip your whole hand through, and I didn't trust mine not to shake.

"I'll let you do it," he said, putting the cream on the counter. As he slid a spoon toward me, I wondered if Samara had told him how I once counted my Cheerios (no more than fifty), then used a tablespoon to measure out the milk (ten spoons exactly). Was that why he didn't want to put the cream in my coffee? Hopefully she told him I don't do that anymore.

"Cheers," Cal said, raising his cup when I sat down across from him. I had no idea what my best friend's husband knew about me. Had Samara told him I'd missed our high school graduation? Not just graduation, the prom and the last ten weeks of school too? Last night, after I went to my bedroom and they to theirs, did they ask each other why someone who'd buried a painful past was so determined to unearth somebody else's?

There was a collage on the wall behind Cal's head—photos of the kids through the years, mashed together in a kaleidoscope of love and joy.

"The boys are so gorgeous," I said, devouring the images.

"Like their mother," he agreed. "What a relief they don't take after me."

"They got the best of both."

"My good luck, her everything else."

People used to say how much like my father I was. I'd always felt a tingle of pride. I'd thought they meant outgoing, optimistic, and fun. Because how could they know we also had selfishness in common? At least according to my husband, who thought this mission of mine was all about what I wanted, quite possibly at the expense of everybody else.

I heard the sound of a car pulling into the driveway. Samara walked through the door a minute later, carrying a pallet of fresh strawberries.

"Whoa," Cal said, getting up to take them from her. "That's a lot of strawberries."

"They were selling them out of the back of a truck; hopefully they aren't laced with LSD."

"I can make an angel food cake when I get back," I offered. "To go with the strawberries."

"Yes!" Samara said, and I knew her enthusiasm was about the cake, not my outing. After a breakfast of poached eggs (prepared by me), they both wished me luck, and I got on the road.

Samara and Cal had a third car—an older Toyota Camry. They called it "the nanny's car," but Samara insisted the nanny didn't need it. I was glad it wasn't too new or fancy. If my dad was cheap with his girlfriend, I didn't want her to think I was rolling in dough. Not that I owed her anything. I wasn't the one who'd slept with a married man.

It was a warm day, and I drove with the windows open even though humidity was terrorizing my hair. I'd stopped coloring it, so it was a bit two-toned—honey-blond at the root, platinum at the tips. I tried to negate the trashy vibe by keeping my makeup simple—a sweep of mascara, a dot of blush, ChapStick instead of gloss. I didn't expect my father's lover to be happy to see me, but I didn't want her to be repulsed.

As for how I felt about her, that was complicated. I had no idea what promises my father had made to his girlfriend of nine years. Maybe he told her he was leaving my mom, or that they had an understanding. My parents had gotten married in the sixties. Marriages were more elastic back then. He could have told her his wife was on board with it or had a boyfriend of her own. My dad was lying to us, I had every reason to believe he was lying to his girlfriend too.

And that was the most upsetting part of this. No matter how you sliced it, Richie was the bad guy. GM and I might have reason to resent one another, but we also had something in common. We loved a man who broke our hearts. Had I known my candy-coated version of my father was a lie? Maybe, but I liked my selective memory. Finding those letters was like a dam breaking. The painful bits that were flooding back were the foul-smelling detritus scraped from the ocean floor, destroying the landscape of his legacy.

I crossed the Mystic River in Somerville, then merged onto Revere Beach Parkway. The trees thinned, and spacious single-family homes became tightly packed row houses. As I passed a pizza place, a gas station, a Dunkin' Donuts, I rehearsed what I'd planned to say. I'd lead with the news: *I'm Richie's daughter. I thought you should know he passed away.* I had her letters with me, to show her when she asked how I knew about her. I had no idea what would happen after that.

I pulled onto the street matching the return address on the envelopes. Fern Street was in a working-class neighborhood on the border of Malden and Everett. It was Monday. If she was a working woman, it was possible she wouldn't be home. Or didn't live here anymore, in which case everyone would be relieved.

I found 16C and pulled up right in front. It was a triplex, with three front doors off a small wooden porch. The slate blue paint looked fresh and inviting, and for a second I let myself believe I might even be welcome.

I got out of the car and locked the door. My heart was thumping in my ears, and I could feel the armpits of my T-shirt growing damp. I cursed myself for showing up empty handed, but then again, I was the one who'd lost someone. If anyone deserved a bouquet of carnations, it was me.

I stepped onto the front walk. The flesh-colored bricks were arranged in a herringbone pattern and bordered by neatly trimmed crabgrass. I'd dressed down, in my Lee jeans and Reeboks, figuring I should at least try to be physically comfortable.

The front-porch steps groaned as I climbed them—four to the top. A pair of bright-red geraniums in plastic pots hung from the rafters. 16A and 16B were on the right, so I turned left, past a small wooden bench and a hip-high pink flamingo. There was a rectangular mailbox bolted to the wall above the doorbell. Individual stickers spelled out the name "MCNALLY," and terror shot up my spine as I realized I might be in the right place.

The wooden front door had a window in it, but the pleated ivory curtain kept me from seeing inside.

I blotted the sweat that was beading on my brow with the back of my hand. I looked down at the flamingo. If I aborted my mission, no one would know but me and him. There were a million reasons not to do this. But I choked them down and rang the bell.

June 18, 1984

Dear Adam,
I told them not to let me hold you. Not because I didn't want to, but because I thought it might mess with my head.

It's been eleven days since they took you away from me. I didn't think I'd miss you, but I can't stop crying. The doctor said it was hormones, but he's never had a baby so what does he know?

I was in the hospital for two days but I think they took you after one, because I asked to see you and was told you were already gone. It's not that I changed my mind—I think you'll have a great life with your new parents. I just wanted to see you to know that you were OK.

I wasn't going to ask your name, it just kind of slipped out. Maybe no one told the nurse that it was a closed adoption, or maybe she thought it was no big deal, but now that I know it I can't stop thinking how you're not just a baby, you're a person. A person with a name and a future that has nothing to do with me.

Everywhere I look I see babies. I guess they've always been there, I just never noticed them. But now that's all I see.

Good God what have I done?

CHAPTER 17
ADAM

Days until training camp: 97

My parents invited Matty to stay for dinner, but he said he had to go. I'm not sure if it was because he didn't want to endure the awkward conversation or because we were having fish, but he left just as Mom was pulling the baked salmon out of the oven.

"Dinner's ready, Adam," Mom called from the kitchen.

"Be right there," I shouted back from the front hall.

Matty slung his backpack over his shoulder. "Thanks for the beta on the AP World test," I said, reaching for the door.

"What are friends for?" He flashed his star-quarterback smile, and I had to make a joke to disguise the rising butterflies.

"A real friend would have choked down fish dinner."

"Not a chance." I opened the door, and he stepped outside. "Good luck with your parents," he said, turning around to look at me. I never really had friends—never had time when I was playing tennis, and then I was too busy getting fat. So I didn't know if it was normal for friends to sit on the bed, knees practically touching, talking about their feelings. We never did that at football practice, and that was my only experience being around kids my age.

"Thanks, I'm gonna need it."

We stood there for an awkward second, him on the porch, me in the doorway, staring uncomfortably at each other. If this was a dumb rom-com, and I was cute like him, the audience might have been rooting for us to kiss.

"You got this," he said in his team-captain voice. Then instead of a pucker, he held out his fist for me to bump.

"See you tomorrow," he said, then turned around. As he strode down my front walk, I got nervous for another reason. I knew my parents loved me and wanted me to be happy. But telling them I needed something they couldn't give me might be too much, even for them.

I often wondered why my parents only wanted one kid. If I was such a blessing, why didn't they try to double their luck? We had a big house, and Dad made good money, they could have afforded to give me a little brother or sister. So why did they stop with me?

It was a lot of pressure being the only child. If I was a dud, they had no backup. I was their sun and their moon. My meltdown was not a passing storm; it was Armageddon. There was no one to take the family baton besides me. Like I said, a lot of pressure.

Matty waved as he got behind the wheel of his mom's station wagon. I was one of the few kids in my class who didn't drive. When everyone was taking driver's ed, I was retooling my serve or my unreliable inside-out forehand, and I didn't want to take it now with a bunch of tenth graders. I waved back, then shut the front door and joined my parents in the kitchen. Mom was setting a pitcher of lemon water on the table. Dad was already seated at his place with his napkin in his lap.

"Everything looks delicious," Dad said, grabbing the pitcher and then filling the water glasses. My parents were trying really hard to normalize food. We ate dinner together every night. Mom stuck to the nutritionist's guidelines—a lean protein, a vegetable, and a clear soup or salad—without making a fuss about it. Every morning she made me sandwiches that looked like everybody else's sandwiches, minus the mayonnaise and cheese. Yes, I got apple slices instead of Devil Dogs, but so did a lot of kids. She didn't nag me to eat a good breakfast, but kept the fridge stocked with fruit, three kinds of nonfat yogurt, and a bowl of prepeeled hard-boiled eggs.

Despite Mom's efforts, I couldn't stop self-sabotaging. Sandy thought I was secretly stuffing my face with junk food because I thought I was unlovable and was trying to give people a reason to reject me. If I kept gaining weight, she explained, I could let myself believe my real parents had dumped me because I was a big fatty. Fear of abandonment was apparently the number one cause of self-destructive behavior. I didn't know if learning why my birth parents left me at a law office would make me feel better, but I couldn't imagine feeling much worse.

"Thanks for making dinner, Mom," I said as if she hadn't done it every night since I was three. I imagined she enjoyed it more back then, when it wasn't so fraught.

"My pleasure."

I couldn't have asked for better parents. They were caring and kind and praised me constantly, even when I messed up. "That test / assignment / opponent was hard," they would say when I got a bad grade or lost a tennis match. "We're proud of you for challenging yourself." I saw how some parents tore into their kids when they fell on their faces. My parents never shamed me. Yet all I ever felt was shame. And no wonder. They wouldn't have bet the farm to turn me into a tennis star if they didn't want me to become one. And no one wants their only son to be gay. I was a disappointment on every front.

"I tried a new recipe," Mom said as she passed me a plate of zucchini. "I baked it in a separate dish so it wouldn't taste like fish."

I looked down at the zucchini spears. Mom had arranged them to look like little hands waving hello, then dusted them with paprika, garlic, and three kinds of peppercorns. I hated that having a mother who made me zucchini art wasn't enough. *Why hadn't someone told them to have a second kid?*

"I read the letters," I said, because I knew they were wondering, and the least I could do was be honest with them.

"I hope they weren't too upsetting," Mom said. And Dad pursed his lips like he was holding his breath.

"That last one . . . ," I started, but then my throat got tight. I felt bad for ruining dinner, but I knew Mom would have let me ruin a hundred dinners if it would help fix me.

"We didn't get them until you were several months old," Dad said. "So we didn't know she was, y'know . . ."

"Struggling with it," Mom said, as if they had a script and he'd forgotten his lines.

"It was a closed adoption," Dad said, even though I already knew that from her letters. "By her request."

"We never met her," Mom added. "We don't even know her name." I knew they were trying to fend off my burning question, but I asked it anyway.

"But doesn't the law firm know who she is?"

"They're not going to tell us, Adam. That was part of the deal."

"But they could relay a message, couldn't they?"

"What message?" Dad asked.

"That I want to meet her."

And there it was. The zucchini fans were starting to shrivel, but I couldn't imagine any of us wanting to eat them now.

"A closed adoption means there's no contact between the families," Dad said. "She's the one who wanted it that way."

"Yes, but if they got her letters to you, then we should be able to get a message back to her," I said like I'd just solved a difficult riddle.

"There's a reason she did it this way," Mom said. Her tone was gentle, like a doctor delivering a fatal diagnosis.

"We don't know her reasons," I insisted.

"Yes, we do," she said. And Dad delivered the final blow.

"She doesn't want to be found."

CHAPTER 18
ADAM

Banks and Murdoch LLP was one block from the Boylston Street T station in downtown Boston. I decided not to call first, because if they were going to say no, I wanted them to say it to my face. It's not that I didn't believe my parents when they said my birth mother didn't want to be found, but how could they know for sure?

I didn't tell anyone I was going, not even Matty, even though he was my alibi. I'd told my mom I was going to his house to study for the AP World test retake, which arguably is what I should have been doing. Everyone in the class failed it, so I hadn't missed anything except the opportunity to commiserate. I'd been a little nervous walking into class after my freak-out, but no one said anything mean. Maybe Matty told them not to? Or maybe they just didn't care enough about me to wonder what was wrong.

My last period of the day was PE. I wasn't on a team, so I had to take general PE with the drama geeks and band nerds. We played kickball. Mr. Drucker put me at first base so I didn't have to move, just stand there with my foot on the bag and wait for someone to throw me the ball. Of course that never happened in band-nerds-versus-drama-geeks kickball. We were so inept on defense, if a kicker made contact, it was an automatic home run.

We finished our game ten minutes before the bell. Drucker let us go early because we weren't athletes, so what did it matter? I had all my stuff, so left right from the field. I hoped having my school backpack with me wouldn't make me look like a stupid kid, but then again, maybe it would help me score sympathy points?

It was a mile from the field to the Harvard T stop. I walked along Memorial Drive, past the hospital, where for all I knew I'd been born. My amended birth certificate had fudged the details of my birth ("to protect the anonymity of the birth parents"). The original existed, but had been sealed by the court, and the only way to get it unsealed was to claim medical necessity. I didn't need a bone marrow transplant, and no judge was going to reunite me with my birth parents because of unsightly weight gain. Someone who knew when, where, and to whom he was born would never understand that feeling like an impostor in your own life is as serious a medical condition as needing a new liver. So there was no point going to court.

I bought two tokens at Harvard Station, then descended the stairs to wait for my train. The Red Line took me across the river to Park Street. I could have walked from there, but the trains were air-conditioned, and I didn't want to arrive all sweaty, so I switched to the Green Line to go one more stop. A little girl with braids tied with ribbons stared at me from the seat across the aisle. I gave her a three-fingered wave, and she buried her face in her mother's armpit. The mom pulled her close without looking up from her book, as if comforting your child was as natural as laughing at a joke.

The stink of the subway gave way to the aroma of gasoline and rotting leaves as I exited the T into lazy downtown. Boston didn't bustle like big cities do in the movies; there were no crowds to get lost in. I reminded myself that I came here to find myself, not lose myself—no chaos was required. The late-afternoon sun cast shadows on the sidewalk that were as long as my odds of success, but I trudged forward with stubborn determination. The letter I had stayed up too late to write was tucked in the outside pocket of my backpack, which I carried over one shoulder to keep my shirt from frothing with sweat.

Number 104 was across the street. I decided to cross at the light because I was already tempting fate; no need to push my luck further. The building was a four-story brownstone with no elevator. Banks and Murdoch was on the top floor. I took my letter out on the third-story landing to have it at the ready, but also to catch my breath. My chest felt tight. I reminded myself it was all in my head, and the tightness subsided.

Banks and Murdoch was now Banks, Murdoch, Goldstein, Reingold, Meyers, and Meyers—at least according to the nameplate next to the door. I wondered if the two Meyerses were related, and also why I cared, as I turned the stainless steel door handle and stepped inside the suite.

The waiting room was a cozy space with a big bay window overlooking the street. A receptionist sat at a wraparound mahogany desk with a computer monitor, keyboard, a bright-yellow coffee cup, and a phone with a dozen clear buttons on it. The bookcase to her right was lined with binders with names on the spines: J. Walton, S. Victor, L. Ezzo. I felt a jolt of excitement. *What if my mom is L. Ezzo and everything about her is right there?*

"Can I help you?" a gray-haired secretary in a Victorian-era blouse asked as I stepped onto the Oriental rug. Her mouth was smiling, but her eyebrows were suspicious.

"I hope so," I said, my confidence already in the toilet. "My mother was a client here. I need to get a note to her." I took a step forward and set my letter on the desk. The envelope was curling up at the sides like a canoe, so I used my palm to try and flatten it.

"There's no name on this envelope," the secretary observed without touching it.

"Yes, I know. I don't know her name. I was hoping you could fill that in. You handled my adoption."

The silver-haired gatekeeper looked up at me over her glasses. "How old are you, young man?"

I didn't know why it mattered, but I answered the question. "Sixteen." She took off her glasses and set them on the desk.

"Wait here."

She pressed a button on the wall, and the glass door to the inner chamber clicked unlocked. She stood up and walked through it, leaving me alone with all those binders. I had the sudden urge to riffle through them, even though I knew the super-secret stuff was probably behind that locked glass door.

I stayed standing as I waited. The phone rang twice, then stopped. I imagined my birth mother calling to say she'd changed her mind, please can she have her baby back? And the gray-haired lady—whose hair wasn't gray yet, because this was seventeen years ago—telling her, "I'm sorry, but a deal's a deal."

Click.

The glass door opened, and the gray-haired lady walked through, followed by another lady in a dark-blue skirt and blazer.

"Hello there," Blue Blazer said from the doorway. "I'm Cynthia Meyers, one of the partners here." She offered her hand, so I stepped forward and shook it. She looked young, thirty at the most. I wondered if the other Meyers was her husband or her dad, but I didn't ask.

"And you are?"

"Adam Michael Ross." For some reason, I thought I should state my full name, but after I said it, I felt ridiculous.

She opened the door all the way. "Why don't you come on back."

"Don't forget your letter," the receptionist said, waving it in the air.

I took my wilted letter from her outstretched hand, then followed Ms. Meyers down a short hallway into a stodgy-looking conference room.

"So, Adam. How can we help you today?" Cynthia Meyers, Esq., asked as she offered me a seat. The room looked more like a cigar lounge than a conference room, with dark-wood floors and heavy emerald curtains. Ms. Meyers, with her cheery, high ponytail and hoop earrings, looked as out of place as I felt.

"As I was explaining to your secretary, my mother was a client here."

"Your birth mother?"

"That's right."

She was still smiling, but she looked skeptical. "How do you know that?"

I was prepared for this. "Because she wrote to me." I opened my backpack and showed her the letters with their address on them. "She sent these to you, but they were meant for me."

I offered her the bundle, but she didn't take it.

"Do you know what a closed adoption is, Adam?"

I stifled the urge to punch her in the face. "I'm not asking you to tell me her identity. I just want you to forward this letter I wrote. Like you forwarded her letters to me."

I pulled the last letter she'd written out of the envelope—the one that started "Dear Adam . . ."

"She wrote to me, see? I just want to write back, that's all," repeating myself, but only because she was making me. I set my letter on the table. "I even put a stamp on it."

Her eyes floated from my letter to the stack from my birth mom.

"Eighteen-cent stamps," she observed. "These are from a long time ago."

"Not that long. And look how many," I said, fanning them out to show her. "I just want to write her back, that's all." I felt a flash of panic. What if she asked me why? What would I say? How do you explain to a person who grew up with all their puzzle pieces on the table that the need to find your missing one is as basic as the need to breathe?

"Once we fulfill our services, we don't typically stay in touch with clients," she said. "And they don't tend to update their contact information with us." I didn't harbor fantasies of my birth mom grabbing me with tears in her eyes and telling me that letting me go was the worst mistake of her life. I just wanted to know why she did it. That it was her *situation* that was impossible, not me.

"She might still be at the same address." I found her can't-do attitude maddening. "There's no harm in trying." I was practically stammering now. *Calm down, Adam . . . calm down.*

"Our obligation is to the client. To protect her privacy."

"I'm not asking you to give me her address. I just want you to mail my letter." I could feel my face getting hot. If I was a cute, angel-faced boy with dimples and a lean physique, would she be more eager to help? Just like the restaurant hostess who seats the beautiful people first and the bus driver who sees me huffing and waving my arms but doesn't wait. This was the story of my life now. And in an uncharacteristic burst of courage, I decided the stakes were too high not to call her on it. "This is about my appearance, isn't it?"

Now it was her face that flushed strawberry red. "What? No—"

"You don't want to tell her I'm looking for her because you think she'll be disappointed how I turned out." I hadn't planned on shaming her, but I also knew firsthand how effective it could be.

"Mr. Ross, I assure you, that's not it at all. We forwarded her letters because that was her wish, and she was our client. You have no such privileges." I could tell from the overly forceful tone of her voice that I had touched a nerve.

"What if I paid you?" It was a bluff, but not really. If she would do it for money, I would find a way to get it. My parents were paying ninety dollars a week for me to see Sandy. If I told them this was the thing that would make me feel better, they would pay.

"It would be a conflict of interest for you to retain our services." I flinched at the notion of a conflict of interest. I was her son. Since when were we on opposing sides?

"Why would she write to me if she didn't want me to write back? You'd just be closing the circle," I said, borrowing a phrase from my AP World History teacher.

"People choose closed adoption for a variety of reasons," Ms. Meyers said, returning to her detached speaking voice. "Often it's to put a difficult chapter behind them."

"Sometimes they want closure too." Was that what I was looking for? Closure? It was the only thing the mother who'd discarded me could give me that the mother who chose me couldn't. But also, what if she didn't have a good reason? And what was a good reason?

I put the letter on the conference table and stood up.

"You think you're protecting her, but she may be just as desperate to know me as I am to know her."

And I left before she could tell me I was wrong.

April 29, 2001

Hello,

I was about to start this letter with, "You don't know me," but of course you do. You were the first person I ever met, and I think about you a lot. I don't know if you think about me, but if you do, I wanted to let you know how to find me, and that I hope one day we can meet again.

I want to reassure you that I was placed in a wonderful family. My parents gave me everything, and I feel very lucky. We live in a big house, I go to a really good private school, and I play sports and have friends. Hopefully this is the kind of life you wanted for me and gave me up so that I would have it.

I found out I was adopted when I was seven years old. I'm not sure when the hollow feeling set in, but it was sometime after that. I thought it would go away, but that hole in my chest keeps getting wider. Maybe it's not fair to tell you that. But maybe you have a hole, too?

My parents gave me the letters you wrote. They really helped. Thank you for sending them.

I hope you'll write back to me, but I'll understand if you don't. I don't know your reasons for putting me up for adoption, and if I've opened old wounds I am truly sorry.
Sincerely,
Adam Michael Ross

CHAPTER 19
JANE

The doorbell was a hip-high, M&M-size button just to the right of the door. I pressed it, but it didn't make a noise, so I had no idea if it worked.

I didn't want to be obnoxious, so I waited thirty seconds before I knocked. Just three times, like a normal person would.

"You lookin' for Ellie?"

I peered over the pink flamingo to see a woman with box-dyed red hair looking at me from the doorway of the apartment next door. She was smiling like I was a welcome sight, so I did my best to smile back.

"Oh! Hi. I, uh . . . I'm not sure I have the right address," I stammered, because I didn't have prepared remarks for a neighbor. "I'm looking for a friend of my father's. He recently passed, and I wanted to let her know." It wasn't the whole truth, but it also wasn't my place to spill someone else's tea.

"I'm sorry for your loss, dear." Her Boston accent was thick, and her teeth uneven and tobacco stained.

"Thank you."

"I don't know where Ellie is. She left about twenty minutes ago. Maybe she was outta milk or somethin'. You wanna come in and wait for her?" She opened her screen door like she assumed I would say yes.

"I don't want to trouble you."

"It's no trouble. We look out for each other, Ellie and me."

I was tempted to leave. I wasn't looking for a woman named Ellie; I was looking for a woman whose name started with *G*. But then it occurred to me that this neighbor may have lived here for a long time and might know the person who lived in 16C before Ellie, and if her initials were GM.

"OK, thank you so much."

"I'm Marsha," she said as she stood back to make room for me to enter her apartment. She pronounced it Maaa-shah—no *r*—and I couldn't help but wonder why her parents would give her a name that she couldn't say properly.

"Hi, Marsha. I'm Jane."

We didn't shake hands, but my shoulder grazed her bosom as I stepped over the threshold. She didn't seem to notice.

"I only have decaf," she warned. "Doctor has me off caffeine."

"Decaf sounds perfect."

"I'm supposed to be watching my cholesterol, but I have cream, I'm not a barbarian."

"Coffee without cream is like shoes without socks."

"Exactly!"

I pressed my back against the foyer wall so she could pass. She was short and round, with a belly that stuck out almost as far as her sizable breasts. She had good posture and a confident stride, and her brand-new Nike running shoes suggested she liked to walk.

"Come on into the kitchen."

Her galley kitchen was small but tidy, with a black-and-white checkered linoleum floor and butcher block countertops. She had the standard smattering of appliances—fridge, oven, microwave, toaster, and yellowing Mr. Coffee coffeepot, which was steaming and three-quarters full.

"I just made it not two minutes ago," she said as she pulled two cups from a high cabinet. "Do you take sugar?"

"No, thank you."

"Good, because I don't have any. Doctor has me off that too."

"I don't think I like your doctor."

"Tell me about it."

Unlike Cal, Marsha took the liberty of pouring cream in my coffee—a generous dollop, in fact.

"Please, have a seat," she said. I sat down at the little bistro table by the window, and she set the mug on the place mat in front of me. I would say that this whole encounter was off script, but I didn't have a script.

"Did you have breakfast?" she asked.

"Yes, thank you."

"'Cause I was just about to put in some toast. I get the bread at Sully's up the street, they make it fresh every morning. Do you like pumpernickel?" Her kindness sent a prickle of shame down my spine. Neither this woman nor her neighbor owed me anything, not even the truth.

"Pumpernickel sounds great, thank you," I said, because a hot cup of coffee and fresh-baked bread is an offer of friendship, and it's rude to snub a friend.

"I'm afraid I only have margarine. Doctor's orders. But once you put the fruit spread on, you can't tell the difference."

She set a jar of raspberry preserves on the table. I didn't have the heart to tell her that her "fruit spread" was loaded with sugar, she might as well just eat the butter.

"Thank you so much, Marsha."

She jabbered about the weather as she sliced the bread and put it in the toaster. "It got so warm. This time last year we had three feet a' snow. You remember?"

"Actually, I live in California now." I got afraid she might start asking why I came all this way to talk to a woman I'd never met, but she didn't.

"Lucky you."

She served the pumpernickel toast on cobalt blue ceramic plates with concentric circular ridges on them.

"I like your plates."

"Oh, I've had these forev-ah." She handed me a butter knife and a napkin, then sat down across from me. "So tell me about your father."

I told her about growing up in Lexington on a street so green it was like living in an enchanted forest. I told her about Dad's plane, how I hated our day trips because I always threw up on takeoff and landing. I told her about going to Celtics games, how I was too short to see but didn't care because that's not why I went. I didn't tell her about the girlfriend, the letters, or the real reason for my visit, even though she'd earned my honesty.

"So who's this friend of his you were hoping to find?"

I took a bite of toast so I could have a few seconds to think. "I don't know her name," I said once I'd swallowed. "Only that her initials were GM and that she lived next door."

I braced myself for her reprimand, but she just smiled and nodded. "Must have been Gina," she said, like it was perfectly normal for a man to have a friend that her daughter only knew by her initials. "Gina McNally, GM." She wasn't suspicious at all. I wondered if that cross around her neck had something to do with her kind and trusting nature.

"Gina McNally lived in 16C?"

"For years. With her sister, Ellie. They lived there together. You can ask Ellie about her when she gets back. We'll hear her. She's in the apartment above me, these floors creak worse than a haunted house."

I wasn't interested in Ellie anymore. "Do you know where Gina is now?"

"Oh honey, she died a long time ago, rest her soul."

And I didn't know whether to feel relieved or disappointed.

CHAPTER 20
JANE

I was going to ask Marsha to tell me more about Gina—*What was she like? Did you ever meet her boyfriend? Or their illegitimate child?*—but before I had the chance, she popped to her feet.

"Ellie's home," she said as the floor groaned above our heads. "C'mon, I'll introduce you." She started for the front door. I took a final swig of coffee, then put my cup in the sink and followed her out onto the porch.

"Ellie! Open up, you got a visitor!" Marsha shouted as she pounded on the door with the palm of her hand.

"I don't want to bug her if she's busy—"

"She hasn't been busy since 1985."

I knew Marsha was eager to help me, but I hadn't thought about what to say to my father's lover's sister—if that's who this was—and would have liked some time to collect my thoughts.

I heard footsteps on the stairs. A second later the door opened, and Ellie McNally appeared wearing a scowl that could curdle milk.

"Jesus, Marsha. You'll wake the whole neighborhood."

"It's ten o'clock, the neighborhood's awake. This is Jane," Marsha said, with a sweep of her arm. "She came all the way from California so be nice to her."

"I'm always nice."

"Ha!" Marsha scoffed. Then to me, "I'll let you two figure out about your dad, I gotta go, my coffee's kickin' in."

She gave me the thumbs-up, then disappeared into her apartment.

"I hope I'm not disturbing you," I said, even though it was obvious that I was.

"I'm sorry, I didn't get your name."

"Jane Wallis. But I was born Jane Berenson."

I watched her face, hoping to see a flicker of recognition at the mention of my maiden name. *Nothing.*

"And how do you know Marsha?" Her tone was matter of fact— more accusatory than confused. Like she knew I didn't.

"I don't," I admitted. "She came out when I knocked on your door, then insisted I join her for pumpernickel toast."

"Sounds like Marsha."

We stood there an awkward beat—me, waiting for her to invite me in; her, waiting for me to give her a reason to.

"I . . . uh . . . flew out from California to try to find a friend of my father's. Her initials were GM, and she lived at this address." I'd been afraid my surprise appearance would make her uncomfortable, but I was the one stammering.

She didn't say anything, so I blathered on. "He recently passed away, and I thought this, um . . . friend, would like to know. I understand you had a sister named Gina?"

"Yes. But she's been gone many years now."

"Marsha told me. I'm sorry for your loss."

"I'm sorry about your father." She was leaning against the screen door, propping it open with her shoulder. Her annoyed expression had softened, and I was struck by how beautiful she was. Her eyes were cornflower blue, and sky-high cheekbones cast shadows in the gentle hollows of her cheeks. Her graying blond hair was pulled back in a messy bun with a few strands tickling her face. I guessed from the grooves in her neck that she was in her early sixties, though she could have passed for much younger. I got a prickle down my arms as I realized she looked a little like my mother—a taller, thinner, slightly more youthful version.

Uncertainty gripped my heart as I grappled with what to say. I didn't have a sister, so it was hard for me to imagine how I would have felt if mine had been involved with a married man. Was she disgusted? Understanding? Did she even know? I finally decided I had nothing to lose by showing my hand. Both my father and her sister were dead. If Ellie didn't want to talk about their relationship, then this was the end of the road.

"My dad's name was Richard Berenson," I said. "Everyone called him Richie," I added, hoping that would spark her memory but seeing no indication that it did. "Anyway, I was going through his things, and I found some letters."

"I don't know anything about any letters." Her face was stone. I should have apologized for disturbing her and let her be. But I had come a long way, and if I didn't do it now, I wouldn't have another chance.

"If I could just show you?"

The letters were in my purse, but I didn't want to whip them out here on her porch. And apparently she didn't want me to either.

"Come in." And I felt a buzz of excitement, because she wouldn't want to see those letters if her sister hadn't written them.

She opened the screen door for me, and I followed her up the narrow staircase to her second-story apartment. In contrast to the triplex's traditional exterior, her unit was modern and airy, decorated in bland neutrals—blond-wood floors, a beige couch, a heather-gray easy chair. The fireplace was framed by caramel-colored marble tiles, and the mantel displayed a single black-and-white photograph of two teen girls: one with dark-brown curls and light eyes, and one that looked like her. I would have asked if the dark-haired girl was her sister, if it weren't obvious. The thought I might be looking at a photo of my dad's "other woman" sent a prickle down my spine. I had to tear my gaze away so I didn't get caught staring.

"Please, have a seat," Ellie said, indicating the couch. "Can I offer you something to drink?"

"No, thank you. I had coffee at Marsha's." It was jarring how formal Ellie was acting with me after being treated like an old friend by her next-door neighbor. But I tried to match her energy as I sat on the edge of the sofa and folded my hands in my lap.

She disappeared into the kitchen, then reappeared a moment later with a glass of water.

"So, California?" She set the glass on a coaster, then sat down across from me.

"Thank you. Yes. I arrived yesterday. I'm staying with a childhood friend." A bead of sweat rolled down my back. I took a sip of water.

"So you're from here?"

"I grew up in Lexington."

"How nice." Lexington was an upscale suburb. A fine diamond to Malden's quarry rock.

"Yes, it was lovely. I was very lucky," I said, trying not to sound like an entitled rich bitch.

"You said you had some letters to show me?"

"Yes. But I should warn you, the content might surprise you." I almost said "disturb" instead of surprise, but she was already disturbed.

I reached into my purse and pulled out the letters. "There are thirty-three of them. The first one is from twenty-seven years ago." I opened the ziplock bag and took one out to show her. "The return address is this apartment."

I set the letter on the table, facing her so she could read the writing on the envelope. I thought she might reach for it, but she barely even looked.

"I'm not sure what you want me to say." She looked positively mortified. And why shouldn't she? I had come here uninvited and accused her sister of having an affair with my dad. But I selfishly pressed on.

"Were you and your sister living here then?"

"We grew up in this apartment. Went to elementary school right across the street." I understood that to mean they were raised here and never left.

"Do you think your sister could be GM?" I didn't mean to sound like a cop interrogating a murder suspect, but I didn't understand why she was holding her cards so close to the vest. The answer was obvious. No one else had lived here in the last twenty years, GM had to be Gina. Was she trying to protect her sister's memory? Because it was a little late for that.

"I'm sorry, Jane. But I can't help you. Perhaps you should leave your father's private correspondence private."

She stood up and jammed her hands in her pockets, but not before I saw they were shaking.

"Yes, you're right. I'll leave it alone," I said, and now I was the one who was lying.

CHAPTER 21
JANE

If there are two kinds of people in the world—those who remember high school as the best days of their lives, and those who hated every minute of it—I was definitely the latter. High school was nothing but pain for me. It wasn't fair to blame my dad for all my misery, some of it was self-inflicted. But I could no longer deny that he had contributed to the crippling insecurity that defined those years. I understood now he'd belittled me because he didn't like himself. But like all children who think their parents are all knowing, I took his criticism as fact. If he said I wasn't smart or skinny enough, then I wasn't. It never occurred to me to be angry with him, because in my mind all he was doing was speaking the truth.

After I graduated, I wanted more than a change of scenery, I wanted a fresh start. I left New England for the farthest place I could access without a visa: Southern California. It was the fall of 1984 when Janie from Lex became UCLA Jane. I even changed my hair—traded my honey-blond waves for Billy Idol–blond spikes. I joined the French club so I could summer in Paris, the ski club so I could winter in Switzerland—anything to have an excuse not to go home. In the end, those trips taught me more than all my classes put together. Not just about the world, but also about myself. Nothing like a trip to the land of Bordeaux and Brie to make you realize fear of butter is a distinctly American phobia, and that it's impossible to enjoy life if you always get your sauce on the side. It was those trips to Europe that inspired me to become a chef. After being taunted by Paris's flakiest croissants and Rome's creamiest carbonara, I decided if you can't beat 'em, join 'em, and enrolled in culinary school.

As I said goodbye to Ellie, I tried to imagine what it was like to live in the same apartment your whole life. I didn't know what happened to Ellie's father, but presumably she had one, and he'd once lived in that apartment too. She never got to experience leaving, only being left behind.

There was no doubt in my mind GM was Gina. Ellie's shaking hands had all but confirmed it. Watching Ellie protect her sister made me think of Kenny—how much he'd suffered because of me. His desire to join the air force at eighteen said it all. I was his sister by blood, but Rowan was the brother he chose. I cringed every time I thought about how I'd nearly soured that relationship too.

"Jane!"

I had just gotten to my parked car when I heard Marsha call my name. She was running down her front walk in those bright-white Nikes. I waved and walked around the hood to meet her on the sidewalk.

"Holy cripes, you look like you just saw a ghost," she blurted. "What happened?"

I knew whatever I said she would relay to Ellie, so I kept it vague. "Nothing, I just . . . I think I may have upset her."

My husband and friends had tried to talk me out of coming here, and I knew now that I should have listened to them. Ellie had every reason to hate my father, and me by association.

I never questioned why my father's girlfriend had written all those letters. She was in love with Richie and was trying to lure him back into her arms. I didn't like it, but I understood it. What I didn't understand was why my father kept them. My parents sold their Lexington house in the early nineties when they moved out west to be closer to Kenny and me. Which means my dad had not only held on to those letters long after the affair had ended, he also packed them in a box and carried them all the way across the country. Did that mean he was in love with Gina too? What if somewhere in apartment 16C there were letters to her from him?

"Gina's death was pretty traumatic," Marsha said. "Their father split when they were babies, and they lost their mother when they were barely out of high school. They only had each other."

"Neither of them ever married?"

Marsha shook her head. "They were working women. Men of our generation didn't like that." She said that last part with a tsk and an eye roll, and I wondered if that was the reason she was alone too.

"How long ago did Gina die?" The question of her child was still knocking around in my brain. If she had one, where was he now?

"Oh, gosh . . . a long time ago now. I remember because she was just a year younger than me. People your own age aren't supposed to die, y'know? It's unnatural."

I flashed back to Jesse McBride. He was just two years older than I was when he was struck and killed by that car. Marsha was right. You remember.

"Do you know what year it was?" I asked.

She did some math on her fingers. "It must have been 1983. No—'84. She died on Valentine's Day."

A shock wave tore through my body. The timing was as logical as it was horrific. She wrote that last letter—the one where she'd told my dad she was pregnant—in the fall of '83. Then four months later she was dead.

"She was such a gorgeous girl," Marsha said. "Tall and thin, like a model, with this beautiful mane of dark hair."

"How did she die?" I braced myself for Marsha to tell me she'd died in childbirth. "Was she ill?" I prodded.

"Not physically." I must have looked confused because she clarified. "Honey, she killed herself."

April 24, 2001

Dear Ellie,

I owe you an apology. It was rude of me to come to your home uninvited. I am sorry I barged in on you like that, you were kind to let me in and talk to me as long as you did.

I was not honest with you. I don't imagine you knew about the letters I brought with me, but as you may have guessed, they document an affair between my father and a woman with the initials GM who I have come to believe was your sister. My father's love life was none of my business, and I would have left it alone if not for an admission in the final letter that pierced my heart. In that very last letter, GM informed my father that she was pregnant, and the baby was his.

I became obsessed with the possibility that I have a half-sibling. I fantasized that my father's lover had the baby and would be open to introducing us. I see now how selfish that was, and I am ashamed that I thought it was in anyone's best interest but mine.

Marsha told me that your sister took her own life in February of 1984. The timing of her death, a few months after writing to my father about her pregnancy, suggests something more tragic than I could have ever imagined.

I am so very sorry for the role my father may have played in your sister's death. That you would even let me in your house under the circumstances is a testament to your kindness and shines a glaring light on my ignorance.

These letters are not mine to keep, and I had no right to read them. I wish I knew a way to honor your sister's memory. All I have to offer are her letters—all thirty-three of them—for you to preserve or destroy as you see fit.

If I had known any of what I know now, I never would have shown up on your doorstep. I wish you peace. May your sister's memory be a blessing.

Kind regards,

Jane Berenson Wallis

CHAPTER 22
ADAM

Days until training camp: 88

"I read the letters from my birth mother," I told Sandy during our weekly appointment. We were perfectly cast in the movie of my life. I was the disheveled patient, lying on her too-short leather couch. She was the bookish psychiatrist, staring down her nose at me from her captain's chair, her graying hair piled on top of her head like a Brillo pad.

"That took courage."

"Meh. Not really. Maybe a little." I didn't tell her it was Matty who forced the issue. I never mentioned his name in our sessions, for obvious reasons.

"How did they make you feel?"

"Like I wanted to kill myself." She looked up from her notepad.

"Adam, you know when you say something like that, I have to take it very seriously."

"Don't worry, I'm not actually going to do it," I assured her. She had a tape recorder on her desk, so I elaborated for the record. "I wouldn't do that to my parents. They paid a lot of money for the privilege of raising me."

She seemed to take offense to that. "You think the only reason your parents would grieve your death is because of the monetary investment they made in you?"

"I don't know." I wavered. "No."

She uncrossed and recrossed her legs, signaling a change of topic. "So what did you think of the letters?"

"They gutted me." I pressed the heels of my hands onto my eye sockets. *Crying on your therapist's couch is so clichéd.*

"I'm sorry to hear that."

"Yeah, well, the truth hurts."

"What specifically did they say that hurt you?" And all this time I thought therapy was supposed to make a person feel *better*, not worse.

"Well, first she wrote that finding out she was pregnant with me was the worst thing that ever happened to her."

"You knew that was a possibility."

"Yeah, but then she wrote that giving me away was also the worst thing that happened to her. So basically I ruined her life twice." *First, open the wound . . .*

"You know that's not your fault." *. . . Then, attempt to tamp the bleeding.*

"I know." *Therapy sucks.*

She changed the cross of her legs again. "How's your eating?" And here was the part where she tried to connect my guilt and my self-flagellation.

"If the goal is to bust out of my clothes, it's going great." I'd stopped weighing myself. The bad days had eclipsed the good days. I didn't need to weigh to know I was failing.

"Do you think reading those letters was a mistake?" I found the question odd, because wasn't it her job to know that?

"Do you?"

"It's not for me to say," she said, then opined, "but I've never subscribed to the adage that ignorance is bliss. Because until you know the truth, on some level you'll always wonder."

If I were sitting up, I would have uncrossed and recrossed my legs. "I wrote to her."

"Wrote to whom?"

"My birth mother."

She tried not to gasp, but I heard her breath catch in her throat. "I didn't realize you could do that."

"I don't know if she'll get my letter, but I dropped it off with the lawyer she hired to find me new parents." I figured I'd better tell her, on the off chance something came of it.

"When was that?"

"A few days ago. After my panic attack but before the World History retake."

"Adam, I have to confess, I worry that you're setting yourself up for disappointment."

"I don't expect her to write back."

"Then why did you write the letter?" She knew I was lying, but I doubled down.

"I don't know. I guess I felt like I had to do something. I mean, I know she's out there. And what if she's eating herself to death just like me?"

"That's the second time you mentioned death."

"Third time, do I get a prize?"

"I have to make you aware of my legal obligation. A person is not allowed to shout 'Fire!' in a packed theater. A patient is not allowed to joke about death in his therapist's office. Got it?"

"Got it."

"So I need to ask you—"

"No, I'm not suicidal," I insisted.

"Are you going to be OK if she doesn't write back?" she asked, because apparently the possibility that I might become suicidal still loomed.

"She's not going to write back."

"Adam, I'm a little worried we're not getting any closer to unpacking your feelings of abandonment," she said, not looking at my protruding stomach but indicating she saw it all the same.

"I wrote the letter for me," I lied. "To get my feelings out. It's not like I asked her to call me."

"Did you put your contact information in it?" These sessions were a pain in the ass to get to, and she couldn't help me if I lied my way through them. So I decided to come clean.

"I don't know how to help myself, Sandy. I want my body back. I want to play football. I mean, really *play*. Not just stand there like a Mack truck. But when I'm alone with my thoughts, all I want to do is eat. I know pigging out is moving me away from my goal. And I hate myself for doing it. But the more I eat, the more I feel like there's no hope. Because no matter how innocent you are, people leave you. I was a baby. She didn't know what I was. I didn't even know what I was."

"What do you mean, Adam? What is it you think you are?"

I could tell her everything else. But I couldn't tell her that. Because she was my mother's friend long before she was my therapist, and I'd been abandoned once before.

CHAPTER 23
ADAM

"How did you do on the makeup test?" Matty asked as he caught up with me outside our AP World classroom. I'd tried to slip out at the bell, momentarily forgetting that slipping through doors was not currently in my repertoire.

"Oh, hey, Matty. Um . . . I got an eighty-six."

It was getting risky hanging out with Matty. If anybody saw how I got all red faced and weird around him, they might tease me, which would make me even more red faced and weird. And then he might remember my fake enthusiasm about life-size Pam Anderson and piece it all together and punch me in the face. So I avoided him. I went the long way to class, ate lunch outside by myself, and—when the final bell rang—ran to the exit like I'd been caught shoplifting. Mostly it worked. But not today.

"Eighty-six? Damn. That's great! I only got a seventy-seven. I blanked on that last question about sub-Saharan Africa." He looked bummed, and a wave of guilt washed over me. Matty was the reason I passed the test, and now I was avoiding him like the plague. But also, he was Matty, and had plenty of not-messed-up friends.

"I gotta get to PE," I said, even though Drucker couldn't care less if I showed up for PE on time, or at all. I started to walk away, but he grabbed my arm.

"Adam, what's going on? Are you mad at me or something?"

I looked down at his fingers pressing into my forearm.

"I just need some space," I said, like he was my boyfriend and we were breaking up. He let go of my arm.

"I don't know what's going on with you, but I deserve better than how you're treating me." If Sandy were here, she would explain to him that my cruel behavior was about me, not him. But she wasn't. And I only had four minutes to get to PE.

"I'm gonna be late."

My shoulder bumped his as I squeezed past him, out the door, and into the hall. He was right. He did deserve better. But I treated people how I felt about myself. That is to say, like shit.

It was raining, so PE was in the weight room. Coach Fitz was the weights coach for all the varsity athletes and hung out there when he wasn't coaching. He waved me over.

"Ross!"

He was standing over a kid doing bench presses. There wasn't room for me next to him, so I had to talk over the bench-presser from across the room.

"Hey, Coach."

"How have you been, all right?" He said the "all right" part like he could tell that I wasn't.

"Yeah, good. Just slummin' in general PE." I tried to keep my delivery light, like going from being an internationally ranked tennis player to playing capture the flag wasn't the epitome of humiliation.

"Am I going to see you at camp this summer?"

"Um, I hope so."

He gave me the once-over. "Don't gain too much weight. Size is good, but we still need you to be able to run." He said it like I could dial my weight up and down like the volume of the radio.

"I'm not trying to gain weight. I'm trying to lose it."

He looked down at the bench-presser. "OK, that's enough." He guided the bar back on the rails, then walked over to me.

"What do you mean you're trying to lose weight? You're not on a diet, are you?" Coach Fitz was about my height but half my girth. Probably one of those psychopaths who got up at five in the morning to run ten miles every day before work.

"I mean, kind of." Yes, I was on a diet. But I was cheating so much it didn't really count.

"You need to cut that out," he ordered. "Diets don't work. They just make you feel miserable. You can't lose weight if you're miserable. What are you tipping them at?"

"Sir?"

"How much do you weigh?"

The bench-presser sat up and looked at me.

"I'm not sure."

"Well, let's go find out."

He beckoned me to follow him into the training area—a small room with a massage table, an assortment of foam rollers, a few trash cans for ice baths, and—most terrifyingly—a scale, which he pointed at like it didn't have the power to ruin my day.

"Go on, it's not gonna bite you."

He was my coach, so I did as I was told, looking straight ahead so I couldn't see the readout.

"You're at two sixty-six," he announced, like it was not a catastrophe. "What's your goal weight?"

"Two fifteen."

"Two fifteen is lean for a lineman."

This was my opening. Maybe it was Sandy's influence. Or maybe I was just too worn out to keep my guard up. Because I told him the truth.

"I don't want to be a lineman. I want to be a wideout."

To my surprise, he didn't laugh. I knew he valued me as a lineman. I also knew three of the team's six wide receivers were graduating and he was thin at the position.

"Two fifteen might be a bridge too far, given where you are right now," he said, and my heart hit the floor. "But if we can get you to two thirty, two thirty-five, we can make you a tight end." And my heart inched up off the ground.

"A tight end?" A tight end is a cross between a lineman and a receiver. Sometimes he stays on the line to block. Sometimes he runs passing routes. It's an athletic position that requires both size and skill. And I got tingles all over because it was the perfect position for me.

"With your height you could be great. And you wouldn't need to lose as much weight. In fact, I wouldn't want you to."

What Coach was saying was almost too good to be true.

"First thing we do is get you off that diet. Diets are bullshit." OK, that was definitely too good to be true. "You need to change the way you think about your training," he explained. "You're an athlete. Stop focusing on what your body looks like and start focusing on what you want it to do. Got it?"

He was sounding like a football coach now, and I loved it. "Yes, sir."

"We eat for performance, not weight loss. The weight will come off as you start to build lean muscle mass. Muscle burns calories. As you build muscle, you'll start to burn fat just standing still."

"That makes sense," I said, because I wanted it to, not because it did.

"There is one dietary requirement I am going to put on you."

He paused for dramatic effect.

"What's that?"

"Water. You need to drink water. Lots of it. I want you drinking all day long. If a teacher tells you you're not allowed to drink in class you come see me, I'll write you a note."

"Water. Got it."

"I'm not kidding, Ross. I'll leave the chemistry lesson to Mr. Pickford, but think of it this way. That excess fat is clinging to your cells like mud on truck tires. You can't flush it out without a shit ton of water. If you're not going to the bathroom ten times a day, you're not drinking enough. Can you do that?"

I wanted to ask about the food, but I just nodded.

"Once we get you moving and lifting, the weight will come off. You're young. You're strong. If you do your part, you will not fail." My heart soared like a churchgoer who just found Jesus.

"Yes, sir."

"How early can you get to school?"

"I'm not sure. Why?"

"I want you in the weight room every day before class. I'm here at seven. Best time to work out is in the morning. All my star players come in the morning."

My heart did a loop de loop. Did he see me as a future star player?

"I'll be there."

"If you're willing to do the work, we'll get you there, Ross. We start tomorrow."

CHAPTER 24
ADAM

When I was little, we had a golden retriever named Barley. Barley was not what you would call a smart dog. He didn't sit, or fetch, or roll over on command. But he was happy. When you walked in the door, he would smile and wag his tail, then jump up on his back legs to give you a hug.

One time Mom left two dozen bagels she'd bought for a church luncheon on our kitchen table. When it was time to leave, the bagels were gone. She asked me if I knew what happened to them, and I remember getting scared that a burglar had come in through the back door and stolen them. Not yet knowing anything about life, I thought burglars were the worst thing that could happen to a person.

The burglar turned out to be Barley. We found him curled up in his dog bed, his belly swollen and hard like the hull of a canoe. He not only ate the twenty-six bagels (baker's dozen times two), he also ate the bag. He farted up a storm for the next three days but lived to eat another day.

Our neighbor's dog, Prissy, was just the opposite. Prissy, like her name, was particular. She had one of those dog bowls attached to a grain chute, so as she ate, replacement kibble tumbled down like an infinite waterfall. Her owners didn't have to monitor her eating, she stopped when her tummy was full.

Until recently, I hadn't given much thought to Barley's and Prissy's contrasting relationships with food. I didn't think Barley had any repressed doggie trauma, and I knew a lot of dogs with similar gluttonous tendencies. Where did this urge to eat everything in sight come from? And why did the fact that animals did it, too, fill me with dread? Which behavior was innate, and which one was learned? If I wanted to have a "healthy relationship with food" (Sandy's phrase), would I have to unlearn or relearn?

The AP World History–class final was a week away, so after my pep talk from Coach Fitz, I came straight home to study. If Matty had organized a study group, he hadn't invited me. Which was just as well, I wouldn't have gone. He would never like me in the way I liked him, and I'd already experienced the ultimate rejection. To be rejected by him would be anticlimactic.

I plopped on my bed and took out my study guide. The history of the world in fifty-six pages. Page one, the Agricultural Revolution: humans learn that they can have control over their food supply by planting legumes, grain, peas, and bitter vetch (whatever that is). According to my textbook, learning how to grow food was the first significant milestone in human history. Controlling food meant controlling not just the supply, but also each other. Food was power. The more you had, the more people would revere you. *Hmm.*

The ability to store and trade food led to the rise of cities. Surpluses allowed people to spend their time developing tools and technologies— rakes, plows, dams, aqueducts—to make the cultivation of food more efficient. Food was at the center of everything. Always. *Hmm.*

I had a sleeve of Oreos in my backpack, but I left it there as I pored through my notes. The rise of city-states led to the rise of religion. Every society from the ancient Greeks to the Crusaders had a god (or gods) that would punish you if you did something bad. If we weren't controlling people with food, we were controlling them with fear. Food plus fear equals absolute power. *Hmm.*

I was reading about how Portuguese traders introduced slave labor to North America (to harvest food, of course) when Mom called me down for dinner. Visions of bitter vetch danced in my head as I descended the stairs. It had been six solid hours since I'd put anything in my mouth, and the dull ache of gluttony had been replaced with an actual appetite.

"This looks amazing, Mom. Thank you," I said as I heaped steamed broccoli onto my plate. She had dusted it with sesame seeds and roasted garlic, and it smelled absolutely delicious. "Mmmm, I love how you seasoned this." Being hungry made the smells and flavors more vivid, and I had a glimmer of hope that maybe . . . just maybe . . . I might find a way to enjoy food again.

"How's the studying going?" Mom asked, as she passed the broccoli to my dad.

"Good. Did you know that the first industrial revolution was all about controlling the food supply?"

Mom snuck a glance at Dad. We didn't really talk about food these days.

"Makes sense, I guess?" Dad said cautiously.

As I ate meatballs brought to me by descendants of cows imported from Portugal, I told my parents about my run-in with Coach Fitz.

"I bumped into Coach Fitz in the weight room during sixth period PE. He wants to help me make a workout routine," I said brightly, momentarily forgetting that Dad hated football and anyone who encouraged me to play it.

"That's good of him," Mom offered over Dad's scowl.

"He doesn't believe in diets," I blurted without thinking how it would go over with the people who'd hired a nutritionist to put me on one. "He thinks exercise is the way to get healthy."

"Well, I would say both are important," Dad countered.

"He said diets make people miserable," not realizing that a person who had never been on a diet wouldn't understand why that was relevant.

"Weight loss is a math problem," Dad said. "You'll lose weight if you burn more calories than you consume." I wanted to tell him what Coach said about how I could burn off my cheeseburger just by standing still, but it sounded better coming from him.

"Well, I want to do both," I lied, because I knew I wasn't winning this argument. "Work out and diet."

"I think adding an exercise plan is a great idea," Mom said.

"He wants me to come in the mornings. That's when the other football players work out. Seven a.m."

"You want us to take you to school at seven in the morning to train with the football team?" Dad's voice dripped with disdain. I shouldn't have said the word football. My ask was doomed from the start.

"That's when he has time to work with me."

Dad shook his head. "Football is what got us into this mess."

I looked at Mom. Silently begged her to disagree with him.

"Your dad's right. We have a plan. We just need to stick to it."

I looked down at my plate. I wasn't hungry, but I knew I'd eat everything on it, then help myself to seconds.

And then after that, I'd go upstairs and eat that sleeve of Oreos.

April 29, 2001

Dear Jane,

Thank you for your note, and for giving me the chance to review the letters you found.

I'm writing because I fear you may have made an erroneous connection and I want to put your mind at ease. Gina's suicide was not connected to any actions of your father. Gina suffered from depression her whole life. It was not her first attempt, only her first successful one.

Also I feel compelled to inform you that, while Gina may have known your father, they were not romantically involved, and it is misguided of you to think her death was related to anything your father may or may not have done.

I hope you can rest easier knowing that the tragedy you imagined did not come to pass. I wish you peace as you process your loss. I hope you can put this unpleasant chapter behind you. I speak from experience when I say it's for the best.

Sincerely,
Ellie McNally

CHAPTER 25
JANE

"When did this letter arrive?" I asked my husband when I returned from Boston and saw it on the kitchen counter, peeking out from between our phone bill and a Bed Bath & Beyond coupon.

"What letter?"

"This one," I said, holding it up. Tarzan stood on his back legs and pawed at my thigh like he wanted to play. I put a hand on his head to tell him I missed him, too, but he would have to wait.

"Today. While you were in the air." My knee-jerk reaction was that he was lying, but then I realized if he didn't want me to see it, he would have thrown it away.

"It's from her."

"Who?"

"The woman I went to see in Malden. The one who knew my dad."

I pointed to the return address. It had been five days since I'd left the thirty-three letters from my father's lover on her doorstep, and while I'd put my home address on the box, I hadn't expected her to use it.

When Marsha told me that Gina McNally had taken her own life, likely when (or because) she was pregnant with my dad's baby, I was so distraught I almost flew home immediately. But Samara convinced me to stay the week, make that cake I'd promised to make. If you want a stunning example of the whole being greater than the sum of its parts, bake a cake. Angel food cake is just five ingredients—flour, sugar, egg whites, cream of tartar, salt—none of them particularly remarkable on their own. But when combined in the right proportions, a whole new life form is created. When I flipped the Bundt pan and the magnificent creation was revealed, the expression on the boys' faces brought my battered heart back to life. As they took turns making disappearing divots with their fingertips, I marveled at how food has the power to delight equal to its power to destroy.

Samara and I spent the week touring our old haunts—the North End for cannoli, Kelly's for lobster rolls, Copley Square for overpriced coffee and window-shopping. After dinner we played games with the kids—Clue, Uno, Operation, Boggle. I studied them when it wasn't my turn. Emma had her mother's pale-green eyes, Brandon her throaty laugh, Henry her widow's peak—they were all offshoots of the original, yet each wholly unique. Samara, Cal, and the kids were like my cake—five amazing beings that combined to make something even more amazing: a family.

Samara asked if I wanted to go to Lexington to see my old house, but I had already cherry-picked the childhood memories I liked; I didn't want to confront the ones I didn't. From the outside looking in, I'd had a charmed existence. I had my own room (with a window seat) in a stately five-bedroom house, went to a fancy private school, got to starve myself while people two towns over skipped meals by necessity. But—true to the cliché—money doesn't buy happiness, only an escape hatch so we don't have to fix what's broken.

I wondered if things would have been different if my dad hadn't had the means to keep a girlfriend on the side. Would he have tried harder to make nice with my mom? Come home for dinner instead of abandoning her to spoil someone else? If Kenny and I hadn't found ourselves tangled up in his lies, perhaps we would have stood by each other instead of taking sides. Solidarity starts at the top. But so does dysfunction. We might not have known Dad was cheating, but we all felt it. Mom's misery permeated our house. I took it personally. Kenny ran away. I didn't know where my search would lead, only that if we were ever going to heal, I had to carry it to the end.

My heart was beating wildly as I opened Ellie's letter. It was obvious from her chilly reception that she was hiding something. Had my heartfelt confession inspired one of her own? What my father had done to her sister was unconscionable, but perhaps she'd come to realize that it's not fair to blame children for the sins of their fathers.

"Well?" Greg asked as I read the letter for a second time. "For God's sake, Jane, don't keep me in suspense."

I handed him the letter. His brow grew heavy as his eyes devoured the words.

"She says Gina and your dad weren't romantically involved," he said, giving me back the letter like that was the end of it.

"That's what she says."

He frowned. "You don't believe her?"

I quoted from the letter. "'While Gina may have known your father . . .'"

"So she may have known him?"

"Why would she tell me that?"

"I don't know. Maybe because she doesn't know for sure."

"Gina McNally's initials are in the return address," I reminded him. "Why would she send letters to someone she doesn't know?"

"Maybe she was covering for a friend," Greg said, then clarified, "a married friend." It was a plausible theory. The letters were signed, "Love, Me." Only the envelopes said GM. My dad had used a personal mailbox to keep from getting caught, but a friend would have worked just as well.

"You're suggesting Gina acted as a decoy?" I asked.

"Or a courier," he said, then added, "for someone whose life would be turned upside down if she got caught." His tone made it crystal clear that I should let sleeping dogs lie.

I thought back to my conversation with Ellie, how prickly she'd been. I'd thought she didn't want to look at the letters because they churned up bad memories. But maybe she simply didn't want to admit she and her sister had played a role in helping my dad betray my mom.

"So you think my dad's lover is still out there?" I asked.

"What I think is that you tried, and you should let it go."

But I had other plans.

CHAPTER 26
JANE

Greg and I met at a burger joint in Westwood Village when we were both undergraduates at UCLA. He tells people it was the Fatburger on Kinross, but I didn't go to places with the word "fat" in their name, so it must have been the In-N-Out around the corner. He recognized me from Spanish lab, so felt entitled to sit down at my table and help himself to a french fry off my plate. He thought the gesture was adorable. That's not the word I would have used, but I didn't send him away either.

By the end of the meal, he'd eaten half my fries and scored a date. Buying me a meal was the least he could do after devouring my food, I'd told Felicia, my psychology-major roommate, who had already learned enough about human behavior to know I wasn't going out with him for french fry reparations.

The night before our Saturday afternoon *cita*, he called to ask if I might like to go rollerblading. When I told him I didn't have Rollerblades, I figured he would pick something less equipment dependent, like a movie. Westwood had the best movie theaters in LA; it was a reasonable guess. But my former-hockey-player, soon-to-be boyfriend was determined to show off his skating skills and arrived at my door with elbow pads and new-in-box Rollerblades that cost way more than my regular-size fries.

It was not the skating skills that dazzled me; it was the extravagance of it all. Besides stopping at Big 5 to buy me Rollerblades, he'd borrowed a car, splurged for premium parking right by the beach, and packed me a water bottle and a granola bar, which he carried in a backpack so he could have his hands free to catch me when I fell (which I did—repeatedly). When I asked how he knew what shoe size I was, he confessed to having asked Felicia, then swearing her to secrecy. How could I turn down a second date after that?

College was a pivotal time for me and my mental illness, and I give Greg a lot of credit for keeping me from slipping back into it. Nothing like feeling loved to make you love yourself. It's not the recommended path to healing, but sometimes the cart can lead the horse. I hadn't realized how my father's put-downs had picked away at my self-confidence until I escaped them. But inexplicably, that didn't make me worship him any less. Perhaps I was suffering from some perverse variant of Stockholm syndrome? Or maybe I was just a girl who loved her dad.

Resentment about what my father had taken from me simmered under my skin as I drove west on Sunset Boulevard toward my alma mater. As the grit of funky West Hollywood gave way to the glitz of star-studded Beverly Hills, the insanity of what I was doing hit me like a blast of cold air. Ellie's attempt to put the kibosh on my search for my father's lover made me even more ravenous to find out what happened to her. She clearly knew more than she was saying. Was Ellie covering for someone? And if so, why?

The main library at UCLA was a majestic brick building on the northeast side of campus, between the law school and the student center. As an alumna, I had lifelong access, but I still felt like an impostor going in there—investigating your father's extramarital affair is not exactly academic research.

I took the stone steps to the library's main entrance two at a time. The lobby was grand, with thirty-foot cathedral ceilings and twin portraits of men with gray hair. Light streamed in from circular windows on the curved ceiling, but I was going to the dark place, both figuratively and literally.

The periodicals were on the basement level. There was an elevator, but the stairs were just beyond, so I took those to avoid inquisitive looks from the coeds in cutoff shorts standing in the alcove.

The marble staircase spiraled down to a carpeted area manned by a uniformed security guard. I had to show ID to get into the stacks. There was no food or drinks allowed, and he checked my purse to make sure I hadn't stashed any Twinkies or sodas in there.

The daily editions of the *Boston Globe* were arranged by date. The oldest was from May 11, 1960—the year the paper was launched. Each roll of microfilm had a week's worth of newspapers on it. The rolls were stored in plain white boxes the size of Scotch-tape refills stacked on wire shelves in impeccably neat rows. If you were a person who appreciated uniformity and order, this section of the library would be your nirvana.

I thumbed through two decades worth of little white boxes until I got to the one I wanted: February 11–18, 1984. I decided to take the next box, February 19–26, 1984, too, in case the news of Gina McNally's death had been delayed.

I threaded the microfilm through the reader and started scrolling. I decided to start my search on February 15—the day after Gina McNally had died, according to Marsha. There was no search function; I just had to scroll until I found something . . . which I knew might be never.

It took me two hours to comb through four days' worth of obituaries. A few people got "featured" obits—an Arlington-area firefighter, a beloved basketball coach from Cambridge, a pastor from South Boston. The other obituaries were two or three sentences: "so-and-so died on such-and-such date after a meaningful life doing this, that, the other thing. He/she is survived by these fine people (husband, grandchildren, a faithful golden retriever, a beloved parrot named Roger)."

After exhausting the obituaries, I scrolled through the local news. Either the suicide of a local-area woman did not make the paper, or Marsha was wrong about the date, because nothing came up. I had already removed the following week's reel from the shelf, so I loaded it into the projector. February 19 was a Sunday, and the paper had five times as many pages as any other day, as if they took the overflow from the week and dumped it into the Sunday paper. I turned on the magnifying tool and settled in to scroll.

I was so focused on the fine print that I almost missed it. There, above a three-sentence article announcing the passing of Angela Damaris Martinez (who died after a long illness) was a photograph of Gina and her sister, Ellie. Marsha was right. Gina had died in February 1984—four months after she'd sent that last letter. But the caption didn't identify Gina's sister as "Ellie."

Because her name was Gabrielle.

May 3, 2001

Dear Mr. Ross,
We hope this letter finds you well.

Our records confirm that your birth mother was a client of this firm.

While we had no obligation to do so, as a courtesy we have forwarded your letter to our client's last known address. We can make no assurances that the letter will find her.

We hope this concludes the matter you came to our offices to resolve.

Respectfully,
Cynthia Meyers, Esq.

CHAPTER 27
ADAM

Days until training camp: 80

I woke up at six a.m. with a sugar hangover. The symptoms were all too familiar: dizziness, brain fog, dry mouth, headache. It wasn't the first time. In fact, it was rare that I started my day without one.

I knew I'd feel better once I started moving, so I got up and went to the bathroom. I didn't look at my reflection in the mirror. I could feel the folds on my neck every time I tilted my head down, so I knew they were still there.

I ran my toothbrush over my teeth, then went downstairs to the kitchen. My parents were asleep, so I tried to be quiet. As I filled a glass of water from the tap, I remembered what Coach Fitz said about fat being like mud on truck tires. So I drank two glasses. But I also knew drinking water wasn't enough. So I went upstairs to get dressed.

I didn't know how many miles it was to school, only that it took fifteen minutes by car, so it was too far to walk. My parents had refused to take me, and I didn't drive. But I knew someone who did.

I glanced at the wall clock. It was 6:22 a.m. *Still too early.* I pulled on a T-shirt and pair of track pants, made my bed, then went back downstairs to pack my stuff for school. Mom usually got up at seven to make my lunch, but I planned to be gone by then, so I made it myself.

I waited until 6:38 a.m., then picked up the phone and dialed Matty's number. Calling his house this early was beyond rude, but I was suffocating in my own skin. Coach Fitz was offering me a lifeline, and I needed to find a way to grab on.

Matty's mom answered on the second ring. "Hello?"

"Hello, Mrs. Carlson. This is Adam Ross. I'm sorry to call so early, but I need to talk to Matty, it's an emergency."

OK, that was melodramatic, but it just kind of came out.

"What kind of emergency?"

Ugh. I knew I shouldn't have used that word.

"Sorry, it's not life threatening or anything," I backtracked, "I just need to get to school and my parents can't drive me. I was hoping Matty could?"

There was a pause. For a second I thought she'd hung up.

"Let me see if he's awake."

Matty arrived at my house at 6:53 a.m. with bedhead and a sleep crease across his cheek. I jumped into the passenger seat before he'd even put the car in park.

"Thanks for coming."

"What's going on, Adam? Why do you have to get to school?"

I could have made something up, but Matty had left his house wearing pajama pants, so the least I could do was tell him the truth.

"Remember a few weeks back when you asked me if I was going to camp?"

"Yeah."

"I didn't answer you because I was too embarrassed."

"About what?"

"I want to go, but not in my current condition."

"What condition is that?"

"Fat."

To his credit, he didn't object to my descriptor.

"I want to be a tight end," I continued, "not a lineman who just stands there and pushes people. But I can't be a skill player if I don't lose weight. Coach said he'd help me, but I gotta get to the gym at seven."

He nodded, like it all made perfect sense. "Then I guess we'd better hurry." He leaned on the accelerator and zoomed through a yellow light. And it struck me that he might actually care not just about getting to school, but also about me.

I glanced over at his face. His eyes were glued to the road, his expression all business. Guilt wafted over me like a bad smell.

"Sorry I've been a shitty friend," I said.

"It's hard to be nice to someone when you're disappointed in yourself," he said. I couldn't imagine Matty being disappointed in himself about anything.

"What do you know about that?"

"My dad's in AA. He used to get drunk and chase me around the house with a baseball bat. That's how I got to be so fast." He smiled at his joke, but I didn't laugh.

"Jesus, Matty."

"He never caught me. Though I did have to run out on the roof one time. He was too scared to follow me out there. But even if he did, I could have jumped, it's not that high up. Eventually he gave up and went to bed."

"Where was your mom?"

"Mom was scared of him too. He eventually admitted he had a drinking problem and got help. Now that he's sober, he blames that shit on feeling bad about himself and, y'know, wanting to take it out on me."

We were nearing the school now. I didn't know what to say so I just stared straight ahead.

"You know about the twelve-step program?" Matty asked, as he turned into the circular drive.

"Not really. I mean, I've heard of it, but I don't know what the steps are."

"First one is honesty."

"Huh," I said, because I kind of just did that. "What's next?"

"Hope."

CHAPTER 28
ADAM

"Ross! You made it. Good boy."

Thanks to Matty's badass driving, I got to school by 7:05 a.m. and to the weight room three minutes after that. Sure enough, Coach Fitz was there as promised, showing two kids on the basketball team how to do a proper dead lift. ("Knees soft, hinge at the hip.") There were also three girls by the free weights, but they were doing their own thing and didn't look up when I lumbered in.

"Did you eat breakfast?" Coach asked as I stood in front of him with my hands on my hips like a contestant in a beauty pageant.

"No, sir."

He shook his head. "You need to eat breakfast. Not a lot, just some carbs to get your blood sugar up. An apple or a piece of toast."

I didn't tell him about the Oreos pumping through my veins, how there was probably enough sugar in my bloodstream to ferment my vital organs.

"Will do, Coach."

"We're not counting calories. We're eating for performance. There's a difference. If you starve your body, it won't perform. Do you understand?"

"Yes, sir." He must have sensed that I didn't really understand, because he kept talking.

"I want you to tune out all those voices that say you're supposed to look a certain way. Athletes come in all shapes and sizes. You're not auditioning for a Calvin Klein ad; you're a football player. Do you understand?"

The image of Marky Mark's eight-pack abs danced in my head. "I think so."

"Most people think there's something wrong with them if they don't look like models," Coach opined. "Get that out of your head. It's made up to make you hate yourself. The diet industry can't sell you a remedy if they don't sell you a problem first."

I hadn't expected to get a sociology lesson, but I tried to follow along. "Yes, Coach."

"Take Larry Bird," he continued. "He look like an athlete to you?"

"I mean, he's tall?"

"Tall and slow with flabby arms. Tiny Archibald is short and fast with legs like spark plugs. They're complete opposites. My point is, you're on your own journey. I don't want you to compare yourself to anyone else. That only leads to disappointment and self-sabotage. You can't succeed if you're chasing someone else's goal."

I got tingles down my arms. Coach's pep talk had shaken something loose. I knew he wasn't talking about tennis, but I couldn't help but wonder if my mission to destroy myself was connected to the shame of betraying my dad. Tennis was Dad's goal, not mine. Once I realized I was only playing to please him, that's when things fell apart.

"We weigh once a week," Coach said, "just to set a baseline. And only here."

"OK."

"I'm serious. You may gain before you lose. Muscles hold water when they're getting stronger. I don't want you to be discouraged by what you see on the scale."

"Copy that."

"I don't want you focused on losing weight. That's a negative goal. I want you in pursuit of positive goals: gaining strength, increasing mobility, running faster, jumping higher, finding your most powerful self. You think you can do that?"

"Yes, sir." I felt like I was on a rocket ship that had just taken flight. I wanted to bottle up everything Coach was saying and drink from it all day long.

"Have you been working out at all?"

"Not really."

"Then we'll start nice and easy. A light, full-body workout to remind those muscles they're still there. Sound good?"

"Sounds great."

"OK, go get loose."

I warmed up on the bicycle—easy resistance, just to get my muscles warm. The first minute was easy. The second, third, and fourth minutes hurt like hell. But by minute five, a few endorphins kicked in, and the heaviness in my legs and chest gave way to a tolerable numbness.

After the bike I did some squats. No plates, just the bar, which weighed forty-five pounds. After three sets of ten, I did three sets of dead lifts for hamstrings, three sets of rows for deltoids, traps, and triceps, and three sets of calf raises. All with just the bar.

"Feeling OK, Ross?"

"Yep." I was more than OK. I was so happy I wanted to cry. My tennis body had been awakened like a bear in springtime. I could feel it stirring, hungry to resurface.

We finished the session with some bicep curls and three thirty-second plank holds, which Coach made me do on my knees "just for the first day." My stomach grazed the ground, but I could feel my abs engage, and I was thrilled they'd found a purpose beyond staying out of the way of my dinner.

"You're an athlete, Ross. You just forgot for a minute there."

He warned me to take it slow ("Don't sabotage your progress by trying to do too much!"), reminded me to drink water ("A hundred ounces per day, minimum!"), then sent me on my way. I know it sounds crazy, but when I caught the sight of my profile in the mirror, I almost thought I looked better. Which was impossible—I'd only worked out once! The body is physical, but body image is mental, and while my physical body had made only minuscule progress, my body image had taken a giant leap.

By lunchtime, I'd drunk three liters of water and gone to the bathroom twice. The fog had lifted from my brain, the stiffness was gone from my joints, I think my eyesight had even gotten sharper. When lunch rolled around, I was actually hungry for a change, not just eating out of habit.

"How was your workout?" Matty asked when he saw me in the cafeteria picking the turkey out of my sandwich. Yes, I was hungry, but I craved protein, not empty carbs.

"Good. Coach has a plan for me."

"If you need rides, maybe I'll start working out in the mornings too."

And my great day just got better.

CHAPTER 29
ADAM

I knew I was in trouble the second I got in my mother's car. There was no "How was your day, Adam?" She wouldn't even look at me.

"Hi, Mom."

"I don't have words right now, Adam." The bones of her hands were visible through her skin as she gripped the wheel.

"Sorry I left without telling you," I said. And then she found words.

"Your father and I were worried sick. Did you know we called the school? The office secretary was the one who told us you were there," she said, then added, "a secretary, Adam," as if saying it a second time made it more outlandish.

"I figured you'd know I went to school."

"And how would we know that? From the note you didn't leave?"

Sarcasm was a new look for my mother. She wasn't exactly sassy. I had to fight back the urge to smile.

"Sorry, you're right. I should have left you a note."

"We'll discuss it when your father gets home." I'd never been threatened by the dreaded "when your father gets home," because I'd never disobeyed my parents. But that night, I got a taste of how the other half lived.

"Adam, what you did this morning was unacceptable," Dad said after he sat me down in a kitchen chair to give me a talking-to. He was as awkward in his role as disciplinarian as I was in the role of bad kid. As he stood over me with his arms crossed like the dad in *The Brady Bunch*, I tried to look as small as possible—hunched my shoulders, hung my head—like Barley after he ate all those bagels.

Mom was making dinner. The sour smell of brussels sprouts permeated the room, amplifying everyone's discomfort. I assume Dad chose to bawl me out in the kitchen because Mom wanted to listen in but was chained to the stove. It didn't feel like the right time to remind him I had enough bad associations with food already; did he really want to make them worse?

"I'm sorry, Dad," I said, without a "it's just that," because that was his thing, and I didn't think now was the time to teach him how counterproductive it was.

"I'm sure your mother told you we learned where you were from the school secretary." I didn't understand their obsession with the secretary, but I just nodded.

"We told you we didn't want you working out with the football coach. You deliberately disobeyed us." I got a panicky feeling, because I knew what was coming.

"He's helping me, Dad."

"Helping you what?"

"Feel better about myself."

"It makes you feel better about yourself to go behind our backs?" I felt like he was intentionally not getting it, but I still tried to explain.

"It makes me feel better about myself to be in the gym."

"Then I'll take you to the gym."

"It's more than just the workout." I didn't want to use the words "spiritual experience," so I didn't finish the thought.

"I don't understand. Isn't that what you do there? Work out?"

"Coach just has a way of making it click."

"Because he told you that you don't have to diet?" *Ugh*, why had I told them that part? My chest was getting tight. I thought about the twelve steps. *First step: honesty.*

"Because he believes in me." Dad's face contorted with anger, and I knew that was the absolute worst thing I could have said.

"I see. So you think no one in this house believes in you?"

"That's not what I meant." Now it was me who didn't have words. How could I tell him Coach Fitz made me feel hopeful and happy without him taking it as a dig against him? Coach had offered me a path to play football. My parents had given me literally everything else.

Mom moved her pan off the stove and turned to look at me. I felt like a caged rat. No matter what I said, they would make it about them and how hard they sacrificed everything to make a good life for me. But I wanted to make my own good life now, in my own way, with the people who let me be me.

"It's just that I'm really connecting with what Coach is saying about how to get in shape. He makes me feel like I can do it."

"In shape for football," Dad clarified.

"What difference does it make?"

"You're a tennis player, Adam. You've been a tennis player since you were six years old." Because of course this was all about tennis.

"I don't want to play tennis anymore, Dad."

"What kind of spell did that Coach put on you?" But Coach hadn't put a spell on me. He'd freed me from the curse of trying to be something I'm not.

"I want to keep working out with him in the mornings."

"Well, we don't approve." And my sixteen-year-old self finally rebelled.

"I don't need your approval. Matty will take me."

I thought he would explode. I braced myself for a "while you're in my house you will abide by my rules" speech. But he didn't say anything. He just turned his back on me and left the room.

I looked at my mom. I thought she would offer words of comfort or encouragement, but she turned her back on me too. So I got up and went to the den to call Matty.

"Hey," I said when he got on the line.

"Hey."

"Remember what you said this morning about driving me to the gym?"

"Ah shit."

"What?"

"I shouldn't have told you that."

"Why not?"

"My mom only let me use her car because you said it was an emergency." *So much for my plan.*

"Right. OK, don't worry about it."

"But I'm saving up to buy my own car this summer," he said. If I was going to have any hope of becoming a tight end, I needed to lose the weight before summer. Otherwise I'd be stuck as a lineman forever. But I didn't tell him that.

"What's after hope?" I asked.

"Huh?"

"In the twelve steps."

"Surrender."

"That's depressing."

"Not, like, to your problem. To a higher power."

I knew he didn't mean my parents, but they were at the top of my personal hierarchy, and I didn't need to surrender, because they had already won.

GINA MARIE MCNALLY

Beloved sister and world traveler

Gina Marie McNally, a lifelong resident of Malden, passed away on February 14, 1984, at the age of thirty-four. Born on February 8, 1950, to Christine Gerrity and Theodore "Teddy" McNally, Gina was known for her generosity, humor, and warmth, which endeared her to all who had the pleasure of knowing her.

Gina was a graduate of Malden High School. She enjoyed a fulfilling career as a stewardess for American Airlines. Her greatest joy was traveling the world and sharing her love of exploring with all the people she met.

A memorial service to celebrate Gina's life will be held at St. Anne's Catholic church in Malden this evening at six o'clock. In lieu of flowers, the family requests that donations be made in Gina's memory to Samaritans Hope of Greater Boston.

Gina faced many challenges in her life, and her passing has left a profound sense of loss among those who loved and cherished her. She is survived by her sister, Gabrielle, as well as numerous cousins, colleagues, and friends.

CHAPTER 30
JANE

"You went to the library?" Greg asked when I stepped away from the stove to show him what I'd found. I'd printed Gina McNally's obituary right from the microfilm reader. If a picture is worth a thousand words, at ten cents, that printout was a bargain.

"Ellie's the blond one," I said, holding up the paper for him to see. "A.k.a. Gabrielle."

But Greg didn't want to look at it. "For God's sake, Jane. This obsession's gone too far. You're acting like a crazy person."

"It was the library, not CIA headquarters," I said, putting the printout on the table and then crossing back to the stove.

He begrudgingly looked down at the photo, then admitted, "She looks like your mother."

"Even more so in person."

I poured a quart of boiling water into a pot of rice noodles, then stirred them with a wooden spoon. Since "retiring" from my job at Scratch Kitchen, I'd started experimenting with East Asian cuisine, and tonight I was attempting pad thai.

"Well, it would explain why she wrote that her sister 'may have known him,'" he said, putting air quotes around the "may have known him" part.

"It explains everything." Who GM was. Why her address was on those envelopes. Why she'd let me in her apartment, but then wouldn't answer my questions. She didn't want to talk about the letters she'd written, but she wasn't about to let me leave without seeing them.

"What are you going to do?" Greg asked.

I tried to imagine how Ellie had felt when I told her I was Richie's daughter. It must have been like seeing a ghost. Imagine living your whole life thinking you got away with something, only to be confronted by it nearly twenty years later.

I was desperate to know why my father had carried on with her for all those years. What he'd promised her. What he'd told her about my mother and the two children they had together. But I'd already decided my next move.

"Nothing," I said.

"Nothing?"

"I already gave the letters back to her. There's nothing more to do."

Calling it quits was easy and hard. Hard, because I still had unanswered questions. Easy, because I couldn't make her answer them.

Before going to Boston, my dad's girlfriend was an abstraction—the faceless villain in a storied cliché. But now she was a person—a person who lived in an apartment devoid of love and joy, who'd lost a sister, who'd loved a man who couldn't love her back. I resented her for how she'd inserted herself between my father and our family, but after seeing her eyes flood with panic at the sight of those letters, I couldn't help but feel compassion for her. In the end, she was the one who wound up alone.

"What about the pregnancy?"

I stuck my head in the refrigerator to look for the various sauces I would combine to coat the noodles—soy, fish, tamarind . . .

"Jane?"

"What about it?"

"Do you still think she had a kid?"

I flashed back to Ellie's Spartan-chic apartment. There were no jackets, shoes, toys, photographs. Plus Marsha had said Ellie lived with her sister, not her sister and her child. Surely she would have mentioned a kid if there was one.

"If she did, there were no signs of one."

"You think she lied about being pregnant?"

I'd considered that possibility. But if she'd lied about a pregnancy to get my dad to leave his wife, he'd find out soon enough. And then what?

"I don't know what to think," I said.

"Are you going to keep looking for him?"

I'd grappled with that all day. That child—if he existed—was part of my story, just as I was part of his. I had planned to tell him only good things about our father—how he had a joke for every occasion, could solve complex math problems without writing them down, made lamb chops on Sundays that were so tender they fell off the bone. I would tell him that we weren't perfect, but just because he was born in secret, didn't mean he had to be alone.

But no, I wouldn't look for him. Not anymore.

"She has my number," I said, then turned my attention back to making dinner.

Ellie may have betrayed our family, but I had to respect her privacy. Most likely, I'd never know what happened after Ellie told my father she was pregnant. I was still curious. But my instincts told me she'd suffered enough.

CHAPTER 31
JANE

Sunday was Mother's Day. Kenny flew in for the occasion, compliments of Rowan and his plane. Rowan's own mother was in Cabo, compliments of Rowan and his wallet. Cindy couldn't come because she was in her eighth month and didn't want to leave the ground, so we had lunch for four at Mom's house. (Unmarried, childless Rowan went surfing in Malibu for the day.)

I'd kept the menu simple—spinach salad with strawberry vinaigrette, pesto chicken-salad sandwiches, and sour cream coffee cake for dessert. It was a beautiful, breezy, sunny day, so we ate on Mom's balcony. Her table was decorated with a too-large bouquet of flowers Kenny had picked up on the way. No one dared suggest we move them, so we jockeyed our heads to talk around them like we were all stuck behind someone really tall at the theater.

I hadn't experienced Father's Day without my dad yet, so Mother's Day was still my least favorite holiday. It's not that I didn't think we should take time out to honor our mothers—of course we should. I just knew that for every mother who got warm fuzzies from a card or box of chocolates, there was someone who spent the day with a sword through her heart; someone who never knew her mother, lost her mother, was unable to be a mother, or found herself accidentally about to be a mother and had to make the complicated choice about whether to go through with it. Mother's Day rubbed our faces in our losses, failures, and tragedies in a way no other day could. And yet here I was, partaking in the ritual, because Mom had enough hurt feelings for a lifetime, and not everything was about me.

"This chicken salad is delicious, Jane," Kenny said as he helped himself to seconds. I had served the tangy, crunchy concoction on store-bought croissants because they were just as good as homemade and making croissants took all day.

"The basil is from our garden," Greg said. Our "garden" was a window box with replanted herbs from the supermarket, but I just smiled.

"How's Cindy feeling?" Mom asked, nibbling at her coffee cake.

"Good," Kenny said, then reconsidered. "Tired."

"You didn't have to come," Mom admonished him.

"She's OK. This is her third, she knows how to pace herself."

"Greg's having his sperm checked," I blurted, and everyone stopped chewing.

"Enjoy that," Kenny joked, then looked at me like *What are you doing, Jane?*

"You know what they say. It takes two to tango," Mom offered. I didn't look at Greg, but I could feel the embarrassment radiating off his cheeks.

"You'll get to the bottom of it," Kenny offered.

"We're not worried," Greg assured him, then changed the subject. "So, Kenny, how long is the flight to Phoenix?"

We chatted about what Mom should see on her upcoming trip to San Diego (Greg recommended a few restaurants in the Gaslamp Quarter, Kenny recommended the Maritime Museum), and then the men cleared the plates while Mom and I retired to the living room. Neither of us sat on the cushion where Dad died, even though that corner of the couch, with its view of the ocean, was the best seat in the house.

"The place looks good, Mom," I said, noticing how she had removed subtle signs of her husband—his coffee-stained coasters, his heavy glass ashtray, his ratty lumbar pillow, his threadbare moccasins. She even replaced the framed photograph of the two of them in Nantucket with a cheery vase from Cost Plus World Market. How interesting that while I was resurrecting memories of my dad, my mother was putting hers to bed. Even our coping mechanisms were at odds.

"It's easy picking up after just yourself." Mom liked to remind me how men of her generation expected the woman to do everything around the house. Greg wasn't like that. I did all the cooking, naturally. But he always helped me clean up. And we split the other household chores evenly. He took out the garbage and washed the windows. I did the laundry and the vacuuming. It was all very equitable. Unlike in my house growing up.

As we waited for Kenny and Greg to emerge from the kitchen, Mom told me about the book she was reading for her book club (*The Secret Life of Bees*), the HOA drama (Shirley Sommers in 404 hadn't paid her dues in six months), the flowers she saw on her daily walks (coneflowers and dogwood, everywhere she looked). As per usual, she didn't ask about my life. Which was fine—it was her day, and I was grateful not to have to lie about what I'd been up to. I hadn't told Kenny about the letters or my discovery, because there was no way he wouldn't tell Mom, and she'd already said she didn't want to know. Plus if he'd wanted to look under that rock, he could have helped me sort through Dad's stuff.

As for what I would have done if my trip to Boston had revealed Kenny and I had a half brother, I guess I'd filed that under "cross that bridge when I come to it." It wouldn't be fair to keep the discovery of a long-lost sibling a secret, but our family was notoriously tight lipped. I didn't know I was going to be an auntie until Cindy's belly nearly knocked over a wineglass at Dad's birthday party. Our family was, and always had been, on a "need to know" basis.

"Who wants coffee?" Greg called out from the kitchen. I'd already had two cups at home, and Mom didn't drink it in the afternoon, so we both said no thanks. Five minutes later we were hugging and saying our goodbyes. Greg and I offered to drive Kenny to Malibu, but Rowan was already on his way in their rental car, and Kenny wanted to take a stroll on the beach to walk off that coffee cake before he got on the road. There was a version of this day where we all went to the beach together, maybe even met up with Rowan for some Frisbee or paddle tennis. It was only an hour flight to Phoenix, and they could leave whenever they wanted, since it was Rowan's plane and he was piloting it.

But no one wanted to linger. We'd had our obligatory meal, and now everyone was going back to their lives. Surfing in Malibu is more fun than brunch, but it made me sad Rowan didn't feel welcome at our table. High school was a long time ago. We'd seen each other many times between then and now—at his and Kenny's graduation from the academy; on Kenny's significant birthdays, twenty-one, twenty-five, thirty; at the air show where they demonstrated what the planes, and their pilots, could do. We were both in Kenny's wedding—him, the best man in tails; me, a bridesmaid in lemon chiffon. We'd even danced. And it was fine. I was fine. The good news–bad news about my upbringing is that it taught me I could heal from anything—a broken heart included.

"Give Cindy our love," I said to my brother as he waved goodbye. We were about to follow Kenny out the door when Mom grabbed my arm.

"Oh, I almost forgot. A letter came for you," she said, then darted off toward the kitchen. I occasionally got mail at Mom's place. We had a joint investment account, and notices announcing stock dividends and changes in interest rates all came to her address. I also occasionally got letters from the charitable organizations we supported—sometimes thank-you notes, but usually requests for more money.

Mom returned with the letter and handed it to me. As I looked down at the return address, my heart dropped to my knees. "Cross that bridge when you come to it" is generally a good strategy, until the bridge appears.

July 12, 1983

Dear Gabba-dabba-ding-dong,
Roses are red,
   Violets are blue,
   Pack your bags,
   We're going to Montreal.
Love,
Richie Rich
P.S. I know that doesn't rhyme
P.P.S. Do you have a passport?
P.P.P.S. Montreal is in Canada

PART 2

SEPTEMBER 1983

CHAPTER 32
ELLIE

I met the love of my life at a high school football game. Malden was playing Stoneham, the rich-kid school two towns over. Our student section, the Blue and Gold, was chanting, "We're gonna fight, we're gonna cheer, we're gonna make you all disappear!" even though by halftime we were losing by twenty-two points.

The shellacking continued in the second half. I don't remember the final score, just that the Stoneham Spartans set a league record for most touchdowns scored in a single game. When it was over, and the Stoneham High students were roasting us with chants of "Malden sucks!" we couldn't get out of there fast enough. I had gone to the game with two girlfriends, but I lost them in the crowd headed for the exits. It was freezing, and my feet hurt, but I didn't have a ride, so I pulled the collar of my coat over my ears and steeled myself for the twenty-minute walk home.

I was halfway across the parking lot when a kid on a bicycle whizzed past me, knocking me onto the hood of a parked car—a two-tone Buick station wagon that I would soon lose my virginity in. I wasn't hurt, just startled and annoyed. I shouted at the cyclist. I'm pretty sure I called him a jerk-off, but it might have been something worse. That's when the guy sitting in the driver's seat rolled down his window. I don't remember the conversation exactly, but it went something like this:

Him: You kiss your mother with that mouth?

Me: That jerk on the bicycle almost knocked me over.

Him: I believe he goes by "jerk-off."

Me: I didn't dent your hood if that's what you're worried about.

Him: Are you OK?

Me: I'm fine.

Him: You need a ride?

Me: I'm not getting in your car, I don't even know you!

Him: My name is Richie Berenson.

Me: And? So?

Him: Now you know me. What's your name?

Me: Gabrielle. But everyone calls me Ellie.

Him: Hello, Gabrielle. Beautiful name. And now I know you.

Life has a funny way of turning on a dime. If I hadn't gotten separated from my friends, if that bicycle hadn't clipped my elbow, if my feet hadn't hurt so much, if it wasn't so darned cold, maybe I'd have a proper husband and a normal life right now. But I never got the diamond ring and the white wedding, just the honeymoon—or rather, multiple honeymoons, way more than your average bride.

Richie wasn't the best-looking guy I had ever met, far from it. He was short and a little doughy around the middle, with a round face and deep-set eyes that were as blue as a sunny day. But it wasn't his looks that ensnared me. The guy was a born salesman; he could charm the socks right off your feet. When I hesitated to accept his offer to drive me home, he assured me he was a "nice Jewish boy" who "wouldn't hurt a fly." Now, twenty-four years later, as my nice Jewish boy let go of my waist and went back to his wife, I couldn't help but wish I was a fly.

Hanscom Field was a private airport twenty miles west of Boston. That's where Richie kept his plane—a single-engine Mooney painted red and white. We'd said goodbye here dozens of times over the years; after trips to Bar Harbor, Barnstable, Myrtle Beach, Miami. Richie loved to fly, and I loved being his copilot. We talked to each other through headsets that looked like giant earmuffs with shiny, jade green shells. They had crescent-shaped microphones that you could swivel between your hairline and your mouth. If Richie wanted to talk to the air traffic controller, he pressed a little button on the boom. Pilots had their own language, like secret agents in a spy movie.

Him: This is November 201 Yankee Lima, requesting taxi to runway 27 Bravo.

Control Tower: Yankee Lima roger. Taxi to 27 Bravo and hold short.

Him: Yankee Lima roger.

Control Tower: Yankee Lima wind is ten knots from the west, gusting to fifteen.

Him: Yankee Lima copy that, ten to fifteen knots. Ready for takeoff 27 Bravo.

Control Tower: Yankee Lima you are cleared for takeoff. Maintain climb to ten one-thousand.

Him: Yankee Lima roger ten thousand.

I willed myself not to cry as Richie blew me a kiss and got into his car. It was the end of Labor Day weekend, but the balmy summer heat was holding on. If he saw the sheen in my eyes, I would blame it on the weather. Richie loved being with me because I was fun and easygoing, not a crybaby. Every time I was tempted to fall on my knees and beg him to stay, I asked myself, *Who do you want to be for the man you love? A clingy, emotional basket case? Or a breath of fresh air?* He wasn't going to leave his wife for more of the same.

I knew loving a married man was a sin, but also that morality is not always black and white. None of my friends approved. But none of my friends knew how unhappy he was in his marriage. Or how happy we were together. People assume the primary purpose of a mistress is sex, but Richie and I loved to just lie, holding hands, on a blanket, listening to Joni Mitchell while we stared up at the sky. We pretended her song about clouds was about us. Richie and I saw both sides too. From our lookout ten thousand feet above the earth, we saw people going home to their sardine cans in the suburbs, crammed together so tightly they couldn't breathe. We're spoon-fed a dream about getting married to live monotonous, obedient lives, but it's not for everyone. Yes, he'd made a commitment, but he hadn't understood what he was committing to until it was too late to unmake it. And I hadn't realized what I had let go until it was too late to get it back.

People think only ducks imprint for life, but sometimes it happens to people too. Richie was my first everything. I'd tried to love other men, but after that post-football-game car ride, Richie was imprinted on my heart. When we graduated—him from Stoneham, me from Malden—I was happy for him when he went off to college, because that's what he wanted, and how could I claim to love him if I didn't let him spread his wings? Georgetown people were fancy, and he was brainwashed to want a fancy wife. And I never held it against him; that's how much I loved him.

He had a Mercedes now, but the love I felt for him was unchanged. I watched him drive away like I did after all our trips together, then started my car. Richie and I always drove to the airport in separate cars. Malden was ten miles in the opposite direction for him, and I couldn't exactly pick him up at his sardine can.

My blouse was damp and stuck to my back as I rolled down my car window. The airport smelled like gasoline and rubber. I'd come to love that smell, and I wanted one last hit before I drove home. We hadn't planned our next trip, but I figured it would be soon. Richie never made me wait more than a few weeks.

I thought all those trips through the clouds had given me a superior perspective on things. But the problem of looking at life from both sides is that real life is not two dimensional, and—contrary to the old adage—what you don't know *can* hurt you . . . can hurt you *a lot*.

CHAPTER 33
ELLIE

"How was your weekend?" I asked my sister as I walked into our apartment to find her sprawled out on the couch. Gina was a stewardess. The two of us spent a lot of time packing and unpacking suitcases.

"Fine. Did two round trips to San Francisco." In the nine years since I'd been back with Richie, Gina never asked where I went, but I told her anyway.

"I was in Nantucket." Nantucket was an island off the coast of Cape Cod. Most people went by ferry. The boat ride from Hyannis took a little under three hours. Plus you had to drive to Hyannis, which could take an hour or more. But Richie could fly us there in forty minutes. And we got to arrive in a plane.

"I hope you didn't bring any sand home in your suitcase."

"I didn't."

"Still, maybe you should open it outside."

Gina had a way of telling me she didn't approve of my life without ever saying it. She wasn't jealous that I got to play copilot to her stewardess, because she'd earned her wings while I'd stolen mine. Those "Welcome to Nantucket" smiles at the terminal were meant for the pilot's wife, not his mistress. But while it may have been true that I'd stolen someone else's man, it was also true that he'd been mine first.

The hardest part about loving a married man is not guilty feelings. I didn't feel guilty. Richie and I were soulmates—we just didn't figure it out until after he'd married someone else. No, the hardest part about being involved with a married man is not being able to talk about it with anyone. Not even your sister. When Gina went to San Francisco, she got to tell stories of bridges peeking through fog, rainbow-colored row houses, the best Chinese food she ever had. But I had to keep my stories about cobblestone streets and yachts as big as 747s to myself. No one would ooh and ahh if I told them how Richie and I had made love in the bluffs of Sconset under the most beautiful sky you've ever seen. The most I could hope for was for my sister and friends to keep their disapproval to themselves.

"Is that a new hat?" Gina asked, looking up from the TV. I'd bought a sun hat with a polka-dot scarf around the brim. It was easier to wear than to carry. I'd forgotten I had it on.

"You like it?"

"I've never seen you wear a hat like that."

I heard the unspoken disapproval in her voice. It was a rich-gal hat—one like Jackie O might wear. We were McNallys, not Kennedys. *Who did I think I was fooling?*

Once my high school flame got into Georgetown, everybody assumed our relationship was over. "You don't go to Georgetown to marry the girl next door," my mother had said, forgetting it was worse than that. I wasn't the girl next door. I was the girl from Malden.

And she was partly right. Richie and I did lose touch for a while, but not just because he was busy fraternizing with a higher class of people. I was busy too. Good grades had earned me a partial scholarship to Boston College, the Catholic university downtown, and I waited tables to make up the difference. If I wasn't in class or studying, I was working. There weren't enough hours in the day to pine for the man who'd left me behind.

I didn't put myself through college to earn Richie back. I went because I'd watched my mother bust her ass cleaning houses for cash her whole life, and promised her Gina and I would be the ones to break the cycle. If we didn't get jobs with pensions and benefits, she'd be mopping other people's floors until the day she died. She still died mopping floors, but not at an age that you would say her daughters failed her.

My degree from BC was in business administration. I graduated with honors and got an executive-assistant job at a medical-device company three weeks after getting my diploma. I didn't like wearing pantyhose in August, but I had my own desk, good benefits, and the self-respect that comes with never having to ask a man to pay for my dinner. I lived at home. Mom wouldn't let us help with the rent. "Save your pennies!" she'd tell me when I tried to give her money. "You don't ever want to be dependent on a man!" I didn't know if she was afraid that I wouldn't get married, or that I would. Or which in her mind was worse.

Our apartment was on the second floor, but we had a small balcony. I walked through the sliding door and set my suitcase on the chaise, opening it outside like my sister had asked. My clothes were damp and smelled of sea air and sex. Richie and I had gotten sloppy about birth control. When we were teenagers and as fertile as rabbits, we always used a condom. But after Richie got married, he didn't want to anymore. I counted the days between my periods and made excuses when I thought getting pregnant was possible. But then I turned forty. And I stopped counting.

Nobody believed my married boyfriend was going to leave his wife. "He's been getting his cake and eating it, too, for nine years," my sister and friends said. "Why on earth would he leave her now?" I wasn't trying to give him a reason, but I was growing weary of all those sideways glances. He never asked if I was ovulating. It was almost as if he was ready for things to change too. When he said he didn't want more kids, I always assumed he meant with her. Because if he meant me, wouldn't he be more careful?

I unrolled my bathing suit and draped it over the railing. There was a piece of seaweed in the bottoms, so I picked it out and let it fall to the grass below. As I shook out my sandals, shorts, tank tops, and tees, I realized Gina was right. There was sand in my suitcase. And if my calculation was right, there was a good chance this trip had left me something else to remember it by too.

CHAPTER 34
ELLIE

I called his house three days after my missed period. I know that seems soon, but my cycle was like clockwork. And this wasn't something I wanted to tell him in a letter.

His teenage daughter answered. I put on my executive-assistant voice as if this was a work-related matter, even though he had an office and his kid would know that's where work calls come in.

Me: Hello, I'm looking for Mr. Richard Berenson, please.

The daughter: He's not home, can I take a message?

Me: Do you know when he'll be back?

The daughter: Hold on.

She put the phone down. I don't know why I didn't hang up. Maybe I wanted to hear her voice? Just once, to know she wasn't better than me.

The wife: Hello?

It's not that I didn't know she was real. Of course I did. I'd seen pictures of her. Their wedding photo had made the local paper, and of course Richie had one in his wallet. I imagined her gripping the phone with her manicured hands, flashing her perfect teeth while her shiny ice-blond hair cascaded over one eye.

The wife: Who is this?

Her voice was nothing special. I don't know why that surprised me. Did I expect her to sound like the Queen of England? Because she didn't. She sounded normal, just like me.

The wife: Hello?

I hung up. Yes, it was a childish thing to do, but Richie was leaving her; the sooner she found out about me, the sooner we could all move on. I know that sounds cruel, but the marriage was over. He wouldn't be spending every third weekend with me if it wasn't. I had Richie's whole heart. At this point, all she had was squatter's rights.

I didn't know when Richie would call, and he had asked me a long time ago to stop calling him at work. I stupidly phoned his office too many times, and the gals who worked for him started to cluck. So now we just wrote letters. It was slow, but also kind of romantic. Once we were officially together, would we still write each other letters? I couldn't help but wonder.

I opened my desk drawer and pulled out a piece of my nicest stationery. I was careful with my words. I decided not to use the word "pregnant." I was certain that I was, but I hadn't done the test yet. So I let it be implied. *I have to see a doctor. I was hoping you'd come with me.* He was smart, he'd get it.

I knew he would scoff at the idea that this baby was God's will—he wasn't Catholic like me. But I didn't want him to think it was an accident. So I wrote, *I can't help but think maybe it's a sign? That it's time to be together out in the open, like we talked about.*

We had talked about it. We'd talked about it a lot. He told me he wanted to wait until his kids were out of high school. The timing was perfect. His nineteen-year-old son had just left for the Air Force Academy, and his daughter was in her senior year of high school. Nine months from now, she'd be graduating, and he'd be free. I reminded him that he had done his duty as a husband and a father, and now his life got to be about him. *You only get one chance at life, you should spend it with the person who brings you joy.*

I didn't want him to think that I'd already made the decision. *This is not something I want to do by myself. I might not want to do it at all.*

That way if he was against it at first, I'd make it seem like he had a say in the matter. I had no doubt I could bring him around. But I thought it best to ease into it.

I didn't want to scare him, but I needed to convey that time was of the essence. *If I don't hear back from you by the weekend I'm going to make the decision without you.*

But I had made the decision. I was having this baby. There was nothing to gain by letting him think I might want to end the pregnancy. *Honestly, I can't see myself ending the life of a child conceived in love. What if he has your eyes?* That last part was an appeal to his ego, but also wishful thinking, because my Richie had beautiful eyes.

I put the letter in a baby pink envelope and sealed it with a kiss. Then I dropped it in the mail. He only lived twenty miles away. If he didn't call, I could just go see him. I had never done that before, but extraordinary circumstances require extraordinary measures.

I got a nervous feeling in my belly as I realized this was the end of an era. I reminded myself that life was change, momentarily forgetting that not every change is for the better.

YOU'RE INVITED!

Janie's Sweet 17th Birthday is here, and we're HAVING
A PARTY!
WHEN: Saturday September 3
TIME: 6PM–10PM
WHERE: Singing Beach, 1 Singing Beach Road,
Manchester-by-the-Sea
WHAT TO BRING: Your favorite libation to share

Bonfire starts at 6PM but come early if you want to swim
We will have hotdogs and s'mores
BE THERE OR BE SQUARE

CHAPTER 35
JANIE

I turned seventeen right before the start of senior year. My birthday fell on the Saturday before Labor Day, so everyone was looking for something to do. Samara wanted to throw me a beach barbecue. I didn't want to have a party that involved putting on a bathing suit. I had gnarly stretch marks on my hips and thighs, and I was beyond self-conscious about them.

"They're not that bad," Samara tried to convince me.

"I have spiderwebs on my ass."

"Just wear shorts!"

The human body has a cruel defense mechanism. After starving it for two years, as soon as I started to eat normally, it blew up like a balloon. My doctor assured me that once it trusted I would feed it regularly, the extra weight would come off. "It's going to store every calorie you eat as fat until it knows you're not going to starve it anymore," he explained. He warned me not to flip out. "I know you're going to be tempted to diet. If you want your metabolism to return to normal, you have to keep eating."

I did what he said and forced myself to eat three meals a day, scale be damned. As my waist and thighs expanded, I traded my jeans for sweats and sundresses. I didn't dare look in the mirror. I wouldn't have believed what it reflected back at me anyway—even when I was skinny, my body dysmorphia tricked me into thinking I was fat. My eyes saw what I didn't want to be, not what I was. The human mind can be cruel too.

I started junior year weighing eighty-eight pounds. By Christmas, I was one hundred and forty-three. I'd gained over fifty pounds in three months by just eating "normally." But I didn't panic. I kept eating. I also started walking and lifting dumbbells in my garage. By spring break, I'd lost ten pounds. Over the next few months, the weight melted off like butter on a hot sidewalk. I was now a reasonably average one hundred and eighteen pounds and holding. I'd thought only bodybuilders and pregnant women could gain and lose that much weight in nine months' time, but apparently it can happen to self-loathing teenage girls too.

"How about we do it at night?" I suggested, hoping for a compromise.

"A beach bonfire!" Samara squealed, clapping her hands. "That's brilliant!"

We chose Singing Beach in Manchester-by-the-Sea because it was the prettiest and had parking. I didn't have a car, but my brother did. His new best friend from Air Force Academy camp was flying in from Colorado for the weekend, and my brother agreed to drive us after he picked him up from the airport. "I was going to take him to the beach anyway," my big brother said so I would know he wasn't angling for an invitation to my party. I remember wondering why Kenny's future roommate was coming to visit the week before they moved in together, but once I met him, I just said thank you.

Samara and I shopped for hot dogs and ingredients to make s'mores, then picked out our outfits. I wore jean shorts and a bikini top, she wore a baby doll sundress with a kerchief in her hair. We shaved our legs and polished each other's toes—hers, red; mine, pink. She'd swiped a bottle of Smirnoff from her parents' liquor cabinet, so I stole a bottle of Tanqueray from mine. When Kenny got home from the airport at three o'clock, we were antsy to go.

"Your brother's here," Samara said as Kenny's Bronco roared up the drive. We ran outside to greet him and make sure he hadn't changed his mind about that ride.

"Hey, Samara," my brother said as he got out of the truck. Then I think he said something about emptying the trunk, or changing into trunks . . . I was so transfixed by the anatomically perfect being that had just gotten out of the passenger seat, I couldn't be sure he'd said anything at all.

"Hi. I'm Rowan," the Godlike creature said. When his eyes made contact with mine, it felt like my entire body had been lit on fire.

"I'm Samara, that's Janie," my best friend said, then stepped on my foot and whispered, "Close your mouth."

"I'm just going to put on my bathing suit," Rowan said, slinging his duffel bag over his shoulder. He was tall with chestnut hair and arms like a prizefighter's—perfectly sculpted and golden brown.

"What do I need to bring?" my brother asked. I couldn't speak so Samara answered for me.

"We have everything, just hurry up and change."

Kenny jogged up the front walk and opened the door for Rowan. As soon as they disappeared inside, Samara pinched my arm.

"Ow!"

"Pull yourself together, woman."

Between the explosive weight gain and weekly doctor's visits, it had been a rough year. If Rowan was the prize for beating my eating disorder, I would have gotten sick all over again. This was more than just a crush. I was that boy skunk from Looney Tunes—the one who's so lovestruck by the girl skunk, his heart shoots out of his chest like a rock from a slingshot.

"Hey! Snap out of it. He's going to think you're a mental patient," Samara said, gently slapping my face with her open palm.

"I am a mental patient."

"Not anymore," she said, then reconsidered. "But if you don't take a chill pill, I might insist you go back."

I was never institutionalized, but the threat was always there—my punishment if I let my weight drop any lower. I saw a shrink every other week, and the whole family had to go to therapy once a month for a year. My breakthrough came not when we healed what was broken in our family (we didn't), but when I accepted it was not my job to fix it. After I'd beaten down my mental demons, there were unexpected physical ones to contend with. Because of my rapid weight gain, puberty hit me like a piano falling out a window. My hormones must have been on overdrive that day, because every cell of my body was buzzing.

"C'mon, help me load the car," Samara said, tugging on my arm.

My heart did the conga as I helped Samara pack the trunk. I had never felt this way before, and for a minute, wondered if there might be something wrong with me. But then I remembered seeing a woman on TV faint when she saw the Beatles. I was gaga, but not at risk of losing consciousness.

"Do you have towels?" my brother asked, stepping out onto the stoop.

"Yes, we have towels," Samara replied. "Let's go!"

Kenny got behind the wheel as Samara closed the trunk. "I call shotgun!" she shouted, then ran around the side of the car and hopped in beside my brother. Before I registered what my best friend had just done, Rowan was standing in front of me, his sculpted chest literally glistening in the afternoon sun.

"Mademoiselle," he said, opening the car door for me. His baby blue swim trunks hugged an ass so tight and round it would have made a volleyball feel insecure.

"Thanks," I squeaked.

As he closed my door and walked to his side, Samara spun around and stuck out her tongue like the lead singer of Kiss.

"I'm dying," I mouthed.

"Happy birthday."

CHAPTER 36
JANIE

"So, Janie . . . is today your actual birthday?" Rowan asked as he slid in beside me. Kenny's Bronco had bench seating in the back, which meant there was nothing between Rowan and me but a few cubic inches of electrified air.

"Yes."

"How old?"

"Seventeen."

I'd had crushes before, on that actor on TV, and Jesse McBride, the basketball star, but this was the first time I'd sat shoulder to shoulder with someone who made my heart beat like hummingbird wings. *Breathe, Janie, breathe . . .*

"I remember seventeen," Rowan said.

"Dude. That was last year," Kenny shot back.

"I'm nineteen."

"Barely."

"Is your brother always a dick?" Rowan asked.

"Pretty much."

He smiled a dazzling Patrick Swayze smile, and my cheeks burned like hot coals.

"So, Rowan, what's your story? Did you grow up with dreams of becoming a fighter pilot and saving the world?" Samara asked. "Or are you just going to military college to get girls?"

"That's a joke, right?" Rowan asked.

"I don't think cadets are allowed to date each other," Kenny said. "Plus I'm not sure our future classmates are Rowan's type."

"Oh? What's Rowan's type?" Samara asked.

"If she likes piña coladas," Rowan said, or rather sang.

"Oh please, no," Kenny said. But Rowan was already looking at me.

"And getting caught in the rain?" I said, and he whooped with delight.

"Janie for the win," he said, then flashed that killer smile. I didn't have to look down to know my blush had spread across my chest. My C-cup boobs were a relatively new acquisition, and my triangle-cut bikini top strained to contain them. Getting curves was the upside to gaining all that weight, and I was happy they'd stuck around after I'd dropped those extra pounds.

The boys continued to take swipes at each other as we turned onto Route 128 toward the shore. Kenny teased Rowan for being "a shameless ho." Rowan teased Kenny for having a "pole up his ass." I laughed too loud at Rowan's jokes, and Samara's eyes in the rearview warned me to cool it. Every time we went over a bump or around a curve, I gripped my toes in my shoes to keep from sliding into him. Even though there was nothing in the world I wanted more than to slide into him.

I'll never understand how a human being can be attracted to someone the moment they meet. We're supposed to be the most evolved beings in the animal kingdom, yet if some random guy looks at us in just the right way, we become as dumb as puppies chasing their own tails. We're not drawn to that one-in-a-million stranger for his mind—I had no idea if Rowan was capable of intelligent thought when I turned into Pepé Le Pew—nor did I care. He was just a jumble of skin, bones, hair, muscles . . . really nice muscles, but still. I'd seen guys with nice muscles before, and I didn't want to hurl myself at them. Rowan's energetic field was like a tractor beam from an alien spaceship, sucking me in against my will. Resistance was futile.

We got to the beach a little after four. It was crowded, but we still scored a good parking spot near the sand. I wasn't normally superstitious, but I took it as a sign that my birthday wish was going to come true. Rowan was only here for the weekend, yet I was already fantasizing about our life together . . . *talking on the phone at all hours, visiting each other on weekends. How would we break it to Kenny that his sister had stolen his new best friend? Would Rowan tell him? Or would I?*

We spread out the blankets, putting heavy things on the corners to keep them from blowing away. I hadn't planned on swimming, but it was hot, and I didn't want Rowan to think I was some sort of princess who wouldn't get her hair wet.

"How does my butt look?" I asked Samara, sticking it in her face.

"Too cute and perky to sit on."

"I'm serious!"

"So am I."

"My stretch marks aren't too gross?"

"You can barely see them. Besides, who cares? Nobody expects you to be perfect, Janie."

I didn't correct her, but that last part wasn't true. If I got a ninety-five on a test, Dad wanted to know what happened to the other five points. If my bed wasn't made, or I left the milk out or crumbs on the counter, Dad told me I was a slob. And then there was the brutal dissection of my body—a headshake when I helped myself to seconds, a raised eyebrow when my pants got too tight. Once he even used his finger and thumb to measure the fat on my upper arm because it was looking "a little thick." If he didn't expect me to be perfect, why did he pick me apart all the time? His criticism hurt, but it didn't make me love him any less—only hate myself that I wasn't good enough for the man I was desperate to please.

"If I go in, do you think it will be obvious that I like him?" I asked.

"Oh, girlfriend, we're way past that."

I thought about Rachel Refsnyder and that day on the boat. How I'd wanted to take off my life jacket but didn't because I was afraid of what my father might say. I'd lost two years of my life obsessing about how I looked. Rowan and Kenny were already in the water. Yes, I had stretch marks. But I also had a life to live.

"Fuck it."

I slid out of my shorts and ran through the hot sand toward the water. The froth cooled my feet as I waded in up to my thighs. There was a set rolling in, but I pushed through, letting the waves crash against my chest. I peeked down at my bikini top to see if it was holding on. Not the best choice for swimming, but there was no turning back now.

As I stood there in the hip-high water, a wave crested in front of me. I sucked in my breath and dove underneath it. The water wrapped around my waist. It tried to pull me back to shore, but I held my ground, frog-kicking with my legs while pulling with my arms. I'd been so focused on what my body looked like, I'd forgotten what it could do. I could swim. I could dance. I could lie in the sand and let the sun warm my skin. All these years, I'd measured my self-worth by how many ribs were showing. Why hadn't anyone told me being happy had nothing to do with that?

The current shifted and pushed me out to sea. As the water rocked me forward, I shot up on the ocean side of the wave. I was past the break line. I leaned back and let my legs float out in front of me, then stared up at the sky. Water tickled my face as my hair fanned out like a lion's mane. I closed my eyes, let the heavy salt water hold me exactly as I was.

"Hey, bathing beauty!" a voice called out, and I opened my eyes to see Rowan swimming toward me. "What are you doing out here by yourself?"

I didn't have much experience with flirting, but I gave it my best shot.

"I'm not by myself. You're here."

"Thank God for that!"

He laughed, so I laughed too.

As my eyes took in his golden skin, full lips, strong hands, I felt a flurry of excitement. Because I remembered that other thing my body could do.

CHAPTER 37
JANIE

I got my period when I was twelve, but when I stopped eating at thirteen, it went away. For two and a half years I was in this state of arrested development. Not a girl anymore, but also not a woman.

The doctor warned me that if I didn't start eating, the damage to my vital organs would be permanent. "You essentially hit the pause button," he'd explained at my weekly weigh-in. "But you can only stay paused for so long. Your reproductive organs will be the first to fail. Remember your body has an intelligence. If it doesn't think it can support reproduction, it will sacrifice those organs to save the rest."

He said it with no judgment, just as a scientific fact. And it scared the hell out of me. I wanted to be perfect, not break down. "So what do I do?" I asked him.

And the answer was simple: "Eat."

As soon as I started gaining weight, my period came back with a vengeance. There were days it was so heavy I couldn't leave the house. But as spring turned to summer, it found its stride, and by my seventeenth birthday, I was as regular as the rising tide.

Fifteen people showed up for my birthday party, but I only cared about the one who wasn't invited. Samara lit the bonfire at sunset, and we were toasting marshmallows and swigging vodka from the bottle just as the quarter moon appeared in the darkening sky. Rowan and I were sitting shoulder to shoulder on a blanket between two of Samara's friends from the track team and my costars from *Hello, Dolly!* Firelight flickered across Rowan's perfect face, casting shadows in the chiseled hollows of his cheeks.

"I haven't had a s'more since camping when I was a kid," Rowan said, twirling his marshmallow-on-a-stick just above the flames.

"I've never been camping," I said. He gaped at me in exaggerated horror.

"I was about to say, what, did you grow up in a cave? But obviously not."

"We were more of a hotel-motel family," I confessed.

"It's not for everybody. You get really dirty."

I tried to imagine my mom with dirt under her fingernails. "My mom gets a manicure every Friday."

"So probably not for her." He was looking at me like I was the most interesting person in the world. I wondered if my friends thought this strapping Adonis was my boyfriend, and if they were jealous or happy for me.

I glanced back at the campfire. "Your marshmallow's on fire."

"Oh, shit!" Rowan pulled the flaming marshmallow out of the flames and blew on it until it went out. He was wearing a shirt, but I could still see his abs ripple with each exhale.

"Want it?" he said, offering me the charred mass.

"No thanks."

He plucked the burned blob off the stick and tossed it in the fire.

"Sticky," he said, wiping his finger and thumb on the blanket.

"Here."

I handed him a bottle of water. He dribbled it over his fingers, then rubbed them together and shook them out. "There. Good as new."

He held out his hand for me to inspect it. I still felt nervous around him, but the Smirnoff took the edge off. I reached for his outstretched hand and turned it over to examine his fingers. We'd been sitting next to each other all night, but this was the first time we'd touched, and the sensation of the back of his hand against my palm made my pulse quicken.

"Nails look good. My mother would approve," I said.

"I'm not interested in your mother."

His voice was low. His eyes were locked on mine. My heart started beating all the way up in my ears.

"Sorry, that was cheesy," he said, crinkling his nose. "You can punch me if you want." Maybe I'd watched too many dumb rom-coms where characters say things like, "I knew from the moment I first saw him that it was meant to be . . ." because, yeah, that's how I felt. If he wasn't *the one*, why did he make me feel like this? I could tell by the way Kenny kept looking at us that he didn't approve. But our attraction was a speeding locomotive, there was no stopping it.

"You want to go for a walk?" I asked, because after six hours of bumping shoulders, I wanted to be alone with him like a dog wants a bone.

"Sure."

I was still holding his hand. He reached for my other one and pulled me up. From across the campfire, Samara's eyes ticked up, and I knew what she was thinking. Rowan was an older boy; there might be expectations. I smiled and winked at her to let her know I was in control. For most people, putting on a bikini was just another day at the beach, but for me it was a breakthrough. For the first time in my life, I felt beautiful. *He* made me feel beautiful. I'd spent my whole life enslaved by other people's expectations, but no more. If I was doing this, I was doing it for me.

To be clear, I was very much a virgin. In fact, I'd only kissed one boy, and that didn't really count because it was during a stupid party game. I had no idea how it would feel to kiss someone I really liked. Or that it would be hard to stop at kissing.

CHAPTER 38
JANIE

Rowan held my hand as we walked along the beach. He had a rolled-up blanket under his arm. I didn't know if anyone had seen him take it, but if they had, I didn't care. I wasn't going to let anyone judge me for wanting to be alone with a hot guy—certainly not on my birthday.

We talked about his home in Colorado. He asked if I liked to ski. I told him I'd only been once—to a place in Vermont called Killington when I was ten.

"I spent most of the day on my butt wiping my nose."

"The first time always sucks," he said, and before I could wonder if he was talking about skiing, he added, "Rocky Mountain snow is a totally different animal." And I breathed a little easier.

"It looks fun," I said. "I wish I was better at it."

"Come to Colorado, and I'll teach you."

Six-month-ago me would never have believed a gorgeous guy like Rowan would want to take me skiing, but seventeen-year-old me dared to imagine it . . . getting all dressed up in puffy parkas, holding hands on the chairlift, cozying up by the fire all rosy cheeked and breathless.

"What was cadet camp like?" I asked, because I thought I'd better change the subject before I got too lost in the fantasy.

He told me about the "mess" and how the enlisted kids taught them to put their knife and fork at three o'clock to signal they were done eating. "That's how the servers know to take your plate away."

"Wow. That sounds so civilized," I said, because I'd just seen *Animal House* and imagined all college dining halls looking like World War III.

"Military school is very regimented," he said. "Some kids need it, I guess."

I thought about Kenny, how he always made his bed and put his shoes away without being asked, and realized he needed it, not to be forced into good habits, but to be somewhere where they were appreciated.

"Kenny wants to be a pilot," I said. "Like our dad."

"Everyone wants to be a pilot," he said. "Otherwise they'd join the army."

"What happens to the ones who don't make it?"

"I don't know. But it's not going to be me."

He stopped and looked at me in a way that made my heart pound as hard as the surf.

"My God, you're so beautiful," he said, his eyes locked on mine. No one had ever called me beautiful, and I nearly cried. He touched my jaw, and I tilted up my chin so he would know it was OK to kiss me.

He tasted salty sweet, like sea air mixed with cotton candy. I got completely lost in that kiss. I didn't realize I was pressing my body against his until I felt him grow hard against my hip. I felt nervous—was this really happening? And then a rush of excitement. Because after not letting myself have cake or ice cream or anything our fathers told us was "bad," I was ready to join the party.

"I could kiss you all night," he said. And I wondered if that was all he wanted to do? Or if he thought that was all *I* wanted to do?

I heard the jingle of a dog collar and looked over to see an older man walking a yellow lab along the shoreline. I couldn't see his face, but I could feel his disapproving eyes on us.

"Let's go put that blanket down," I said, indicating a grassy area up the beach. Rowan raised an eyebrow at me. "You're the one who took it," I reminded him, because why pretend we didn't know why?

He reached for my hand, and we walked toward the dunes.

"How about there?" I said, pointing to a little trough between two mounds of sand, just wide enough for our blanket and tall enough to hide us.

We walked to the spot. He spread the blanket, then sat down and reached for me. "Come on down, the weather's fine," he said.

I knelt down in front of him. He pulled me into his lap, and the world melted away as we kissed under the quarter moon.

"I can't believe I met you," he said, running his tongue along the inside of my upper lip. "You're, like, the most beautiful girl I've ever seen." And then he laughed a little. "God, I sound like such a dork."

"I like dorks," I said, then ran my fingertips down his arm. His skin was smooth like polished marble. He grabbed my hand and pressed it to his chest.

"Stop me if I do anything that makes you uncomfortable," he said, tilting his head back to look me in the eye. "I mean it. I want you to remember this birthday as the best one ever."

"It already is," I said.

He smiled that dazzling movie-star smile, then laid me down like he was putting a baby in a crib.

"Is this OK?" he asked. I must have nodded because a second later he was lying beside me, his body pressed against mine. I tried to relax as his tongue explored my mouth. I was nervous—I had never been with a guy like this. And elated—because, good Lord, if I was going to be with a guy, this was the one.

His hand peeled back my bikini top. I closed my eyes as he caressed my breast. I felt my nipple get hard. He brought his mouth down to meet it.

A tiny voice in me tried to tell me to hit the brakes. I was a beginner. I'd only been on green runs, and he was skiing double blacks. But I reminded myself that voice wasn't me, it was all those other people who tried to control me with all their "shoulds"—you should look like this, you should act, do, *be* like that. Maybe if I wasn't so gaga for him, I would have trusted we had plenty of time to discover each other, it didn't all have to happen in one night. But in that moment, he was as irresistible as hot fudge after a long, cold winter, and I wasn't going to deny my hunger any longer.

He raised his head to look me in the eyes. "This isn't your first time, is it?" And the lie just popped out.

"No."

Maybe I was afraid if I told him I was a virgin he would freak out and run away. Or maybe I was just self-conscious about being "the little sister." I was in such a hurry to close the book on the girl who tied herself in knots to be perfect, I didn't stop to think about the risk I was taking. And not just the emotional one.

Now that I'd given him the green light, things picked up speed. He unbuttoned my shorts. I lifted my butt off the ground so he could slide them down my legs. As he took off his shirt, I reached for the waistband of his swimsuit, and he helped me peel it from his hips. The sight of his naked body made my cheeks burn red hot. A more confident me would have known I had nothing to prove, and that a good and decent man like Rowan would like me just as much if we waited. And if he were more sure of himself, he might have suggested it. But he wanted to please me as much as I wanted to please him, and we were both too young and stupid to know rushing to have sex wasn't the way.

His body was hard and heavy as he lowered it on top of mine. I felt pressure between my legs. I tried to relax into it, but how do you relax when the most gorgeous man you've ever seen is lying on top of you? This was the moment I should have asked about birth control. We both should have asked. But like I said—young and stupid.

His breath was hot against my ear as he rocked back and forth. I felt my body move with him, like a surfboard on a wave. My eyes floated over the gentle curve of his back, my tongue tasted the sweat on his cheek. I knew I should just close my eyes and let myself get lost in the feeling, but this was my first time, I wanted to remember every second of it.

"I'm sorry," he said when it was over. "Usually I go longer." He rolled onto his side, and I turned on my hip to look at him. "You OK?"

I nodded and smiled, and he smiled too.

"I wish we didn't live so far apart," he said, and I felt a pang of sadness when I remembered he was leaving.

"Me too."

"I feel really connected to you, Janie."

A tear rolled down my cheek, and he wiped it away with his nose. "Sorry," I squeaked. I didn't mean to cry. I guess I was just overwhelmed by the enormity of the moment. Like why people cry at weddings. Getting married is a happy occasion, but it wouldn't be the beginning of something if it wasn't the end of something else.

"I love that you can cry in front of me," he whispered in my ear. Then, to lighten the mood, "Unless you're crying because you hate me." He bit his lip in an exaggerated grimace.

"I could never," I said. And through it all, I never did.

"Your brother's not going to be pissed at me, is he?" And I understood that I shouldn't tell him. And I wouldn't. But he was going to find out soon enough.

To: Martin Pearl, MD

From: Better Health Laboratories, Inc.

RE: Medical Record #A45882
This letter is to inform you that the quantitative pregnancy blood test for your patient (medical record A45882) was positive. The hCG level in her blood was 100 mIU/mL, which is indicative of pregnancy.

A quantitative pregnancy blood test measures the amount of human chorionic gonadotropin (hCG) in the blood. hCG is a hormone produced by the placenta after conception.

We recommend you schedule an appointment with your patient to discuss the results of the pregnancy test and do an ultrasound to determine the gestational age.

Our lab is open and can answer any questions Monday–Friday between 8AM and 4PM.

Regards,

Tina S.

(lab technician)

CHAPTER 39
ELLIE

He called me four days after I sent the letter.

"Synergy Scientific, Ellie speaking," I said as I always do. It was just after lunch, and my colleagues were hurrying back to their desks with their Cokes from McDonald's and coffee from Dunkin'.

"Gabs, it's me."

Richie was the only person who called me Gabrielle. Or Gabs. Or Gabalicious, Gabba-dabba-do, Gabba-dabba-ding-dong. He liked to be different. Which of course he was, no matter what he called me.

"How can I help you?" My desk was in the lobby area—there was always someone listening. It's not that we weren't allowed to take personal calls, I just didn't want my coworkers all in my business. I could talk more freely to my boyfriend in a few months when we were official.

"We need to talk. Can you meet tonight?"

"Yes, absolutely. Is there a time that works best for you?"

"Seven-ish. Can we do your place?"

Gina was out of town—San Francisco again.

"Yes, perfect."

I got off work at five. Traffic was heavy, so I didn't make it home until a little after six. I had some mozzarella sticks in the freezer, so I popped them in the oven, then whipped up some spinach and artichoke dip. I cursed myself for not having the makings of a proper dinner, then reminded myself he wasn't with me for my cooking.

I didn't have time to wash my hair, so I wrapped it in a towel before I turned on the shower. As I undressed, I checked my underwear for blood to make sure my letter hadn't been a lie. The shower door got foggy with steam, so I slipped in and rinsed off, then shaved my legs so they'd be smooth to his touch.

I decided to dress for comfort, in buttery, wide-leg silk trousers and a *Flashdance*-inspired off-the-shoulder top. My period was officially a week late. I wouldn't show for another three months, but I liked the message that loose clothes sent.

I had what I'd planned to say all worked out. Gina would take this apartment—she could more than afford it; we'd both been saving money for years. I thought three months' notice would be enough for her. That would take us through the holidays. If she wanted more time to find a roommate or work out her finances, I could give her until February, but I wanted to be settled in our new place by then. I didn't want to be carrying boxes in my third trimester, I wouldn't even be able to get my arms around them!

I assumed we would rent until his divorce was finalized and he knew how much alimony he had to pay. Then we would buy what we could afford. I'd always wanted to live in Boston, in one of those brownstones off Newbury Street . . . or Beacon Hill, with a view of the river. I'd work until the baby came in June, take the summer off, then go back to work in the fall. I didn't want to be a kept woman like his wife. I knew how it made him nuts that she was dependent on him for every penny. Plus I liked my job and couldn't see myself sitting home all day.

My makeup was melted, so I washed my face. He was used to seeing me au naturel, and it's not like this was a date. He was coming over to discuss our future. I know he wanted to wait until both of his kids were out of the house, but I was forty-one. This baby was a year early, but also twenty years late.

The doorbell rang at 7:07 p.m. I scampered down the stairs in slippered feet to let him in.

"Hi," I said, a little breathless, and not from the stairs.

"Hi." He didn't smile, but I tried not to read too much into it. Uprooting your life—even for the woman you love—is complicated. What kind of man would he be if he didn't take it seriously?

"Come on up."

We didn't kiss on the stoop, but we rarely did. I had a nosy neighbor. Marsha was sweet, but I didn't want her in my business.

"Can I get you something to drink?" I asked when he stepped into the living room. I obviously wasn't drinking, but he looked like he might need one.

"Nah, I'm good." He was dressed for work, in pleated trousers and a pin-striped button-front. I could see the outline of his undershirt on his upper arms. I wasn't used to seeing him like this, and the realization that our relationship was about to change gave me a little thrill. I was finally going to be the woman who greeted him at the end of every day—the partner, not the accessory.

He didn't sit, so I didn't either. He had called this meeting, but I decided to be the one to get things started.

"I take it you got my letter." I smiled at him, so he would know everything would be all right. We weren't stupid teenagers. We were adults. We were in love. This was a happy milestone.

"I know it's probably a bit of a surprise," I continued. And that's when he finally spoke.

"How could you let this happen?" His tone was accusatory, like he thought I'd done it on purpose.

"It's always been a risk," I said, because maybe on some level I had? In the past, if I thought I was ovulating, we'd abstain or do other things. It wasn't foolproof, but at least I tried. Until I didn't.

"How far along are you?"

I didn't know why that mattered, so I just shrugged. "I haven't had an ultrasound yet."

"Was it Nantucket?"

"What difference does it make? We're going to be together by next summer anyway." That was our plan. We'd discussed it. But I figured it couldn't hurt to remind him.

"We never said anything about a baby, Gabrielle," he said, using my given name like an angry parent scolding a child.

"I'm just as surprised as you are." Panic was nipping at my insides. This conversation wasn't going how I'd hoped. "Sometimes Mother Nature has her own plan." I almost said God but stopped myself just in time.

He didn't say anything for a long beat. For a second, I thought he might be coming around. Until he reached for his wallet.

"Here's a thousand dollars," he said, pulling out a wad of bills. "I called a clinic in Brookline, that should be more than enough."

He tossed the money onto the coffee table. The sight of those hundred-dollar bills was as terrifying as a live grenade.

"You want me to get rid of it?" I tried to shame him by using crude words.

"Maybe your sister can go with you," he said, dodging the question. "I'm sorry, but I obviously can't."

Fear and anger collided in the center of my chest. There was only one reason he couldn't take me. My sister had known it all along.

"You said you were going to divorce her as soon as the kids were out of the house. We had a plan, Richie."

"It's complicated."

"What's so complicated?"

"Divorce is expensive. I can't fly you around if I'm paying her half my salary."

I loved traveling. But I loved him more. I didn't care if I couldn't be his copilot anymore as long as I had him.

"I don't need to fly around to all those places," I said. "I just need you." That wasn't entirely true. I needed this baby too. Needed to not be "the other woman" anymore. Needed the man I loved to come home to me. To *us*.

"You can still have me. Nothing needs to change. I just . . . I can't walk out on my family." I shook my head. My father had walked out when Gina and I were much younger than Richie's kids. Men could do whatever they wanted. This I knew firsthand.

I thought back to the night we met in that freezing-cold parking lot, how God had put him right where I needed him. "We can be a family, Richie," I said, trying to keep my voice from shaking. "Like we were always meant to be."

He looked down at his shoes. "I made my choice, Gabby. I'm not saying it was the right one. I just . . . I can't abandon my kids. They'll hate me."

My anger turned to outrage. "But you can abandon this one?"

"You can't abandon something that doesn't exist yet. We made a mistake. A mistake I need you to take care of."

And there it was. The stunning admission. I was, and would always be, just a plaything to him. Like that airplane.

"Get out," I said, scooping up the money and then shoving it into his chest.

"Gabby, please. It doesn't have to be like this."

"GET OUT!" I let go of the money. Crisp one-hundred-dollar bills tumbled to the floor.

"This is the hormones talking, this isn't you."

"You told me your marriage was over. That you were leaving her. You lied to me!" I kicked at my hush money. A few bills floated up in the air.

"I thought I could. But it's not just about her. Things at home are complicated—"

"Stop!" I couldn't stand to think of him running to the kids he had with *her* while running away from ours. "I wanted to do this with you, but I'll do it alone if I have to." I didn't mean it as a threat. I was forty-one years old. I didn't have much runway left. And I meant what I said in the letter. This child was conceived in love. I had enough to give for both of us.

His blue eyes got hard as they locked onto mine. "Raising a kid on your own is hard," he warned, like he was some sort of expert.

"My mother raised two."

"I know you want to punish me," he said, "but that's not a reason to go through with this."

"Punish you? By having your baby? Since when is that a punishment?"

"It's obvious you want to hurt me. And I understand why." I shook my head. If I wanted to hurt him, I would have pushed him down the stairs.

"You're such a narcissist. Do you even hear yourself?"

"Do *you* hear *yourself*? 'I can do this on my own, I don't need anybody!'" he mocked.

"I *don't* need anybody," I said. "I've never had anybody."

"For the last ten years you've had me." And I almost laughed.

"Nine years. And I hardly *had* you. At best, I had you on loan."

"You had the important part." He put his hands to his heart. I almost punched him.

"You need to go now."

"Look, Gabs. Nothing has to change. We can still go on trips together. Like always."

"No, you're wrong. Something did change," I corrected him. "And that something is me."

CHAPTER 40
ELLIE

"Ellie?"

My sister came home at two a.m. to find me sobbing on the couch. Normally it was me who walked in to find her red faced and crying. The stress of all that air travel and lack of sleep sometimes got to her. But tonight she was going to have to talk me off the ledge.

"My God, what happened?" she asked, even though she already knew.

I told her about the pregnancy, and how Richie had lied to me about leaving his wife. To her credit, she didn't say "I told you so," even though she had.

"He wants me to have an abortion," I said through my tears. "He tried to give me a thousand dollars, but I wouldn't take it."

"So you want to have the baby, even without him?"

What I wanted was for him to come running back, say he was sorry, tell me that we would be together now and forever.

"I think so," I wavered.

"Are you absolutely sure you're pregnant, El?"

"I'm a week late," I said. "And I'm never late."

"You were with him in Nantucket?" she asked. But then she saw my face. "Right. Of course you were."

I looked away, because the next part was hard. "He doesn't love me, G. Never did."

She kindly tried to object. "You don't know that—"

"Yes, I do," I interrupted. "It's so obvious now. He was never in love with me. He was in love with his own freedom. I was just a warm body along for the ride." Saying it out loud made my body quake with rage. It was so obvious. Why hadn't I known it until now?

"I'm sorry he hurt you," she said, then opened her arms and pulled me into a hug. She smelled like Aqua Net and stale airplane. I suddenly felt guilty for dumping on her after a long day at work.

"I'm tired," I said, because I knew she was too.

"Let's go to sleep," she said. "We'll figure this out in the morning."

She helped me up. I climbed into bed without putting on pajamas. The thought that I could raise a child with my sister who traveled the world for a living was absurd and deeply unfair to her. She didn't sign up for this. She'd been trying to yank me from that relationship since the moment it started.

I thought about my mom. I imagined her sitting on the edge of my bed, shaking her head in disappointment. How was I going to keep my full-time job with health care and benefits now? Who was going to raise my child while I was working to afford club soccer and college? I had savings, but that money was supposed to buy me a house so I didn't have to work myself literally to death like she had. I wasn't lying when I said I could have a baby by myself. But was it wrong to want more for my child than what I could give?

Somehow I managed to fall asleep. When I woke up the next morning, Gina had already gone to the drugstore.

"One line, it's a false alarm. Two lines, I'm going to be an auntie," she said, handing me a pregnancy test kit.

"I don't know if I can do this, G."

"You pee on it. It's not complicated."

"Not that." My job didn't offer sick days or daycare. *Good God, what was I thinking?*

"Do the test," she said. "Then we'll figure it out."

I went into the bathroom and looked at my reflection in the mirror. Thanks to my hairdresser, you couldn't see the grays popping through my blond hair, but hair dye couldn't help the purple circles under my eyes or the lines that were forming on my forehead and neck. If a woman had a prime, I was past mine.

I sat down on the toilet and stuck the stick between my legs. The box said it could take up to two minutes for the result to come in, but fifteen seconds later, those two parallel pink lines confirmed what I already knew.

I pulled up my pants and flushed the toilet. Ten seconds later, there was a knock on the bathroom door.

"Well?" Gina said, poking her head in. I held up the stick. She nodded but didn't smile.

"What am I going to do?"

"You're going to have a baby," she said simply, because we were raised that when God gives you a miracle, you don't give it back.

Tears streamed from my eyes as my heart flooded with shame. I was supposed to be the one to break the cycle. But instead, I was not only repeating the mistakes of my mother almost exactly, I was also dragging my sister down with me.

"I know this is not how you wanted it, sis," Gina said. "But we have to take what God gives us."

I was beginning to wonder about the things that God had given me. A deadbeat father. A single mom who died too young. A man who couldn't love me. "You live the life you make," my pastor used to preach during Sunday service. But some people are given shiny tools and golden opportunities, while some of us are born in a hole with no shovel to dig ourselves out.

"I'm going to live in this apartment my whole life," I said, chucking the stick in the trash.

"And what's so bad about that?" Gina asked.

I shrugged. How could I tell the person in the same boat as me that our lives sucked? Surely she knew. She was a stewardess. She saw how the other half lived. She served them cocktails.

"You think things would've been better if you'd married Richie?" my sister asked.

I shrugged again. "I wouldn't be alone."

"Right. Just like his wife wasn't alone when he was on Nantucket with you."

She made no attempt to hide her disapproval. I was part of the problem, because men like Richie couldn't cheat on their wives if women like me wouldn't let them.

"I know I did this to myself, you don't need to rub it in my face." I pushed past her into the living room.

"I'm sorry, Ellie," Gina said, following on my heels. "I don't mean to be unkind. But I see it every day."

"See what?"

"Do you know how many pilots are married but have a squeeze on the side?" she asked. I didn't, but I knew she wouldn't have asked if it wasn't a lot.

"At least the wife gets a credit card and her mortgage paid," I said, even though she wasn't asking who had it worse.

"Is that what you want?" she asked. "A sugar daddy?"

"Well, we'd be better off." I spread my arms wide, indicating the cramped apartment we'd called home for our entire lives. "We can't let them save us, and we can't save ourselves. So what do we have left?"

"I don't know, Ellie," she said. "Each other, I guess?"

Her eyes found mine. And I knew, just like our mom had, we would make this work. I let myself cry. Not with self-pity, but with gratitude. Because *each other* had always been enough.

CHAPTER 41
ELLIE

I was forty-one, so my pregnancy was considered high risk. My doctor referred me to a fancy-shmancy guy at Harvard Medical Center, where all the best doctors were. Dr. Pearl was known as the OB to the stars—well, their wives, anyway. Apparently it wasn't unusual to see a seven-foot-tall basketball player from the Celtics in his waiting room. Unless it was basketball season; then the wife would be in the same boat as me.

I'm not a sports-star wife, so it took me a month to get an appointment. By my calculations, I was eight weeks pregnant by then—far enough along for an ultrasound to reveal an embryo the size of a grain of rice. And a flickering heartbeat—if my baby had one. Apparently at my advanced age, it was not a given.

My appointment was in the afternoon, so I went to work in the morning, like always. My boss was cool when I told him I had to leave early for a "doctor's checkup." It was far too soon to reveal the reason for the appointment. I had been at the company for almost twenty years, but there was no reason to think they'd consider a baby born out of wedlock anything other than an inconvenience.

Richie was leaving messages for me all day and night, but I had Gina delete them off the answering machine. He also came by the house twice. The first time Gina was there and sent him away. The second time

I was home alone. He rang the bell over and over again, but I ignored it. Marsha, my neighbor, finally came out and threatened to call the cops. My heart ached to see him. But Gina and I had made a pact that unless he showed up with a copy of his divorce papers, he was not allowed in. And we both knew there would be no divorce papers.

At three o'clock on the dot, I said goodbye to my coworkers, then got in my car to drive to Cambridge for my three-thirty appointment. I was warned Dr. Pearl spent as much time with a patient as they needed (code for he runs late), but I still wanted to be on time. The parking in that neighborhood would be ridiculously expensive. If I were coming back to work after, I would have taken the T so that his lateness wouldn't stress me out.

I wasn't showing yet, though I'd gone up a bra size and had to retire a few of my blouses. So far my morning sickness had been pretty mild, though it wasn't limited to the morning; I don't know why they call it that. No one seemed to notice I was drinking ginger ale instead of coffee and nibbling crackers throughout the day. Besides needing to go to bed at eight o'clock every night, I felt pretty good. Sometimes my belly hurt, but I figured that was just growing pains. There was something growing in there, after all.

The days were getting shorter and colder, and I was grateful for sweater weather because it could prolong my secret. I still hadn't worked out what I would tell people when they asked who the father was. It was too late to invent a fictional boyfriend, and I didn't want them to think I'd had a one-night stand—though that was probably more palatable than the truth.

Dr. Pearl's office was in a small brick building on the edge of Harvard Square. As I suspected, the parking was crazy expensive, but I found a metered spot right across the street, so I snagged it, grateful for any chance to save a few pennies.

The building had three stories, but Dr. Pearl's office was on the ground floor and had its own separate entrance. I felt a little nervous going in there by myself, but felt better when I saw only one man in the waiting room. A couple of women looked up and smiled at me, but most just kept their noses in their magazines. I reminded myself they had no idea what I was and smiled back.

"Checking in?" the dark-eyed receptionist asked.

"Yes. Gabrielle McNally?" It came out like a question, as if I needed confirmation that I was allowed to be there.

"Dr. Pearl is running about half an hour behind, but if you could get started on this paperwork?" She slid a clipboard across the counter.

"Of course."

I found a seat next to a woman with a belly as big and round as a beach ball. She must have seen me staring because she offered an explanation.

"Twins."

A jolt of terror went through my body. *Good God, what if I'm having twins?*

"Wow. Congratulations," I mustered, then sat down to fill out the forms. There were eight pages of questions. The first three were easy: name, age, date of birth. But the fourth gave me pause. *Why do they need to know my marital status?*

I thought about skipping it, but that would just call more attention to it. Surely I wasn't the first woman to have a baby out of wedlock. It was the eighties, not the fifties.

I checked the appropriate box, then moved on to the medical questionnaire. That section was pretty easy. I hadn't had any diseases or surgeries, I basically just checked "no" for everything. But the next section was problematic. My pen hovered over the words "name of father." I couldn't leave it blank. There was also a block of questions about his health history. I didn't think Richie had any congenital health conditions, but I'd never asked.

I decided to use the name of my on-and-off boyfriend in college, John Callahan. I answered "no" to all the questions about his medical history. I didn't want them asking a bunch of follow-up questions, and it's not like they could do anything if he had, in fact, been exposed to any chemicals or environmental hazards.

I signed the form, then checked it over to make sure I hadn't missed anything. I was just about to get up to hand it in when the door to the examination area opened, and two women stepped into the lobby.

The first one was young and couldn't get out of there fast enough. I barely caught a glimpse of her as she scurried toward the exit. But the other was as familiar to me as a recurring nightmare. With that shock of platinum hair and perfect Cupid's bow lips, I could have picked her out of a police lineup.

"Would you like to make your next appointment, Mrs. Berenson?" the receptionist asked.

"No, we're all set," Richie's wife said curtly.

As she followed the young woman out to the parking lot, I wiped a tear from my cheek. I'm sure other pregnant women had cried in that waiting room, but not for the same reason as me.

September 10, 1983

Dear Janie,
Well, they cut off all my hair. Kenny's too, but his was already short, so the change wasn't so dramatic. I think you'd like it. Some of the guys' heads are lumpy, but mine's not so bad.

Training is intense, but I don't mind. Makes the days go fast. The nights are long. We have to have lights out by ten. Leaves me lots of time to think about you.

I know we only had that one weekend together, but I feel really connected to you. I don't think I've ever laughed that much with someone I just met, or maybe ever. I hope you don't mind, but I told Kenny that I like you. It's not like he didn't already know. He's not mad or anything. I just figured if I'm going to come visit, I need to be honest that it would be to see you.

I know it's your senior year and there will be lots of parties and prom and all that. I don't expect you to wait for me or anything (but you can if you want to!). I just wanted you to know that I'm thinking about you. Maybe we could plan a visit? You probably have to be home for

Thanksgiving, but if you want to come over winter break, I'll take you skiing just like we planned.

If you don't write back I won't be offended. Long distance relationships are hard. You're probably too busy for a boyfriend anyway. But hey, you can't blame a guy for trying, right?

I hope you write back. But if not, I hope you have a great year and a great life.

Love,

Rowan

CHAPTER 42
JANIE

I took the test at Samara's house. Samara's family only had one bathroom for five people, but it was still more comfortable than doing it at home. When two lines appeared, I wasn't surprised. You don't spend three years scrutinizing every inch of your body and not know when there's a baby growing inside it.

"We gotta go tell your mom," Samara said. And that's when I started crying. Because now I not only had to cop to my stupidity, I had to ask for help. My parents had already paid a fortune in medical bills for my eating disorder. If they weren't already tapped out, this would send them over the edge.

And then there was the Rowan piece. We had been writing to each other for the last six weeks. Sometimes his letters came clipped together in one fat envelope; sometimes he splurged for multiple stamps to spread them out. It was like a Jane Austen–era love affair, bubbling with sweet anticipation. He told me about his niggling knee pain, his struggles with calculus, how much he missed his dog. I told him about failing my driving test, setting the chem lab on fire, shopping for shoes. The sex act that kicked it off had faded to an afterthought. Until that day when it took center stage.

Samara stood by my side when I went to talk to my mother. Actually, I let the two pink lines do the talking. I thought she would scream and yell like when Kenny and I broke her crystal vase playing Wiffle ball in the house, but she just nodded and said, "I'll make you an appointment." Maybe she thought she was doing me a favor by being so calm. Whatever the case, I was too angry with myself to be disappointed in her.

I didn't have an OB-GYN, so she took me to hers—a Dr. Pearl in Cambridge. She got me an afternoon appointment so I didn't have to miss school. "This doesn't have to disrupt your studies," she'd said, as if that was our top concern.

Dr. Pearl's nurse ushered me back as soon as we arrived, as if my mother had told her she didn't want anyone to see her teenage daughter sitting in the waiting room. My mom filled out the paperwork in the exam room, occasionally looking up to ask me questions like "How much do you weigh now?" and "When was your last menstrual period?"

After about fifteen minutes, a nurse came in to collect the paperwork and hand me a thin cotton gown. "Everything off, open in the front." I wondered if there was some secret code on my file that indicated I was a cliché, because I swear I saw her roll her eyes as she walked out of the room.

My mom had the decency to look away as I got naked. We sat in silence for another twenty minutes before Dr. Pearl entered wearing a white coat and a serious expression, like he knew this was the worst day of my young life.

"Hello, Elizabeth," he said, shaking my mother's hand.

"Dr. Pearl," she said, bowing her head like he was royalty.

"You must be Jane," he said, looking at me.

I nodded. He offered his hand, so I shook it.

"Are you OK if your mom is here during the examination?"

"She's a minor," my mom said, as if she knew I wanted her to leave.

"At seventeen, she has autonomy over her medical decisions, and a right to privacy."

"It's fine," I said, because I didn't want to make trouble. "She can stay."

"How are you feeling, Jane?" Dr. Pearl asked, turning his back to my mom.

"OK," I lied.

"Morning sickness?"

"Not too bad."

"Let's have you lie down," he said, extending the table so my feet wouldn't dangle. He held my hand while I leaned back as if I was already too pregnant to do a reverse sit-up on my own.

"I'm just going to feel your abdomen," he said, then opened my gown and gently pressed on my belly.

"Everything feels normal. Breasts tender?"

"A little."

He reached for what looked like a large tube of toothpaste. "Your menstrual calendar suggests you're about eight weeks along, but an ultrasound will give us a more accurate picture."

He flipped the cap open, then spread an absurd amount of clear goo across my abdomen.

"It won't hurt, I promise. Just really gooey."

He spread the ultrasound gel around with a small wand the size of my dad's electric razor. A grainy image the shape of a shelled peanut appeared on the monitor. He spun it so I could have a better look.

"That's an eight-week-old embryo," he announced.

The wand was pressed to my abdomen. I had no reason to doubt that peanut embryo was inside me, but I still asked, "That's in my belly?"

"Well, in your uterus. Want to hear the heartbeat?"

"Let's not confuse things," my mom said. But I pretended not to hear her.

"Yes, I'd like to hear it."

Dr. Pearl turned a knob on the base of the monitor, and the room filled with the *boom-boom-boom* of my unborn baby's heart. For the first time since I found out I was pregnant, I wasn't scared or full of shame. I was in awe.

"It's so fast."

"It will slow down in about six weeks."

"We're not here for a biology lesson, Doctor," my mother piped up. "I was told you could do the procedure here in office."

"Is it your wish to terminate the pregnancy?" Dr. Pearl asked me, removing the wand from my abdomen. I could feel my mother's eyes on me. Obviously I was in no position to have a baby. Not that I wanted to. Of course I didn't want to. After everything I'd done to my body, there was no way I could ask it to grow a baby.

"Yes, I'm sure."

I thought of Rowan. I hadn't told him—an accidental pregnancy is not something you write in a letter. And the only phone at the academy was in a shared space where everyone could hear. Maybe it was wrong to keep it to myself, but what was the point of telling him? What the hell was he supposed to do, marry me? That wasn't happening. Our fairy-tale romance was over; it would never recover from this. Why hurt him when I was hurting enough for us both?

"We do those appointments first thing in the morning," he said as he wiped the goo off my belly with a scratchy paper towel. "My nurse will schedule it. It will have to be in the next four weeks; I can't do it after the first trimester. Sooner is better. Less chance of complications."

"Does she have to miss school?" my mom asked. And all the air went out of the room. *That's what she wanted to know?*

"Well, I wouldn't think she'd want to go to school the day of the procedure," he said. "We administer a mild sedative, it takes several hours to wear off." He flicked the intercom. "Hannah, can you come in, please?"

"How long until she can go back?" my mother asked, then tried to make it seem like I was the concerned one. "It's her senior year. She doesn't want to miss."

"I usually recommend at least a day or two to recover," Dr. Pearl replied. "She'll have some bleeding for about a week. Like a menstrual period but heavier."

"Maybe we can schedule it for a Friday, then?" She looked at me like *Good idea, right?*

There was a light knock on the door; Nurse Hannah peeked in a second later. The doctor waved her in, then turned to look at me.

"Hannah will take care of your scheduling. If you have any questions between now and the day of the procedure, don't hesitate to call."

I don't know why I started crying. I wanted to do this. I *had* to do this.

"It's natural to be frightened," Dr. Pearl said, handing me a tissue. "If you're having complicated feelings, we recommend you find someone to talk to. These are big decisions, Jane. No one should have to go through them alone."

My mother was sitting right there, so why did he think I was alone?

"Jane's a smart girl," my mom said. "She just made a stupid mistake."

He patted my arm, and then I understood.

CHAPTER 43
JANIE

We made my appointment for seven a.m. the following Friday. When I told Samara, she insisted on coming with me.

"You'll be late for school," I warned.

"It's fine," she said. Which was true. Samara had already applied early decision to Harvard. Once they said yes—which they would—her grades wouldn't matter.

"What did you tell your parents?" I asked when she showed up with her overnight bag.

"That your cat died, and I was sleeping over so you wouldn't be alone."

"That's a little too on point," I said.

"Nobody died, Jane. It's a medical procedure."

She was right, of course. The peanut inside my abdomen was just a cluster of cells. It's not like it had eyes, or a nose, or a consciousness. Like a seed you plant in the garden. In fact, that's exactly how big it was—the size of a seed. Yes, it had the potential to grow into something, but only if the farmer did her job.

"Are you scared?" she asked, after we changed into pajamas and crawled into bed.

"To be honest, it doesn't feel real."

"You're in denial."

"Probably."

There was a long silence. I thought maybe she fell asleep. Then—

"Did you tell him?"

"Tell who?"

"Rowan."

Not only had I not told Rowan, I'd stopped writing to him altogether.

"No."

She didn't say what she thought about that, and I didn't ask.

"Well, good night."

"Good night."

I told myself I was being generous by not telling him, but the truth was, I just couldn't deal with it. The emotions that were pulsing through me—terror, regret, shame, grief—were too intense to process, so I checked out. Maybe that's why I didn't get mad at my mother for acting like this was just another problem that needed to be dealt with. Because I was acting the exact same way. I assumed she'd told my dad, but he hadn't said a word either. I had no idea what he thought of my predicament and knew better than to ask.

My mom woke us up at six a.m., and we were in the car by six fifteen. Samara sat with me in the back and held my hand the entire way. We got there just as a nurse in scrubs was unlocking the front door.

"Good morning," she said to me.

"Good morning," my mom replied.

"You can come on back," she said, beckoning me through the lobby toward the door to the treatment rooms. My mom tried to follow, but the nurse wasn't having it. "Just her."

Mom's face reddened, but she didn't say anything.

"We'll be right here," Samara assured me. And then the door closed, and I was alone with the nurse in the empty hallway.

"How are you feeling, Jane?"

"Fine," I said, because there weren't words for what I was feeling.

I followed her to an office at the end of the hallway. "It's our policy to have you sit with a counselor to go through the consent form," she said, indicating for me to go inside. A woman in a pastel pink sweater was sitting in a high-back chair facing the door. She stood up as I entered.

"This is Kate," my escort said, indicating the woman. "She's going to ask you a few questions before we proceed."

"Hello, Jane," Counselor Kate said.

"Hello."

"I'm a registered nurse specially trained to guide you through the procedure you have chosen to have today," she explained. "Please, have a seat."

The room was set up like a living room, with a couch, a coffee table, and two upholstered chairs. I sat on the couch, and she sat across from me on one of the chairs.

"How are you feeling?"

"Fine, thank you."

"Glad to hear it," she said with a smile. "Because you're not yet eighteen, I need to ask you if you would like to have your mother present."

"She doesn't have to be here?" I was a little confused why they'd left her in the waiting room.

"Only if you want her to be."

But also relieved. "No, I'm good."

She picked a clipboard off the coffee table. "The doctor will walk you through the medical procedure. I just have three questions I need to ask first. We have to make sure you are one hundred percent comfortable with your decision to be here today. But first, do you have any questions for me?"

I shook my head no.

"OK, then I'll start with mine. The first one's a yes or no. Do you understand that you are pregnant, and the medical procedure you are about to undergo will terminate that pregnancy forever?"

"Yes, I understand." I wanted to tell her that was two questions, but I was pretty sure she already knew that.

"OK. Question two. Also a yes or no, but if you have feelings around it, I'm happy to talk through them with you. That's what I'm here for." She paused to take a breath, then asked, "Have you informed the father of your decision to have an abortion?"

I felt a flicker of nervousness, like this might be a trap. If I said no, were they going to tell him? I didn't fill out the forms, my mother did. And I never told her who the father was. But maybe she figured it out. No, there was no way. Even if she knew it happened at my party, there were lots of boys at the beach that night. Good God, what if I needed his permission? This baby—or embryo—was at least partly his. Not that he could grow it into a person without me.

I decided to answer the question with a question. "Does he have, like, a legal right to know?"

"Not at all," Counselor Kate assured me. "We just want to give you an opportunity to talk about your feelings about including him in your decision. But it's your decision. He has no say in it. You don't have to tell him that you're doing this, or even that you're pregnant."

I exhaled a sigh of relief. "I see. Then no, I didn't tell him, and I don't plan to."

She smiled and nodded like that was a perfectly acceptable answer.

"Third and final question, but this one's not a yes or no. What was your process for deciding to terminate this pregnancy, and are you certain this is the right decision for you?"

"My process?"

"Yes. Your thinking process. We want to make sure you are the one who made this decision, so we'd like to know how you made it."

I didn't recall making a decision. When I told my mom, she responded by making me an appointment—no conversation necessary. My dad never brought it up, I couldn't even say for sure if he knew. We were a family who buried difficult things, why should this be any different?

Counselor Kate's pen hovered over her clipboard, waiting to write down my answer. "Well, I'm still in high school," I started, "so it's not really possible for me to have a child. I mean, it's not fair to my parents. I'm not ready to, well, I mean, I'm still a kid myself. And also it costs money, and I don't have any. Plus I plan to go to college next year. So yeah, I can't really do that with a baby."

"All that makes perfect sense. What about the second part of my question? You can answer that yes or no."

"Sorry, can you repeat it?"

"Are you certain that having an abortion is the right choice for you?"

"To be honest, I always thought it was the only choice."

"Is that a yes, then?" In my mind, I was on a road that only went in one direction. There was no turning around. There were also no exits. One destination. And this was it.

"Yes, it's the right choice for me."

"Wonderful. Thank you for answering my questions." She slid the consent form across the table. My eyes were blurry with tears, but I held them back.

"Sign at the bottom, and we'll get you ready for the doctor."

"My mother doesn't have to sign?"

"Nope. Just you."

She handed me a pen. As I held it in my hand, the finality of this hit me like a bomb exploding. I knew it would be easiest for everyone if I just got this over with—easiest for me too. And I was ready for things to be easy. But I couldn't shake the feeling when I saw that grainy peanut . . . heard that thumping heartbeat . . .

I repeated her question in my mind. *Are you sure this is the right choice for you?* Sounds crazy, but I hadn't known I had a choice. I'd had so many people in my head telling me they'd only love me if I looked and acted like they wanted me to, I'd forgotten my life was about me.

By all outward appearances, I had beaten my eating disorder. I'd stopped starving myself, but I was a long way from loving my body. I still felt guilty when I ate, had to force myself not to skip meals, avoided looking in the mirror because I didn't trust the image being reflected back at me. I savored the letters from Rowan, but they weren't enough to silence all the self-destructive thoughts. Who was I trying to be perfect for? What did being perfect even mean?

I knew I couldn't ask my parents to take care of a baby, but I couldn't help but wonder, if I gave my body a chance to do something amazing, maybe I'd stop wanting to destroy it.

I hovered the pen over the paper. Everyone was waiting for me. But I couldn't sign.

"Is something wrong, Jane?"

I put the pen down. "Can we talk about my other choices?"

May 01, 2001

Banks and Murdoch, LLP

100 Boylston St.

Boston, MA 02116

Dear Miss Berenson,
We hope this letter finds you well.

 Some time back, you mailed us a bundle of letters intended for the child you offered up for adoption through this firm. Per your request, we forwarded those letters to his last known address. That child, now a young man, recently came to see us with a letter for you.

 After some consideration, we felt it was our duty as facilitators of the adoption to forward his correspondence to you, as we forwarded yours to him.

 Per our agreement, your identity remains confidential.
If you have any questions please feel free to contact us.
Kind Regards,
Cynthia Meyers, Esq.

PART 3

SPRING 2001

CHAPTER 44
JANE

"When did you get this?" I asked my mom as I stared down at the return address. Our Mother's Day brunch had been uncharacteristically pleasant . . . until she handed me that letter.

"A few days ago. Debbie Potter forwarded it on with a nice note." Alan and Debbie Potter were the couple who bought my parents' Lexington house when they moved to California. I didn't imagine they got much of our mail anymore, given that my parents hadn't lived there for almost a decade. "Apparently the Morettis next door finally convinced them to cut down those pine trees we planted. They were sick of blowing needles off their roof."

I turned the letter over in my hand to see it was still sealed.

"It's addressed to you," Mom said, "so I didn't open it." Her breezy tone suggested she'd either forgotten why my father had brought me to the law firm of Banks and Murdoch eighteen years ago or had no idea who they were.

"Who's it from?" my husband asked, peering over my shoulder. Poor Greg probably thought it was about the half sibling I'd gone in search of, because he didn't know about the other child. How could he? It was our family's best-kept secret.

"Did you see where Kenny went?" I asked my mom, ignoring my husband's question because I didn't want to lie, but I also couldn't tell him the truth.

"Probably toward the beach," Mom said, and I took off running.

"Jane?" Greg called after me, but I didn't stop. "Jane!"

Mom's condo was two blocks from del Rey beach. You could drive there, but the most direct route was to take the dirt path that wound behind the complex. I guessed that's where my brother had gone, and felt a wave of relief when I saw him crossing the street.

"Kenny!" I called out, but he didn't hear. I sprinted into the intersection, clutching that letter like a winning lottery ticket. When we were kids, Kenny and I got along pretty well by sibling standards. Things got chilly when I got sick and dragged him into family therapy, but after my seventeenth birthday, our relationship fell off a cliff. I told myself he was jealous I'd captured the attention of his new friend. But of course it was more complicated than that.

"Kenny!"

My brother turned to look at me as I ran up onto the curb. "Jane! What's wrong?" I thrust the letter into his chest. "What is this?"

"It's from the law firm that handled my adoption."

Kenny was one of four people who knew about the baby. Well, three, now that my dad was dead. But Samara was two thousand miles away, and my mom had buried it so far underground you'd need an oil rig to get to it.

"Why would they be writing to you now?" Kenny asked, because it was a long time ago, and none of us thought we'd ever hear from that law firm again.

I had no idea, so I shook my head.

He turned the envelope over to see it was still sealed. "You haven't opened it."

"You do it."

"Here?" We were standing in the middle of the sidewalk. Cars were whizzing by, though I hadn't noticed until now.

I pointed to a grassy area with a dog run and a few benches. "Over there."

He put his hand on my back and steered me toward one of the benches, but I was too amped to sit.

"You sure you don't want to do it yourself?" Kenny said.

I nodded. "Yes, I'm sure."

We were a block from the beach. The air was thick with humidity, and the envelope had wilted from the moisture. Kenny opened it along the crease. Inside were two letters paper-clipped together.

"There's two letters," he said. "Top one's a cover letter."

"Read the cover letter. But don't tell me if it's something bad." It was a ridiculous thing to say. Of course it was something bad.

Kenny pressed his lips together as he read. I watched his face for clues, but it revealed nothing.

"Well?"

His eyes were shiny, but his voice was soldier steady.

"Apparently your son went to talk to the lawyer."

My son. No one had ever called him that.

"He's not my son," I corrected him, because I had given up that responsibility long ago.

"He wrote to you, Jane." He held up the second sheet of paper.

I shook my head. "How could he do that? He's not allowed to do that. It was a closed adoption."

"It doesn't say 'Dear Jane,' just 'Hello.'" He turned it toward me, but I looked away. I didn't regret my decision to carry that pregnancy to term, but I also never wanted to think about it again. I even lied on my medical forms, checking "no" when they asked if I'd ever been pregnant. I didn't get counseling after giving up my baby because I didn't want anyone to know what I'd done. The only coping mechanism I had was to imagine the person who'd given birth to that child wasn't me.

"Do you want me to read it?"

"No," I said, then backtracked. "I don't know."

The memory of those agonizing nine months unleashed like a storm. Watching my newly flat stomach get round like a barrel. Taking the T to Dr. Pearl's office by myself because my mother wanted nothing to do with it. Seeing the grainy image on the monitor evolve from peanut to person. Hearing the heartbeat grow slower and stronger. Tying sweatshirts around my waist to hide my girth. Switching to baby doll dresses when the weather got hot, praying the wind wouldn't blow and reveal my shape. I'd mastered the art of hiding my weight gain the year before not knowing it was a trial run.

Through it all, besides the occasional "How are you?" my father kept his feelings about my colossal fuckup to himself. Maybe he thought I'd suffered enough. Or maybe he was too mortified for words. I was in my fifth month when he picked me up early from school to take me to meet with the lawyer. "I spoke to a lawyer about your predicament," he said when we got into the car. "Your mother and I aren't equipped to raise another child. I assume when you decided to go through with this, you knew it would end in adoption?" He said it like a question, so I nodded. And then I was sitting at a shiny dark-wood conference table, signing the life that was growing inside me over to a couple who wanted him as badly as my parents did not.

I entered my eighth month during spring break of my senior year. I was signed up to join a class trip to Washington, DC, but going anywhere was out of the question. My mother made up some mystery illness, told my principal I would have to finish out the year at home. I missed my senior trip. I missed my prom. I missed my graduation. Cloaking my body had been stressful, but the period of isolation that followed was an abyss.

Babyboy 23634 was born on June 7, 1984, at 9:02 p.m. in Mount Auburn Hospital to "anonymous mother" and "father unknown." I was given a spinal epidural to block out the labor pain and a steady drip of Percocet to block out the grief. Even in my narcotic haze, I knew I had done something terrible. But also something wonderful. There was no space in between.

"Read it to yourself first," I told my brother, then sat down on the bench and put my head in my hands. As Kenny read the letter in silence, I raced through the possible reasons Babyboy 23634 might have written to me. *Is he sick and needs his medical history? Did his adoptive parents die? Is he in trouble? On drugs? Or just want to know why I would bring him into the world then never want to see him again?*

"He says you wrote to him," Kenny said. "Is that true?"

"I wrote some letters, yes," I admitted. "A long time ago. It was stupid. I was a mess." I thought back to the haze of my isolation, when all my friends were celebrating their last days of school and first days of summer, and I was trapped at home. I didn't remember what I said in those letters, only that I never should have sent them.

"He says they meant a lot to him," Kenny said, sitting down beside me on the bench.

"So is that it?" I asked. "He wrote to thank me for the letters?"

I looked at Kenny, hoping he'd lie to me. But that was not Kenny's way.

"He wants to meet you, Jane."

The hypocrisy of looking for my dad's child while hiding from my own was not lost on me. But it also made perfect sense. I was trying to do for my father's kid what I wasn't able to do for mine. Like a shitty parent who becomes the world's best grandparent, or an addict who becomes a sponsor, I was trying to make amends for my mistake by correcting someone else's.

"The lawyer says you have no obligation to do anything," Kenny said, flipping back to the cover letter. "Your contact information is still confidential. You don't even have to acknowledge receipt of his letter to you."

"What else did the boy say?" I asked, hoping somewhere in his letter he said he'd be fine no matter what I did.

"Just that he has a nice family and he's grateful. And . . ." Kenny tried to suppress the catch in his voice. "Sorry."

"What? What did he say?"

"He says he's sorry if he opened old wounds."

Kenny held out the letter. I let my eyes graze the words. *I think about you a lot . . . I hope one day we can meet again . . . I'm not sure when the hollow feeling set in . . . maybe you have a hole, too?*

We sat there in silence for a beat. The wind was blowing my hair in my eyes and mouth, but I was too in shock to push it away.

"He seems like a nice kid," Kenny finally offered.

"Did you ever tell Rowan?" I asked. There was a period when Mom wasn't even going to tell Kenny, but I was in my third trimester when my brother came home for spring break, and there was no way to hide it from him. He never asked who the father was because he already knew. He saw our fingers threaded together that night at the beach. The stolen kiss goodbye the next day when he left. All it took was simple math to figure out the rest. We didn't talk about it then and hadn't talked about it since. But there was no hiding from it now.

"No, I never told him," Kenny said. If he was anyone else, I might not have believed him. But Kenny was the most disciplined person I'd ever known. If Mom asked him not to tell, he didn't. "Did *you?*"

The idea that I would tell Rowan that I'd had his baby was as reasonable as it was absurd. Reasonable because he had a right to know he'd fathered a child. Absurd because as soon as it was over, I wanted to forget it ever happened. Later, once I'd processed what I'd done, I rationalized that he was better off not knowing. I told myself I was being generous, and I believed it because I was practiced at lying to myself.

Like a lie, silence grows more dangerous the longer you let it fester. The time to confide in Rowan was the day I found out I was pregnant. But I didn't. I *couldn't.* Maybe it was vanity that stopped me. I didn't want him to imagine me with a ginormous belly or think of me as a dumb kid—I was already self-conscious about being the little sister. Or maybe, after everything I'd been through, I just didn't have it in me to do something hard.

He kept writing to me, even though I'd stopped writing back. I don't know what those last few letters said because I never opened them. And then—predictably—his letters stopped. He probably figured

I didn't like him anymore, but nothing was further from the truth. I liked him so much I wanted to spare him the agony and humiliation that had consumed me.

"Jane?" Kenny asked again. "Did you ever tell Rowan about the baby?"

"No."

There was a long silence. It was Kenny who finally said it.

"Well, maybe it's time."

CHAPTER 45
JANE

"You don't have to make any decisions right away," my brother said, leaning forward to find my eyes. Kenny and I were sitting on the bench beside a fenced-in dog run, where a golden retriever with muddy paws was playing fetch. "This has been buried for seventeen years. You can take a few days to decide what you want to do."

While it was true I didn't have to write back to the boy or tell Rowan he existed, now or ever, there was a difficult conversation that couldn't wait.

"There's someone else I never told," I said as the golden dropped a tennis ball at his owner's feet. The sun slipped behind a cloud, and I shivered as a cool breeze rolled over my bare shoulders.

"You mean besides Rowan?" Kenny asked.

"Yeah. Greg," I said glumly. It was one thing not to share a painful memory from my distant past. At worst, that was lying by omission. But he was going to ask what was in that letter, and if I didn't tell him, that would be lying to his face.

"Wait. Greg doesn't know you had a baby?"

"Nobody knows. Just you, Mom, and Samara." The fact that I hadn't told Greg I'd been pregnant while we were seeing a fertility specialist probably sounds insane, but trauma makes people do insane things; that's what makes it trauma. That wound was deep and had been stitched over by years of denial. Yes, it was cruel to keep it from him. But it was crueler to ask me to bleed out all over again.

"It's nothing to be ashamed of, Jane," Kenny said, because sometimes brothers know things, even when you try to keep them hidden.

"Really? Then why did Mom pull me out of school?"

"I don't know. Maybe she was trying to protect you."

I thought about Mom and all the secrets she'd tucked away. She had every right to keep what she knew about Dad's affair to herself, but I should have told her about what I was doing to learn what became of it. Should have told Kenny too.

"Kenny," I started, "there's something I need to tell you. About Dad." I thought this would be a difficult conversation, but he made it easy.

"I know Dad had a girlfriend," he said flatly, as if it were as obvious as the sky was blue.

"How?"

"He told me." I felt my eyebrows arch up. "Oh yeah. A long time ago."

"Like, how long ago?"

"I don't know, twenty years maybe?"

"What!?"

He leaned back on the bench, then told me the story without a flicker of emotion. "Yeah, he was driving me to baseball, and 'Walk This Way' by Aerosmith came on the radio. He started tapping his fingers and singing along. I was like, 'Since when do you like Aerosmith?' And he said, 'My girlfriend turned me on to them.'"

"Jesus, Kenny."

"I don't know if he was trying to show off or what," Kenny said. "But, yeah, I knew about her."

"How come you never said anything?"

Kenny shrugged. And I realized I'd had it all wrong. All these years I thought my brother disappeared into military life because he was angry or jealous. But when you don't know how to lie, the only way to protect someone is to leave. He ran away not to punish me but to protect me from the outrage and disappointment our dad had caused him.

"Did Mom know?" I asked.

"We never talked about it. But I would imagine so." My brother's alliance to my mother suddenly made perfect sense. Of course he chose her. How could he not, given what he knew about our dad?

"How did you find out?" Kenny asked.

"I found letters in his desk when I was cleaning it out."

"I was wondering if he kept them." And I felt my eyebrows arch even higher.

"You knew about the letters?"

"Yeah, he showed them to me."

"What the fuck, Kenny?"

"I dunno, maybe he was trying to normalize it." I tried to imagine my dad showing love letters from his mistress to his teenage son like they were some sort of found treasure.

"Did he show you the one where his girlfriend said she was pregnant?" And now it was his eyebrows that floated up.

"No, I didn't know about that one."

"Do you think we have a bunch of half siblings wandering around?" I asked.

"Nothing would surprise me with him."

"Don't you want to know?"

"Not really."

"If you found out today that we have a half sibling," I pressed, "you wouldn't want to meet them?"

"Do we?" he asked. And I wondered if he kept closer tabs on me than I'd thought.

"I have no idea."

"I know how disorienting this must be for you, Jane, but remember, Cindy was married before me. Her husband wants nothing to do with their kids. I'm their father. And I'll be as much a father to them as I will be to the little one on the way. Family is what you make, not what you're born into."

He leaned over and put his elbows on his knees. His face was pointed toward the ground, but I still saw his pained expression.

"Kenny, what is it?" I thought he was angry at me for siding with our father while he was running around on our mom. It was inexplicable that she'd tolerated his cruelty, but then again, hadn't I done it too? Like a battered wife who makes excuses for her violent husband, I'd let my father demean me because I thought I deserved it. Was I following Mom's example? Or is it just human nature to want to be loved by the person who can't love you back?

I was about to apologize for my ignorance. I knew as soon as I found those letters that I had chosen the wrong side. But as I opened my mouth to speak, Kenny raised his head to meet my eyes.

"I was a really shitty brother." His jaw flexed as he bit down on his anguish. "I'm sorry, Jane. I should have never let that happen to you." He leaned back on the bench and stared out at the horizon. And I knew this wasn't about our dad anymore.

"You had nothing to do with what happened with Rowan," I said.

"I'm not blind. I saw how he was looking at you."

"It's not like he dragged me off like a lion with its kill. I liked him."

"You were seventeen."

"Yes. And if you had told me not to go with him, I would have told you to fuck all the way off."

He turned to face me. His eyes were rimmed with regret. What happened was not remotely his fault, but I could never convince him of that. My heart cracked down the middle. Kenny had suffered so much. I was so paralyzed by my own trauma, I never considered what it had done to him.

"When I found out, I wanted to kill him," he said.

"Why didn't you?"

"Because he was in love with you."

I opened my mouth to object, but the words got stuck in my throat. Because if someone had asked me back then, I would have said I loved Rowan too. Which to my grown-up ears sounded insane. We were kids. What did we know about love?

"Then I wanted to kill *you*, for blowing him off," he said. "Until I found out why."

The crack in my heart broke wide open. I thought about all the letters we'd written—dozens of them, like star-crossed lovers in a Merchant Ivory movie. It was still a stretch to call what we had "love," but it was not trivial either. Perhaps it could have grown into something? If fate hadn't intervened.

"I can't believe you never told him," I said, because I couldn't imagine seeing him every day and not saying something.

"Yeah, well, right back at you." And that stung. Because I should have. "Plus Mom told me not to say anything to anyone, ever."

"But nothing to be ashamed of," I said, parroting back his words to him.

"You can't let them tell you how to feel, Jane. No one gets to tell you. Not your mother, not your father, only you get to decide."

It was an easy thing to say, but so hard to do. For so many years, I'd let other people make me feel unworthy of the life I'd been born into. If only I'd been able to tune out the voices that demeaned me—not just my dad's, but the commercials and fashion magazines that made us all feel like we would never be pretty or skinny enough—how different would my life be now?

I looked out at my golden retriever friend, lying on his belly, wagging his tail. His joy was palpable. It was great to be evolved with a big brain and an opposable thumb and all that, but sometimes it felt like we humans spent our childhoods collecting insecurities, and our adult lives trying to shed them.

"Greg's here," my brother said. I followed his gaze to see Greg's car pulling into the parking lot.

"What do I say?" I asked, because I wasn't ready to face him.

"He's going to want to know what's in that letter, Jane."

I had to tell him. We were trying to have a baby. After everything we'd been through, it was unfair to keep him in the dark.

"Rowan's picking me up at Mom's at four. We'll wait for you. In case you want to tackle that too."

Somehow, Kenny knew I was going to write to that boy. That I couldn't leave him with pages missing from his story like our dad had done to us. And I couldn't do that without telling Rowan first.

Kenny tried to hand me the letter. "Here."

"You take it," I said, pushing his hand away.

"You're not going to show it to him?"

"Not yet." Greg was walking toward us. I waved and forced a smile.

Kenny tucked the letter in his pocket, then turned to greet my husband. "Hey, Greg."

"Hey, Kenny," he said to my brother. Then to me, "You want to tell me what's going on, Jane?"

Over Greg's shoulder, Kenny gave me an encouraging nod.

"Let's talk in the car."

CHAPTER 46
JANE

Greg's Acura was parked under a towering palm tree on the beach side of the lot. The sun had fought its way out from behind the clouds and warmed my arms and chest as I followed him toward the car.

Greg opened the passenger side door for me, and I climbed inside. I told myself telling him I'd birthed a child seventeen years ago didn't have to change anything between us. I expected him to be stunned, but I hoped once his shock and anger faded, he would be relieved that I'd been pregnant, because that suggested I could be again.

Greg got behind the wheel and started the ignition. "I'm just going to crack the windows," he said as he opened his and mine a few inches.

I couldn't look at him, so I stared straight ahead. The bike path that hugged the lot was teeming with bikers, joggers, parents pushing strollers. On the sand just beyond, families played beach volleyball and tossed Frisbees. Mother's Day was a happy day for so many, I longed for the day it would be for me too.

He turned off the car. I could feel his eyes on me, demanding an explanation. But where to start? He knew about my childhood illness, my father's infidelity, the intimate details of my menstrual cycle . . . Not telling him about the child I had birthed and given away was a glaring omission from the story of my life. I imagined his reaction something between wounded and mortified.

"It's from your father's girlfriend, isn't it?" he said. "The letter you just got."

"No." It's not that I'd forgotten about Ellie and the child she may or may not have had, it just had momentarily disappeared in the shadow of this other stunning development.

"Then who?" Greg asked. "The kid?"

There was a sharp edge to his voice. I couldn't blame him for being upset. Running out of my mom's apartment without a whiff of explanation was unkind, and I imagined it left him feeling hurt and confused.

I tried to ease into it. "I'm afraid it's more complicated than that."

"Where is it?" he asked.

"Where's what?"

"The letter that sent you running from your mom's condo like a bat out of hell."

"Kenny has it."

"Why don't you want me to see it?"

I forced myself to look at him. His mouth was tight, his eyes hard. "I'm sorry I ran off, but this is difficult for me," I said, hoping the apology would soften his anger.

"I told you, you never should have opened that can of worms, Jane. People find out you have a rich family and they want their fair share."

For a second I thought I'd misheard him. *He thinks this is about money?*

"First of all, we're not rich," I started.

"Your mother is."

"Second of all, that's not what the letter was about." I was trying to create space to explain, but we were already steeped in misunderstanding. Once again my evasive behavior had made a bad situation worse. Why hadn't I learned?

"People need to let bygones be bygones," he said. "The past is the past."

"No one's coming after anyone's money." I felt myself starting to panic. I couldn't blame him for having the wrong idea—I'd left him in the dark.

"Your dad's girlfriend is not the victim here. You are," he said. "You and your mom."

"This is not about anything my dad did, Greg. Please, just let me explain." I was desperate to pivot the conversation. But then he did it for me.

"Why did you tell them I was getting my sperm tested?"

Because I'm an insensitive clod, I almost said. But his defensive tone made me wonder . . .

"Are you?" I asked. "Getting your sperm tested?"

And he went silent.

"Greg?"

"What's the point? We both know it's you."

And there was my opening—so wide I could have driven a truck through it. But I needed to address this other issue first.

"Hormone shots are painful and can have brutal side effects," I said, even though he already knew this. "The next logical step is for you to get tested. I'll go with you if you want," I offered, because we were in this together.

"I can have an orgasm without your help," he snapped back.

"So when are you doing it?"

No answer.

"Have you made an appointment yet?"

Again, no answer.

"It's been three weeks since we saw Dr. Chen."

"I've been busy," he said, even though the clinic was open nights and weekends, and he could be in and out in ten minutes.

"Having a kid is a lot more time consuming," I said, because if he didn't have time for a ten-minute appointment, how on earth would he handle having a baby?

"Maybe it's time we read the writing on the wall, Jane."

My heart nearly stopped. "What writing is that?" He didn't speak or even look at me. "Greg?"

"If it's this hard, maybe it's not meant to be."

Not meant to be. His words hovered in the air, so noxious I nearly choked on them.

"So that's it? We're giving up then?"

"It's always been more important to you than it is to me."

I couldn't imagine my life without children. Yes, we'd been trying, but there was so much more we could do. It was unfathomable to me that he would give up this easily.

"Why did we go see Dr. Chen if you had no intention of taking her recommendations?"

"Because you asked me to," he said. "But it always felt . . . I don't know . . . disingenuous, I guess."

"Were you hoping she'd just say we should give up?" I asked, because why else would he go to all that trouble?

"I'm sorry, Jane." His voice was getting quieter as mine was growing frantic. "I'm not spending a bunch of time and money to force a baby into the world that I don't even want."

And there it was. The stunning admission that perhaps I'd known all along. It was wrong of me to lie to him, but he'd lied to me too. He'd said he wanted a family. We had that conversation before we said "I do." Perhaps on some level, we both knew we'd never been fully honest with each other. He told me what I wanted to hear, and I held back what I thought he didn't.

A tear rolled down my cheek. I turned away from him and stared out my window, at two little boys daring waves to tickle their toes. Maybe if I hadn't already felt love so fierce it could split the sky in half, I could have conceded too. But having a baby was an experience I wanted to have again, this time for keeps.

But now more than ever I couldn't tell him that.

CHAPTER 47
JANE

"Where are you going?" Greg asked as I opened the car door.

"I'll meet you at home," I replied. Pungent sea air rolled over my skin and swirled with my grief. In less than a month, I'd lost both my grip on the past and my dreams for the future. I felt like someone dropped me in the middle of the ocean with no compass and no port in sight.

"I'm not leaving you here by yourself, Jane," Greg said, like we were in a combat zone not upscale Playa del Rey.

"Kenny will give me a ride," I said. Or my mother would. Or a taxi would. My crisis was existential, not logistical.

"It's not like we didn't try."

I couldn't bring myself to look at him. We'd barely scratched the surface of trying. A third of the time it's the man, and it was almost certain that we were in that third. But I couldn't tell him how I knew that now.

"I need some time to process, Greg." I shut the car door and started across the parking lot. I didn't know where I was going, besides away from him and this devastating new reality.

"I love you, Jane," Greg shouted out the car window. I waved in acknowledgment but didn't say it back.

I was thirty when Greg and I got married. My baby fever didn't start raging for another two years, but once it started, it burned hot. Maybe it was buying a house that awakened it, because what's the point of making a home if you aren't going to have a family? Or maybe the memory of a love that filled every crevice of my heart finally got too persistent to ignore. Whatever spurred it, once I let my desire for a baby out of the starting gate, it would not relent until it reached the finish line.

Greg was amenable, but I was definitely the driving force. When people asked him if he wanted kids, he sometimes joked, "I'll regret my life either way, but it's fun trying." When I called him on his indifference, he would assure me it was just trying to take the pressure off. But maybe I should have listened to what he was saying instead of hearing what I wanted to be true.

It was a five-minute walk to my mom's, but I took an extra lap around her neighborhood, past thick ficus trees, hot-pink bougainvillea, dogwood in full bloom. On this Mother's Day, I tried not to think about how many more times I would have to smile through this holiday while dying inside. I knew plenty of childless people who were happy and fulfilled. Some of them derived great meaning from careers in education, medicine, the arts. Some of them expanded their minds through books and travel. I knew a person could live a life of service without being in service to a child of her own. I also knew I didn't want that to be me.

I peeked at my watch to see it was almost four o'clock. Rowan would be at my mom's to pick up Kenny soon, if he wasn't there already. I tried to anticipate what the young man who'd written to me would ask about his father. *Where is he now? Are you still in touch with him? Why doesn't he want to meet me?*

As I approached Mom's condo, I rehearsed in my mind how I'd dodge those questions: *Your biological dad is a super cool guy, but I never told him about you.... Why not?... Because I didn't want to burden him—not that you were a burden! That's not what I meant! The reason I didn't tell him is because I was scared—no, not scared, you're not scary. I guess the real reason is that I'm a lying asshole. Aren't you glad you wrote to me?*

Mom's building had an electronic keypad, so I punched the code and let myself in. As I took the stairs to her second-floor unit, I flashed back to Greg's comment about her being rich. I never discussed my mom's finances with Greg. My dad had left her comfortable, but she wasn't loaded. And what did he care what happened to her money? Was he worried that if someone came after it, we'd have to help? And isn't that what family is for?

It occurred to me that I'd gotten my priorities all wrong. I'd been so obsessed with finding my father's *other* family, I'd ignored what he'd done to ours. To Kenny. To my mom. To *me*. I tried to imagine what it was like for Kenny, watching in silence while I snubbed our mother and fawned over our father. Why didn't he tell me Dad was betraying us? Did he think I wouldn't believe him? Or was he just being kind because he knew how much those motorcycle rides and Celtics games meant to me, and to knock my father off the pedestal I'd put him on would have been like pushing me off a cliff?

And what about my mother? What must it have been like for her, knowing there was another woman but choosing to keep the family together? All those times she failed to stick up for me felt different now that I knew she wasn't sticking up for herself.

And then there was what my father had done to me—chipping away at my self-esteem one mean remark at a time. Was he hard on me because he felt bad about himself? He certainly had reason to feel ashamed of his choices.

Mom's front door was locked. My key was in my purse on her kitchen counter, so I rang the bell.

"Hey," Kenny said when he opened the door.

"Hey."

"Where's Greg?" he asked as I stepped into the foyer by myself.

"I sent him home."

"Didn't take it well?"

"I didn't tell him." His eyebrow ticked up. "Believe it or not, we have bigger problems."

"Sorry, sis." His face flooded with compassion.

"A conversation for another day," I said.

"Anytime you want to talk, I'm here." A few weeks ago, I never would have confided in Kenny. But now that the hard edges of misunderstanding had softened, I realized how much I'd missed my big brother.

"Thanks, Kenny." I would have a lot to unwind in the coming weeks, and knowing he would be there for me made my heart swell with gratitude.

"What do you want me to do with this?" he asked, flashing the corner of the letter that was sticking out of his pocket.

"Is he here?" I asked, unsure what I wanted the answer to be. No, I didn't want to tell Rowan how I'd betrayed his trust all those years ago, but it wasn't fair to him or Kenny to sit on this secret any longer.

"He's in the shower. He was surfing all day and didn't want to fly home with sand on his balls."

"Thanks for that image."

My brother smiled, which made me smile too.

"What are you two doing skulking in the hallway?" Mom said, peering at us from around the corner. "Come in and sit with me."

Kenny took a step back so I could pass, then followed me into the living room. I went to sit on the couch, but as I stepped in front of my mom, she put a hand on my shoulder.

"We knew this day might come," she said.

I looked at her in surprise.

"I told her who the letter was from," Kenny said.

Mom never wanted me to have the baby. She'd tried for weeks to talk me out of it. I braced myself for an "I told you so," but she surprised me again. "Just keep listening to your heart, Janie. It's always known the right path."

And I didn't know if she was talking about what I did all those years ago, or what I was about to do next.

CHAPTER 48
JANE

"OK, sorry! I'm ready," Rowan said as he emerged from the bathroom looking straight out of *Top Gun* in cargoes and a tight white tee. I stood up, and he stopped short. "Oh! Jane! I thought you'd left."

"Hey, Rowan," I said with a little wave. His hair was wet and his face sun kissed, just like that fateful day at the beach.

"Ro, do you think we could delay our departure a little, maybe leave in like an hour?" Kenny asked.

"You're the one with the pregnant wife," Rowan reminded him.

"I just wanted to hang with my mom a little longer," my brother said, then looked at me like that was my cue. In a day of difficult conversations, the one I needed to have with Rowan promised to be the hardest, but there was no getting out of it now.

"Want to go for a walk?" I asked my brother's friend, because I needed to talk to him in private and couldn't exactly ask him to go into the bedroom with me.

Rowan looked at Kenny, like *Is that cool with you?* And Kenny gave him the thumbs-up.

"OK sure, let's go for a walk."

Rowan opened the door for me, and we walked in silence down the stairs and out the side door by the courtyard. Water was cascading out of the hot tub into the pool. I let the gentle *whoosh!* wash over my frazzled nerves.

"Beach?" I asked as we approached the cut-through.

"Sure."

The path was wide enough for us to walk side by side, so I paused so he could catch up.

"How was the surfing?" I asked, as if kidnapping a man I hadn't been alone with for nearly eighteen years was perfectly normal.

"I have water in my ears," he said, then tilted his head and gave it a shake. "Every time I move my head, it sounds like popcorn popping."

"That's the worst."

"Turns out I'm not much of a surfer," he confessed.

"Was this your first time?" I asked.

"And maybe my last."

"Well, at least you can knock it off your bucket list."

"Done and done."

The path opened up. As we merged onto the sidewalk, he asked, "What's on your bucket list?"

I pretended to think about it while I swallowed the lump in my throat. There was really only one thing on my bucket list, and the likelihood of me getting it had just plummeted.

"I've always wanted to see the pyramids," I finally said.

"Oh, yeah, totally worth it."

"You've been to Egypt?"

"When I was stationed in the Gulf, we took a day trip to sneak a peek. Blew my mind." I'd forgotten Rowan had served during the Gulf War. Kenny and I weren't talking much back then.

"It's hard to believe something that old still exists," I said.

"Yeah, they're incredible," he agreed. "What else?"

"Alaska."

"Alaska? Really?"

"Still haven't been camping," I said, wondering if he remembered he'd once teased me about that.

"You can do that there. Lots of wilderness."

"You've been?"

"A couple times. If you go far enough north, there are days in the summer when the sun never sets."

We crossed the street at the light, then picked up the bike path. We were a few hundred yards from the ocean now. The late-afternoon sun was low in the sky, casting shadows as long and dark as our past.

A few shadow lengths in front of us, a couple merged onto the path. Her hand was jammed in his back pocket; his arm hugged her shoulders as his fingers played with her hair. They walked in perfect lockstep, as if to music only they could hear. Their rhythmic footfalls lulled me into the memory of that stolen dance at Kenny's wedding. Greg and I were newly married—less than a year. My new husband wasn't much of a dancer, so he left me to group dance with a circle of Kenny's friends. When Prince's "1999" gave way to a sappy Whitney Houston song, the dance floor cleared out. My eyes searched the crowd for Greg. But landed on Rowan.

For a tense second, neither of us moved. And then, without a word, he extended a hand toward me. I had already snubbed him all those years ago by ignoring his letters; it felt heartless to do it again. As his hand found the small of my back, I rested one hand on his hip and the other on his shoulder. As we danced, I let my cheek rest on his lapel so he wouldn't see my tears. That was the first time we'd touched since my birthday weekend. The only time.

"It's kind of a trip being on the beach with you again," he said, and I felt heat spread across my cheeks. That dance was meant to mend the tattered edges of our past, and here I was about to tear it open again.

"Yeah, that was quite a night." My heart was thundering in my chest. He'd teed me up perfectly. I was on the edge of the cliff. All I had to do was jump.

"I was so nervous around you," he said. And I stopped in my tracks.

"No, you were not."

"Oh yeah. When your friend . . . what was her name?"

"Samara."

"Right, Samara. When she jumped in the front seat, I nearly crapped my pants."

"You weren't wearing pants," I reminded him.

"That's true," he conceded. "I still have that bathing suit." I must have looked at him funny because he added, "It's vintage now."

Rowan was easy to talk to. It was such a nice day. And I was about to unleash a storm.

"Rowan," I said, turning to face him. His eyes had caught the sun and shone bright against his tanned skin. "There's something I need to tell you."

His eyebrows ticked up. "Should I be sitting down?"

"Ideally."

He pretended to look for somewhere to sit, but there was only sand. "I don't think your mother's plumbing can handle any more sand. Is it OK if I stand?"

My heart was thumping in my ears. I knew he was trying to keep things light, make this easier for me. But I couldn't get the words out.

"Jane, what is it?"

"I don't know how to tell you this," I started. And I really didn't. And maybe I shouldn't. Maybe Greg was right, I should let bygones be bygones.

"I ruined everything," he interrupted.

"What? No." I shook my head. "Why would you say that?"

"We just met," he said. "I came at you at Mach 10 when we should have just taxied for a while."

"Is that a pilot's metaphor?"

"Mach 10 is really fast."

"I was as into it as you were," I reminded him.

"That's what I thought," he said, "but then you stopped writing. At first I thought maybe you met someone. But Kenny would have told me that. Then I thought maybe your friends or your mom got to you and convinced you I was a creep."

The moment was now. I had to take it.

"No one thought you were a creep," I said. "That wasn't the reason I disappeared."

"Then why did you?"

I could feel my eyes fill with tears. The sun burned hot on the side of my face. I swallowed my fear and spoke the words for the very first time.

"Rowan, I got pregnant that night."

I forced myself to look at him. A tear was rolling down my cheek, but I didn't wipe it away. More were coming. A lot more.

"Jane, I . . ." His voice trailed off. His eyes were vacant. His face was ash. "Why didn't you tell me?"

"It was stupid. I should have. I didn't want to bother you with it, I guess?"

He took a step away from me and put his hands on his head.

"Wow. Jane . . ." He stared at the horizon in dumbfounded silence. I had blindsided him. "I don't know what to say."

"I should have told you," I said. "I just, I don't know. You were in the air force. I figured you had more important things to do."

"How could you think anything could be more important than that?"

I didn't know, so I just shrugged. The memory of showing my mother that positive pregnancy test played in my mind. "I'll make you an appointment," she'd said. As if a simple procedure could make the whole thing go away.

"Does Kenny know?" he asked.

"Yes."

He considered that a beat.

"I can't believe I'm still alive."

Poor guy, he thought that was the worst of it. The longer I waited to tell him the rest, the harder it would be. So I forced myself to look at him, then blurted it out.

"I had a son, Rowan. *We* had a son. I'm a horrible person for not telling you. The lawyer said I didn't have to, and I thought, well, why should this blow up his life too? It was selfish and if you hate me I deserve it and I'm sorry. Oh God."

I fell to my knees. The enormity of the lie I'd lived for nearly eighteen years hit me like a car crash. I folded over my legs and let the sobs course through my body.

I'm not sure when he put his arms around me, just that we stayed like that—me crying, him holding me—for I don't know how long. I knew beachgoers were staring, but for the first time in my life, I didn't care what anyone thought . . . except for Rowan.

"I'm sorry, Rowan," I said into his chest. He waited for me to stop sobbing, then leaned back on his feet to look at me.

"What happened to him?"

"I put him up for adoption."

"Is he . . . does he know how it happened?"

"No. The adoption was closed."

"So you're not in touch with him?"

"No. I only just now found out where he is. He's with a good family. He's doing well."

He nodded slowly, like he was trying to imagine it.

"I know it's a lot," I said in what was possibly the understatement of the year.

He didn't react. His face was eerily still. I couldn't tell if he wanted to cry or punch me in the face.

"I'm sorry you went through that alone," he finally said. His voice was flat, like he didn't know what to feel. Betrayed by my silence. Hurt that I hadn't trusted him. Flabbergasted that he was partly responsible for bringing a human being into the world. There were so many emotions to choose from.

"I'm sorry. I know it must be a shock."

He nodded, then rose to his feet and took a step away from me.

"I, uh . . ." His voice caught in his throat. He took a second to find it. "I think I'm going to need some time to process this, Janie."

My heart broke wide open. To hear him call me by the name I went by back in the day was a cruel reminder of what could have been. "Yes, of course."

I wanted to tell him about the letter, but he just asked for time. I wanted to give it to him, but also, I'd waited long enough.

May 21, 2001

Dear Mr. and Mrs. Ross,
My name is Jane Berenson Wallis. I live in California now, but I am originally from Lexington, Massachusetts. I recently received a letter from the law firm Banks and Murdoch in Boston, accompanied by a letter from your son, Adam.

My former lawyer asserts that your son is the child I put up for adoption on June 7, 1984. If you have an adopted son born on this date, could you contact me?

In his letter, Adam stated a desire to meet me. I would like to connect with you before I take any next steps.

Sincerely,
Jane Berenson Wallis

CHAPTER 49
ADAM

Days until training camp: 66

"You're down eight pounds, Ross," Coach Fitz said at my weekly weigh-in. I was coming to the gym every morning before school. When my parents said they wouldn't drive me, I borrowed a bike from Matty's brother and rode the six miles. The first time, it took me almost an hour, but now I was doing it in half that.

"It's a start I guess?"

"I don't want you to fixate on the number," Coach warned. "It's how you feel in your body that counts."

"Yes, sir."

"How are you feeling?"

"I feel good, Coach."

Maybe eight pounds doesn't sound like a lot, but there were other changes too. My previously amorphous arms were starting to crease where the muscles intersected. I wouldn't call it definition just yet, but there were hints that it was coming. The fanny pack that used to protrude over my belt was now more like a flap steak. I was sleeping better, thinking better, even seeing better. My body wanted to be fit. And my mind was catching on.

"Just remember, Ross. Good things beget more good things," Coach said. "The better you are to yourself internally, the more external things will fall into place."

I thought maybe the external thing he was hinting at was a spot on the team as a skill-position player, but there was no way I was asking.

Matty lived a mile from school, and track season was over, so he'd started coming to the morning workouts too. After biking (me) and running (him), then lifting for forty-five minutes, we needed showers. During the season, I was able to disappear in the crowd, but the locker room was pretty empty before school, and if we didn't want to be late for class, we had to get naked at the same time.

"I lost too much weight during track," Matty said, looking down at his concave stomach as we got dressed after our showers.

"I got some extra I could give you." Two months ago, I never would have joked about my weight. But now that I had taken control of it, it felt good to poke fun at myself. But Matty didn't laugh.

"I look like a Barbie doll." He seemed genuinely upset, and it struck me that maybe I wasn't the only one who worried about his weight.

I didn't want to stare at his naked body, so I just said, "You're not skinny," because anything more specific would have made me sound like a perv.

"I've been doing too much cardio," he said. "Hopefully now that I stopped running track I can get some muscle back."

I tried to check him out without checking him out. The truth was, he looked like I did when I was playing tennis. Lean and fast and ripped all over. I would have sold my soul to look like that. But I tried to be supportive because, as I was learning, everybody feels insecure sometimes.

"You'll bulk up by camp. Just keep coming to morning workout. And eat your Wheaties."

"You're looking better," he said, and I tried not to blush. I'd slipped my boxers on as soon as I'd gotten out of the shower, but he could still see the rest of me.

"Thanks," I said. Then pulled on my shirt before things got weird.

Mom didn't pick me up from school anymore now that I had the bike, but we still all ate dinner together. They didn't comment on my changing shape, but I knew they noticed it—otherwise they'd still be pressuring me to stop working out with Coach Fitz. We weren't fighting—it was more like a cold war. As long as I continued to lose weight, I was winning.

I biked home after sixth period PE. Finals were coming, and I wanted to go to my room to study. But when I walked into the house, my mom and dad were sitting at the dining room table waiting to talk to me.

"Adam," my father said. "Come here, please."

I slid my backpack off my shoulder and walked toward the table. I thought they were going to tell me I needed to give the bike back, but I was planning to start jogging to school soon anyway, so I readied myself to return their punch with one of my own.

"Please sit down," my mom said.

"Did I do something wrong?" I asked as I slid into the chair as far away from them as possible.

They looked at each other, and I knew it was going to be bad.

"We got a letter in the mail today that is, frankly, very disturbing," Mom said. Her hands were resting on a folded-up piece of paper. Next to it was an envelope. I tried to make out the return address, but I'd sat too far away.

"Did you go to the law office that handled your adoption?" Dad asked.

It was too late to lie to them. Not that I wanted to lie. I had every right to go see those lawyers. Plus I had no idea if anything would come of it. For all I'd known, they'd thrown my letter in the trash.

"Yes," I confessed.

"What's with all this sneaking around?" Mom asked. "First to the gym in the mornings, now this." She put her hands in the air, palms up, like she was carrying two hostess trays.

"It's not that you went," Dad said. "It's that you did it behind our backs. Don't you feel like you can trust us?"

This was kind of about them not being able to trust me, but I didn't correct him.

"I'm sorry," I said. "I know I should have told you." And I was proud of myself that I didn't add an "it's just that" like he would have done. And what do you know? He said it for me.

"We know you want to find your birth mother."

"We would never stop you from looking for her," Mom said. "Why do you think we gave you the letters?"

A ball of sadness formed in my throat. They were right. I should have told them.

"We just would have liked to be a part of that decision," Dad said. "Why didn't you come to us?"

It was a fair question, and I tried to answer it honestly. "I guess it was just something I wanted to do on my own." I knew that was only a part of the truth, but how could I explain that sometimes teenagers have to rebel to become what they really are? Brave, not afraid. Hopeful, not hopeless. A football player, not a tennis player. And yes, that last thing, which I was working up the courage to say out loud.

"I'm sorry," I said again.

"We're disappointed you went behind our backs," Mom said. "But if that's what you want, we support you." And then she unfolded that piece of paper and slid it toward me.

"What's that?" I asked, afraid to take it from her.

"It's a letter from your birth mother," Mom said. "She's ready to make contact, if you are."

My heart thumped as I looked down at the letter. *Dear Mr. and Mrs. Ross* . . . At first I was confused about why she'd written to my parents and not me, but then I realized asking their permission to make contact was a sign of respect, and I felt like even more of a schmuck for going around them.

I picked up the letter and read it twice. "Her name is Jane," I said, not really to anyone. "Jane Berenson Wallis." I didn't know very many people with three names, except from my history books. Harriet Beecher Stowe, Coretta Scott King, Sandra Day O'Connor. Was she famous? Or was having three names a California thing? That's where she said she lived, which also seemed fancy.

"She was just Berenson before she got married," Mom said, and I tried on both versions of my name. Adam Berenson, if she wasn't married then. Adam Wallis, if she was.

"You think she's the right person?" I asked, because I wanted to be sure.

"Seems so," Mom said.

"I imagine the law firm made sure before they forwarded your letter to her," Dad added.

"What do we do now?" I asked. And my mom smiled beneath sad eyes.

"That's up to you."

May 28, 2001

Dear Mrs. Wallis,
We can confirm that our son Adam was born on June 7, 1984, and that he visited the law offices of Banks and Murdoch with a letter to his birth mother, which we have every reason to believe is you.

He understands that his adoption was closed, and that you are under no obligation to meet him. We respect your privacy, and appreciate how you handled our son's attempt to make contact.

We invite you to call us if and when you feel ready. You'll catch us at home at eight o'clock eastern time most weekday evenings.

Sincerely,
Marvin and Gloria Ross

CHAPTER 50
JANE

"You don't need to cook for me every night, Jane," my mother said as I arrived at her condo with two bags of groceries. I'd been staying at my mom's all week. After all the baby drama, Greg and I both needed some time apart. His confession that he didn't want to be a father was a devastating blow. Not because he hadn't been honest with me—I'd be the worst kind of hypocrite if I judged him for that. Because I wanted a child, and I couldn't have one if he didn't want one too.

"Actually, Greg's coming over," I said to explain why I'd bought so much food.

"Greg's coming here?"

"I thought maybe we could all eat together, then he and I could go for a walk."

She looked at the watch she couldn't see, then the clock on the wall. And then she slipped on her shoes and headed for the door.

"Where are you going?"

"To a movie."

"You don't have to leave." I didn't mean to kick my mom out of her own house, but I understood why she wanted no part of my reunion with Greg.

"I'll be back in a few hours." She waved over her shoulder and walked out. Things were still bumpy between Mom and me, but now that I knew what she'd gone through, I understood why she'd been so detached. Her husband was not just cheating, he was in a yearslong affair with another woman. It's easy to say she should have left him, but it's complicated when you have kids—more so when one of them is sick. Did she stay for us? For me? Or, like me, did she love Richie so much she was willing to suffer through his cruelty just for a little piece of him now and again?

It was already after five o'clock, so I got to work preparing dinner. As I chopped the carrots into little wheels, my thoughts turned to the letters that led to the unraveling of my life. Clearly my mom knew about them, otherwise she would have cleaned out Dad's desk herself. I didn't ask her if she knew what they said, just as she didn't ask me why I went to Boston after reading them. Or what the boy had written in his letter to me. So far we were both protecting our traumas. I didn't want to poke at her wounds any more than she wanted to poke at mine.

I poured the vegetable stock into the pot and turned the heat down to simmer. Greg and I had spoken briefly every day, just to let the other know we were OK and make a plan to have "the talk." Kenny had been checking in with me too. He tried to assure me Rowan understood why I disappeared into myself during that fraught time. He also begged me to keep Rowan in the loop about my plans to meet the son we had together, if I made any—which I hadn't . . . yet.

I went into Mom's spare bedroom and peeled off my yoga clothes. After four years of marriage, I didn't need to dress up for Greg, but I wanted him to know that I cared enough to comb my hair. My heart fluttered in my chest as I curled my eyelashes and dabbed my lips with gloss. Was I nervous because I was afraid of what would happen if I stood my ground about becoming a mother? Or that I wouldn't be able to?

The doorbell finally rang at 5:55 p.m. I removed the beef stew from the burner and answered the door.

"Hi."

"Hi."

"Come on in."

Greg was dressed for work, in pleated trousers and a light-blue button-front. I noticed he'd gotten his hair cut, but didn't assume it was for me.

"You look nice, Jane."

"You too."

He stepped inside, and we shared an awkward hug.

"Is your mom here?"

"No. She went to a movie."

"Ah."

"I made stew, but it can sit. Shall we talk in the living room?"

"Sure."

He followed me into the living room, which for some reason I'd dusted and vacuumed earlier that day. I sat where I normally sat, and he took Dad's former place with the view of the beach.

"I owe you an apology, Greg," I said, because the silence was more uncomfortable than what we had to say.

"No—" he objected.

"Please," I said, quieting him with my hand. "When I ran off after getting that letter, I didn't think about how that would make you feel. It was unkind to shut you out like that, and I am very sorry I did that to you."

"It's OK," he assured me. "You're allowed to have private correspondence."

"I don't mean to be secretive."

"Every marriage has secrets."

My heart thumped in my chest. For a second, I thought he was going to tell me he had a secret family too. But then he explained.

"The truth is, I've never really been high on having kids. I thought maybe that would change, y'know . . . after we got married."

"But it didn't."

"I'm sorry, Jane."

"You don't need to apologize for not wanting something."

He pressed his lips together, like that's not what he meant. "I'm sorry for what it means for us." He tried to smile, but his eyes revealed how much it hurt to say that.

I felt a cloak of sadness descend upon my shoulders. I couldn't make him want a child any more than he could erase my desire to have one. There was no middle ground.

"So where do we go from here?" I asked.

"The thought of living apart from you breaks my heart." His voice cracked, but he didn't cry. "I would say we should give it some time, but if you want to get pregnant . . ."

He didn't need to finish that sentence. I was thirty-four. At thirty-five a pregnancy becomes high risk. And it gets harder every year after that.

I thought about telling him about my teen pregnancy, how my memory of bringing life into the world fueled my desire to do it again, this time for keeps. But it didn't seem relevant. We were talking about the dissolution of our marriage—the future, not the past.

There was so much I wanted to say, but I couldn't find words. We were breaking up. He had already decided. Part of me wanted to grab him and hold on with all my might. The other part felt grateful he'd said the hard part so I didn't have to. Our diametrically opposed needs were the definition of irreconcilable differences. The fissure that had opened could not be bridged.

"I don't have any regrets, Jane. I hope you don't either?"

And then the tears came. I couldn't stop them. They rolled down my face like river water. Greg got up and knelt beside me.

"I know this is hard. For me too." He slid onto the couch next to me and put his arm around my heaving shoulders. "You taught me everything I know about love," he said, taking my hand in his. "I'm so grateful to you, Jane."

The panic that had exploded in my chest swirled to the pit of my stomach like falling snow. The love I shared with Greg was fulfilling and beautiful, but somehow I knew it only scratched the surface.

"Thank you for saying that," I said. And beneath the sorrow of my marriage ending, I felt a tingle of hope that we'd made room for something good.

CHAPTER 51
JANE

"Well? How did it go?" Mom asked when she came home from her movie and saw me sprawled out on her couch. "He's not still here, is he?" Her eyes darted from the living room to the kitchen and back.

"No. He left."

"And?"

"It's over." I'd been saying those two words on repeat for the past two hours, but speaking them out loud was surreal.

"Oh, honey." Mom set down her purse and sat next to me on the sofa. "Are you OK?"

"Not really." Emotion knotted in my throat. I pressed the heels of my hands into my eyes to tamp my tears.

"What happened?"

There were many possible answers to that question, depending on how far I wanted to go back. The first blow was probably a year ago when Greg urged me to quit my high-stress job at Scratch Kitchen. I'd taken it as a sign that he wanted me to rest so we could make a baby, but in retrospect, I wondered if he was just tired of cooking for himself—he didn't marry a chef to eat alone every night. Then came the scheduled sex. When romantic dinners turned to pleas to "just get it over with," the spark between us became a wet rag. And then came the final blow:

his confession that it was all theater, because he never really wanted a kid, and if I did, it would have to be with someone else.

"He doesn't want to have a baby with me," I said, because that was the thing that couldn't be overcome.

"Maybe after a few weeks he'll come back around."

I appreciated my mom's optimism, but you can't become a father as a favor to someone else. "I don't think so, Mom. He was pretty definitive."

"Well, then, you're better off," she said brusquely. "Now you can find someone who does."

I felt a pang of irritation. It was so my mom to "look at the bright side" me. "Can you let me mourn for a little bit here?"

I thought she'd walk away, but she didn't. "I'm sorry, Jane. I'm not good at hand-holding. But that doesn't mean I don't care." She put a hand on my shoulder. And my irritation softened.

"I'm sorry I'm such a train wreck."

"You're not a train wreck."

"I've cried so much this past week my tears could fill your swimming pool." I thought my joke would make her smile, but instead her face grew serious. "I'm not really going to cry into your swimming pool," I assured her. Again, no smile. She looked down at her hands, started fiddling with her rings. "What is it, Mom?"

"I should have been more compassionate," she said, without looking up. "Back then."

"I know you didn't approve," I started, but she made a stop sign with her hand.

"I need to confess something horrible." Her eyes locked on mine. The intensity of her gaze made my stomach knot with dread.

"I know it's not fair," she said, "but I blamed you for driving him to her." My breath caught in my throat. I didn't know what was more unsettling—that she knew about the girlfriend or that she thought I had something to do with my dad having one.

"Our homelife was messy," she continued. "The drama . . . your illness . . . it was too much for him."

The knot in my stomach tightened. If I wasn't already lying down I might have doubled over.

"But it was nonsense," she said, and I could breathe again. "Your father's dalliances started long before you got sick. Plus you were a child. If you weren't right in the head, we were the ones who made you that way." Her lip quivered with regret. I reached out and gave her hand a squeeze.

"I think it was mostly him, Mom." Yes, my dad was hard on me—sometimes outright mean. But I couldn't remember my mom ever belittling me. Even as she was enduring her own heartbreak.

She shook her head. "I should have stood up for you, Janie. But I was afraid . . ." Her voice trailed off. She took a deep breath and looked me in the eye. "You have to understand. I'm from a generation of women who never learned how to speak up for themselves. We went to college to find a man, and got married to be taken care of by him. I saw what your father was doing to you. But I felt powerless to stop it. Because he was doing it to me too."

I thought back to all those arguments behind closed doors. I thought they were about money. But really they were about what making the money meant—Dad thought the person who worked for it could do whatever he wanted—including cheat.

"How'd you find out about the girlfriend?" I asked.

"He told me about her."

"What?!"

She shrugged. "He wanted me to know he had someone waiting in the wings. Every time I told him to shape up, he'd say, 'Gabrielle likes me just as I am.'"

"You knew her name?" I'd spent weeks trying to solve the mystery of GM when all I had to do was ask my mother?

"Sometimes I wished he would just leave me for her already," she said. "I can't for the life of me tell you why he didn't. She was much more understanding than I ever was."

I thought about the sad woman I'd met in Malden. The soulless gray-and-beige landscape of her home. I was about to admit that I had gone to see her, but my mother preempted my confession. "I have no idea what became of her, and I don't care."

The knot in my stomach bloomed into full-blown bewilderment. I don't know what was more astonishing—that my father had wooed us all into worshipping him, or that three intelligent women would let themselves fall under his spell. I wondered if she'd known about Ellie's alleged pregnancy. I was dying to know what became of it, but she'd just made it clear that she didn't want to talk about it, so I didn't ask.

"I'm sorry for what you went through, Mom."

She sighed and shook her head. "The culture back then was so toxic, it practically dared men to step out on their wives," my mother said, giving me permission not to hate him. "He felt trapped by the need to provide . . ."

"And we felt like we had to be perfect for him in return," I said, finishing her thought.

"That's the American dream for you."

I thought back to those weekly manicures, how her hair and nails were always perfect. Mom never had a job beyond taking care of us kids. Did that mean she went to all those beauty appointments just to please him?

"I'm sorry I wasn't there for you in the way you needed me, Janie," she said. "You deserved better."

"Maybe we can be there for each other now?" I suggested, because Greg was right about one thing: the past was the past. But we could make a different future.

"I'd like that."

I sat up and wrapped my arms around her. Mom stiffened. She wasn't a hugger. But she did her best to hug me back.

"Are you going to go meet the boy?" she asked. I hadn't shown her the letter, but I imagined she knew the gist of it from Kenny.

"You think I should?"

"Oh, Jane," she said, taking my hands in hers. "You've always known better than me what to do."

June 3, 2001

Dear Rowan,
It feels strange to be writing to you after all this time, but there's something I need to share with you, and I thought this would be the best way.

The son I put up for adoption seventeen years ago recently sent me a letter through my former lawyer asking if I would be willing to meet. While I have no obligation to do so, I was moved by his heartfelt words. For many years, I thought that having this baby was all about me. But I realize now I was wrong. I want to do what's best for everyone involved, including you.

I've been in touch with his parents but won't agree to the meeting without your blessing. I'm currently separated from my husband and staying with my mom in Playa Vista when you feel ready to talk.

I cannot overstate how sorry I am for the distress I have caused you. You never gave me any reason not to trust that you would stand by me. I have only my own foolish pride to blame for the painful turn things took.

Kindest regards,
Jane

CHAPTER 52
ADAM

Days until training camp: 55

My mom had sent a letter to my birth mom inviting her to call after eight, so every night after dinner, I snuck into the den and checked the phone for a dial tone—not like a crazy person, like a perfectly normal person who pats their pocket to make sure they have their keys before they leave the house. Nothing crazy about that.

"What are you doing?" my dad asked when he caught me one night.

"I was going to call Matty to ask about the math homework," I lied. "But I just remembered we don't have any."

Dad looked suspicious, but he didn't say anything. I'd lost fourteen pounds, but it looked like more because I was also putting on muscle, which takes up less space in your clothes. To his credit, Dad didn't pretend not to notice. I even got an occasional "You're looking good, Adam," and I would give Sandy all the credit because he liked her way better than Coach Fitz. Truth is, I can't say why I'd stopped binge eating. Maybe talking to Sandy *had* helped. Maybe it was Matty's friendship. Maybe it was Coach Fitz's daily pep talks and the dream of playing football. Or maybe I just stubbornly wanted to prove I could do it my way, because I was nothing if not stubborn.

"Should we play a game?" Mom asked one night after a dinner of roasted chicken and Broccolini. We hadn't had a family game night since before I quit tennis, and I couldn't help but take the suggestion as a sign that our cold war was thawing.

"Boggle?" my dad asked. I would have preferred charades, but Dad needed a win, so I gave it to him.

Dad went to get the game while Mom and I finished clearing the table. I was putting the water glasses in the dishwasher when my mom touched my arm. "It's only been two weeks," she said. "Don't give up hope."

I straightened at the word *hope*. Was that the magical elixir fueling my progress? When I was playing tennis, I didn't feel hopeful about my future because winning at tennis was my dad's dream, not mine. I played out of fear of disappointing him, which makes you act the same way but feels really different. Getting in shape again, playing tight end, meeting my birth mom—these were all things that I wanted for myself. And I felt hopeful as hell. Was that what this search was all about? Finding out who I really was so I could stop living in fear of disappointing everyone else?

Dad passed out pens and paper, then sat down in his seat at the head of the table. I glanced at the clock. It was 8:03 p.m. I hadn't checked the phone line, but ten out of ten times it still worked, so I forced myself to stay put.

"No three-letter words," Dad reminded us, because it had been a while since we'd played, and just because he'd let me quit tennis didn't mean he was going to let me coast through life.

He shook the box, then opened the lid and flipped the egg timer. "Go!"

I looked down at the sixteen letters arranged in a four-by-four square. Dad was already scribbling. But I was entranced. The universe works in mysterious ways, but also sometimes it doesn't, because right there in the middle of the box were the letters *G A Y* all facing the same direction—toward me.

"It's always too many vowels or not enough," Mom said, but I couldn't see past that word to know which unfortunate configuration this was.

"At least we didn't get the dreaded *Q*," Dad said.

Dad's hand was scribbling, but mine was frozen over my paper. Mom must have noticed I was sitting there with my jaw in my lap, because she asked, "Adam? What's wrong?" And I just blurted it out like you curse when you stub your toe.

"I'm gay."

Dad stopped scribbling. For five full seconds, it was so quiet you could hear the sand falling in that egg timer.

"Does it feel scary to say that?" Mom finally asked. It was an odd thing to say, unless she was projecting?

"Does it scare you to hear it?"

She looked at my father, then back at me. "We were a little worried at first." *Wait. At first?* "Because we knew things would be harder for you."

"You knew?" I asked, because I wasn't even one hundred percent sure I knew until a few months ago.

"Not definitively," Dad said.

"We didn't want to assume," Mom added.

"We figured you'd tell us when you were ready."

I felt a little dizzy. "Since when did you know?"

Mom and Dad looked at each other again.

"When Matty started coming around," Mom said. "He's such a nice boy," she added, and I felt my face flush red hot.

"There's nothing going on there," I said. "Matty and I are friends."

Mom smiled but didn't apologize for her bananas remark. "There's no rush to figure it out."

"Adolescence is a time of discovery," Dad said, like a sex ed teacher. "Your mom had a girlfriend when I met her."

My jaw dropped from my lap to the floor.

"It was the sixties," she said with a shrug. "Also Wellesley is all girls. When in Rome . . ."

Dad chuckled like he thought smashing my world open like a piñata was hilarious.

"So . . . it wouldn't freak you out?" I asked.

"We love you no matter what," my mom said. "Gay, straight . . ." She looked at my dad like they'd rehearsed this.

"Tennis, football," he said, right on cue.

"We're sorry if we put pressure on you to be a certain way. You have every right to lead the life you want."

"You don't owe us anything, Adam," Dad said. "We feel really grateful we got to watch you grow into the amazing young man that you are."

I had an absurd thought. All this time I was worried I wasn't enough for my parents, maybe they were worried they weren't enough for me.

"I'm not looking for my birth mother because I'm disappointed in you," I said. "You're great parents. I'm not trying to replace you."

"We never thought that was the case," Mom assured me.

"We know we aren't perfect, but we hope you know we did our best," Dad added.

I wanted to say something profound about not knowing where I came from feeling like a rock in my shoe. How some days it hurt me, and some days I didn't even know it was there. But then, at exactly 8:13 p.m., the phone rang, and I felt a flicker of excitement that I was finally going to get a look at that rock.

June 8, 2001

Dear Jane,
I have not been totally forthright with you. But you probably know that by now.

I wanted to thank you for returning my letters to me. My relationship with your father was complicated. I loved him. But he was not mine to love, and I was selfish to carry on with him as long as I did.

I am not writing to offer excuses for our behavior or ask for your forgiveness. My reason for writing is to inform you that, contrary to what my letters may suggest, I did not have a child with your father. If it was the hope of finding a half-sibling that brought you to my door, you are looking for someone who doesn't exist.

I hope this brings you closure and peace going forward.
Sincerely,
Ellie McNally

CHAPTER 53
JANE

Santa Monica airport was twenty minutes away, so I got up at six a.m. I'd packed the night before. I was only planning to be in Boston for two days, but I wasn't sure what you wear to a reunion with a son born in secret, so I wanted to have choices.

I tried to be quiet so as not to wake my mom, but when I went to the kitchen to make coffee, she was already at the counter pouring me a cup.

"You didn't have to get up, Mom."

"I wanted to see you off," she said. "Big day." She poured in a dollop of cream, then handed me the cup. Six weeks ago, if someone had said I was going to move in with my mother, I would have told them they were out of their mind. I wouldn't say we'd become best friends, but I understood that she had trauma, and she had forgiven me for imposing mine on her. It wasn't perfect, but it was a start.

Greg and I had gone from talking daily to every few days to hardly at all. We hadn't made any decisions about who got what in the divorce, but our separation definitely felt permanent. During my daily walks on the beach, I often thought about how he'd warned me that looking under rocks might trigger an avalanche. Having your life blown apart is never easy, but if it was built on a foundation of lies, perhaps it's for the best.

"How are you feeling?" Mom asked as she filled her mug.

"Tired," I said, evading the real question.

"You can sleep on the plane."

We both knew that was unlikely, but I nodded and smiled just the same.

I glanced at my watch. It was almost six thirty. "I'd better go."

"Good luck," Mom said, then hugged me like she meant it.

Santa Monica airport was a small, private airfield on the border of Santa Monica and West LA. I drove myself and parked in the pay lot beside the terminal. My pilot was waiting for me at the entrance, next to a flagpole flying the American and the California-state flags.

"Morning, Jane," he said.

"Hello, Rowan."

It was Rowan's idea to fly me to Boston; I never would have asked. He'd insisted it was "the least he could do," and while I'd told him he didn't owe me anything, I accepted his kind offer.

"How was the flight from Boulder?" I asked.

"Easy breezy."

The plane was a small Learjet—bigger and more powerful than any airplane my father ever flew, but tiny compared to a commercial airline. Rowan must have gotten up in the middle of the night to be here by seven, but he looked bright eyed and ready.

I boarded the plane in the front by the cockpit. Rowan held my arm as I walked up the two-step metal staircase—more like a ladder than stairs, with chains instead of rails.

"You want to sleep or copilot?" he asked.

"Whatever's best for you," I said, not sure if I hoped he would banish me to the cabin or want me by his side.

"I'd love the company," he said, handing me a headset. Rowan and I had talked twice in the last three weeks. He'd called me right after he'd gotten my letter to offer to take me to Boston, then once more to confirm the plans. We'd kept our conversations short and transactional. Not that there wasn't a ton more to say. It remained unspoken that the boy he was taking me to meet was his son too. He didn't express interest in meeting him, and I didn't want to put him on the spot. So it just hovered there in yet another high-stakes game of "cross that bridge when we come to it."

I took a seat in the copilot's chair. I had been in the cockpit of my dad's four-seater dozens of times as a kid, and just like back then, I was mesmerized by all the knobs and buttons.

"Do you know what all these buttons do?" I asked as a wave of nostalgia washed over me. I was sure I'd asked my dad the exact same question. His wizardry in that cockpit was one of the reasons I'd worshipped him.

"I hope so," Rowan said, then smiled like he'd told that joke before.

He had me hold his clipboard while he went through his preflight checklist. When all systems were go, he turned on the red beacon light, warning anyone nearby to stand clear.

"All clear!" he said, then fired up the engines.

As we taxied across the tarmac, I reflected on how much my life had changed in the last month. I was separated from my husband and heading toward divorce. I was living at my mom's and talking to my brother almost daily—about his students, his kids' shenanigans, what was for dinner—nothing heavy, just normal sibling stuff. I was nervous about my uncertain future, but I also felt connected to my family and myself in a way that had never felt possible.

Rowan squared up on the airstrip, then hit the gas. The acceleration pinned me against my seat as we hurtled down the runway. A few seconds later, I felt the earth drop out from under us. I looked out the window to see the ground peel away. My chest got tight as I felt the weight of what I was about to do. As we ascended into the clouds, I wondered why, in four years of marriage, I'd never confided in my husband about having had a baby. Was I afraid of how I'd feel about myself if he disapproved? Or afraid of how I'd feel about him?

After we reached cruising altitude, I ventured into the cabin to have a nap. I wound up sleeping almost the whole way there. Rowan woke me right before our descent.

"You want to see your fine city?" he asked.

I got up and clipped in beside him. As the Boston skyline came into view, my heart swelled with emotion. I'd fled my hometown because of all the painful memories there—discovering I was pregnant, hiding my body for nine long months, then having my baby ripped from my arms. I'd tried to forget that horrible chapter of my life. And here I was, flying headlong back into it.

I watched Rowan's face as he worked the controls. The curve of his jaw had gotten sharper since I'd run my fingers along it all those years ago, but his skin was still shiny smooth. When Kenny told me Rowan was once in love with me, I thought he was nuts, but Samara probably would have said the same thing about me. Yes, it was puppy love, but I couldn't help but wonder what it might have grown into if we'd given it a chance.

We touched down at Hanscom Field at two thirty. Rowan hangered the plane, then we picked up our rental car at the terminal. There wasn't time to go to the hotel before my four o'clock meeting, so we drove straight to the address Adam's parents had given me. I pointed out landmarks to fill the silence—the burger joint with the best fries, the pond we used to swim in . . . anything to avoid talking about how we got here and what might happen next.

We pulled onto Adam's street. I stopped blathering as the gravity of what was about to happen descended on me like a rocket landing.

"Do you want me to come in with you?" Rowan asked as he glanced down at my fidgeting hands. I couldn't tell if he was asking because he wanted to meet Adam or because he was worried I might collapse.

"I don't know," I said, wiping my sweating palms on my thighs. Adam was expecting his birth mother, not his father. But I didn't want to shut Rowan out for a second time. "Do you want to meet him?"

"He wrote to you," he said, not answering my question.

"Because he didn't know about you." I glanced up at the street numbers—sixteen . . . eighteen . . . we were almost there.

"I'm here to support you, Jane," he said, and I was reminded that he'd brought me here as reparations to his best friend, even though his best friend had arguably betrayed him too.

"It might go badly," I warned.

"Is that your way of asking me to come in? Or not to come in?"

"I'm just thinking out loud." The house was up on the right. I pointed. "There it is, number forty-four."

Rowan pulled over and put the car in park.

"So? What are we doing?" I asked, unsure what I wanted his answer to be. Things were complicated between us. It might get uncomfortable. Hell, it was already uncomfortable.

"I feel like you should have some time alone with him," he said, and I felt a prickle of relief.

"What are you going to do?"

I must have looked worried about his safety, because he said, "This is Cambridge, not Kuwait."

"Right."

"If you decide you want to add me to the mix, I'll come back. But don't feel obligated."

"That doesn't really feel fair to you," I said, because this young man was his son as much as mine. Why did I get to decide?

"He's been part of your story for eighteen years, Jane. I didn't even know he existed until a few weeks ago. You should have some time to get to know each other without me getting in the way."

"OK," I agreed.

"Call me when you're ready to be picked up," he said, tapping the Razr phone clipped to his belt.

"OK," I said again.

"Good luck, Jane."

Without thinking, I leaned over and hugged him. Then I got out of the car to meet my son.

CHAPTER 54
ADAM

Days until training camp: 32

For some reason, when I heard my birth mother was coming, I imagined us meeting in a back alley under the cover of darkness. But that's not how it went down. In fact, it was one of the most proper occasions our home had ever seen, down to the freshly baked shortbread cookies and the cozy around the teapot.

Mom spent the whole day cleaning. I helped her by taking out the trash and sweeping the garage (yes, she made me sweep the garage, that's how worried she was about disappointing my birth mom). It was my fault. I was the one who'd suggested our family wasn't perfect by writing that letter; it was only fair that I help rectify that impression.

We decided to wait until school was out before we did the meet and greet. Mom didn't want any disruptions during my finals. My second-semester grades would be the last ones colleges would see before my applications went in, it was important they didn't suck.

I'd been working out faithfully every morning—biking or running to school, then lifting for thirty to forty-five minutes before class. Coach Fitz was right. By focusing on what my body could do, not what it looked like, the negative self-talk melted away. My muscles remembered what it felt like to be strong and were reemerging with a vengeance. My legs had morphed from sourdough rounds to braided challah. Even my abs were starting to peek through. I had eight-and-a-half more pounds to go to reach my goal. If I continued at my current pace, I would get there with a week to spare.

"I'm going for a run with Matty," I told my mom after the garage floor was dirt- and debris-free. I was still mortified that my parents had thought Matty and me were a thing, but I tried to put it out of my mind. Matty had grown into a great friend—my best friend. I still thought he was a babe, but so what? Plenty of people live with crushes they never act on.

"She's coming at four o'clock," my mom reminded me, as if I hadn't been counting the minutes. It was like Coach said: positive thinking attracts positive results. Maybe it was a coincidence that my birth mother appeared once I took control of my weight and my life, but maybe it wasn't.

Mom had warned me not to have any expectations. "Just because she's coming for a visit doesn't mean she wants to have an ongoing relationship," she said when the date was set. And I told her that I knew that, even though I had no idea what to expect or even what I wanted to happen. Was I hoping I would feel an instant connection to her? Or that I wouldn't feel any connection at all?

I slipped on my Nikes, then jogged to the park at the end of my block. Matty was already there, stretching out his legs. He was only doing cardio a couple times a week now. And drinking protein shakes before bed. He was working hard to gain the weight I was trying to lose, and I supported his goals as he supported mine.

"You ready?" he asked, as I jogged over to him.

"Let's go."

We settled into an easy pace, probably about an eight-minute mile. Summer humidity had crept in, and I was sweating within a few strides.

"So?" he said as we jogged across the park. "Today's the day."

"Yup."

"You ready?"

"I was born ready."

"Ha!"

A few months ago, I would have been nervous as hell to meet my birth mom. Not because I was ashamed of my appearance. Because I thought I needed her to turn me around. That's a lot of pressure—the opposite of "no expectations." Funny thing, once I set out to find her, it clicked that maybe I had the ability to solve my own problems all along. I'll never know if my courage to go see that lawyer was what emboldened me to talk to Coach Fitz and come out to my parents, but maybe it was intertwined.

As we ran side by side, Matty and I chatted about the end of school and our goals for senior year. Matty knew he wasn't Division 1 material, but he held out hope for D3. "You, on the other hand, could leave us all in the dust."

"I haven't even played one season at tight end," I objected.

"Yeah, but you're an athlete. A better one than I'll ever be."

His praise embarrassed me, so I just let the comment hover.

We ran in silence for the next mile, down streets lined with leafy maple trees and spring flowers in full bloom. All around us, couples held hands and walked dogs. I wondered what they thought when they saw us. Two guys out for an afternoon jog? Or something more than that? I wasn't ready to sing it from the rooftops, but I didn't feel the need to keep my gayness a secret anymore either. Just because it would never be Matty didn't mean that I would never find someone who liked me the way I liked them. And if my so-called friends couldn't handle that, well that was their problem, not mine.

We looped around Cambridge Common, then started heading back. My body felt hard and fast. I wasn't even breathing heavy. I had a long way to go to be elite again, but for the first time in over a year, it felt within reach. Dad still wanted me to go back to tennis, but he was leaving it alone, at least for now. He even apologized for being such a dick about my morning workouts. Not an admission that he was wrong, but it still felt like a win.

"I gotta cut out," I told Matty as we reached my street. "She'll be here in half an hour."

"Good luck," my best friend said.

I went full tilt for the last half mile, putting my endurance to the test. My lungs burned as I ran up my front walk, but I was grateful for the pain because it meant I was challenging myself.

"Adam! There you are!" my mom said as I walked in the front door. "You'd better go get showered. She'll be here any minute." She was wearing a dress with flowers on it, and I was touched she'd gussied up for the occasion.

I took a shower, then toweled off and pulled on a pair of chinos that I was thrilled to be able to fit in again. The doorbell rang as I was buttoning up my shirt. I looked in the mirror—really looked. Because this was the last time I would see myself in a vacuum. Did I have her eyes? Her lopsided smile? Were her arms long like mine? Would I see myself differently now that I knew where I'd come from?

I heard my mom's footsteps as she walked toward the front door to answer it. I tucked in my shirt, then headed downstairs to find out.

CHAPTER 55
ADAM

I paused on the stairway as Mom answered the door.

"Mrs. Wallis," I heard her say. "Thank you for coming."

"Please, call me Jane."

"Gloria."

"Nice to meet you, Gloria." From my perch twelve stairs up, I could hear their voices but not see their faces. I had risked my parents' wrath to get that letter to my birth mother, but now that she was here, I was paralyzed with fear. What if she didn't like me? Or I didn't like her? When she was just an idea in my head, she was perfect. But nobody's perfect.

My father emerged from his office. I saw him check his hair in the hall mirror before sidling up beside my mom.

"Hello, Jane, I'm Marvin. It was good of you to come."

"Thank you for inviting me."

"Please come in."

I saw my mother take a step back. And my other mother take a step forward. I retreated up one stair so they wouldn't see me watching.

"Shall I take my shoes off?" my birth mother said. Her voice was smooth and sweet, like maple syrup.

"Oh, it's fine."

"I'm happy to."

My birth mother bent over to untie her shoes. I could see the top of her blond head. Her hair was kind of two-tone, but not in a trashy way. It was thick like mine and grazed her shoulders as she stood back up.

"I thought we could have tea in the living room," my mother offered.

"That sounds lovely," my other mother said.

"Adam just got out of the shower. I'm sure he'll be down in a moment. Please, right this way."

I had a sudden urge to run. I thought about her letters. The ones she'd signed with an *X*. Something about not wanting to reveal herself so that I could imagine her—and myself—however I wanted. But it was too late for that now.

She turned away before I saw her face, but I could tell by the way she held herself that she was pretty. She wasn't skinny. More like slender, with proud shoulders and an athletic shape. She was taller than my adopted mom—most people were—but definitely not an Amazonian queen. Five foot five or six at the most.

Her back was to me as she followed Mom into the living room. She was dressed casually, in white pants and a fluttery top. Blush, I'd think you'd call it. Not pink but not red, something in between.

"Did you make these?" I heard her say, and I guessed she was talking about the cookies.

"Yes. Last night. I'm not much of a baker."

"Adam?"

I looked down to see my dad staring up at me.

"You OK?"

I had to join them now, he'd said my name too loud for my moms not to hear him.

"I'm coming."

He waited for me at the bottom of the stairs.

"If you don't want to do this—"

"No, it's fine. I'm fine."

He looked down at my feet, which were bare. "You want me to get you some socks?"

I didn't think my birth mom would be offended by me walking around in bare feet in my own home, so I shook my head no. "I'm good."

We stood staring at each other's feet for a beat. I felt a stab of guilt for judging him for all those qualified apologies ("I'm sorry, it's just that . . ."), because isn't to be understood what we all want?

"I'm going to go join them," he said. And then he left me there with my bare feet and wet hair like some sort of savage.

"You're a chef?" I heard my mom ask. And then my newly unearthed mom said something about using Irish butter to make the cookies more yellow, and I knew I had to go in there, because who the hell wants to eat yellow cookies?

"Hello," I said, standing in the doorway. My birth mother looked at me but didn't stand up, and I knew she was as surprised by my appearance as I was by hers.

Because we looked exactly the same.

Same widow's peak. Same pool-water blue eyes. Same dimpled chin. Same full lips. It was like looking in a gender-swapping, time-bending mirror, except she had bigger boobs and less upper-lip fuzz.

"Adam, this is Jane," Mom said to be polite, because she knew I knew her name. I'd read her letter forty times.

"I'm Adam," I said, to save Mom the trouble.

"Nice to meet you, Adam."

I nodded dumbly. I was the one who requested this meeting, but now that it was underway I was at a complete loss for words.

"Jane was just telling me about her favorite shortbread recipe," Mom said, as if they were old friends. "She's a chef!" I knew nothing about the handoff. Had they spoken to each other all those years ago? Used secret code names instead of their real ones? Blindfolds to protect their anonymity? Who interviewed whom? And which one had rank, the baby donor or the baby recipient? "She makes hers with Kerrygold butter," Mom added. "They come out golden yellow."

"But I'll take chocolate chip over shortbread all day and night," my birth mother said—*My first mother? My original mother?* I didn't know what she was to me, but I was right there with her about chocolate chip.

There was a beat of awkward silence. Mom finally stood up and said, "Your father and I are going to step out for a few minutes," then hooked her arm through Dad's and made good on her promise.

I couldn't just stand there and stare at my birth mom like she was an animal at the zoo, so I parked my butt in the chair across from her and waited for one of us to figure out what to say. My heart was beating all the way up in my ears. Her lips were pressed together like she was holding her breath, and I wondered if she was wigging out too.

"Is this weird for you?" I finally asked, because I had requested this meeting, and it was rude to just sit there.

"Super weird," she said. And then her eyes welled up. "But not in a bad way." Her voice squeaked like she was trying not to cry, which made me want to cry too.

"Could we like, walk or something?" I asked.

"Yeah, let's do that."

And now I wished I'd let my dad get me some socks.

"I'll be right back."

I bolted out of the room, nearly knocking down my parents who'd been hovering by the door like it was the first day of kindergarten and I was five.

"Are you OK?" Dad asked like he always did after I lost a match or got a bad grade. He and my mom had caught me every time I'd fallen, like parents are supposed to. And I would have said so, but Jane was waiting.

"We're going for a walk," I said. They looked worried, so I added, "Don't worry. I know where home is."

CHAPTER 56
ADAM

We walked in silence down the path. It was wide enough for both of us, but she let me go ahead. I waited for her when we reached the sidewalk, and we turned and started down it, careful not to let our shoulders touch.

"You're younger than I thought you'd be," I said, because my parents were much older, and I'd expected her to be gray haired and weathered like them.

"I had you when I was seventeen," she said. "So yeah, I was young." I didn't know where we were going. I figured we could just walk in circles until we ran out of things to say.

"How did that go over with your parents?" I asked, trying to imagine the reaction if I got a girl pregnant—probably shock, given what they knew about me.

"Not so good."

"Thank you for not terminating me," I said, imagining it was on the table.

"You're welcome," she said, confirming it.

We passed a neighbor walking his little yippie dog. I wanted to point at her and shout, "Check me out, I found my birth mom!" but I didn't, because I wasn't sure how I felt about it yet.

"Must have been a tough time," I said, hoping I sounded sympathetic. I tried to imagine juggling pregnancy, precalc, and all the other bullshit we have to deal with in high school, and my respect for her shot through the roof.

"For the record, I'm really glad I did what I did," she said.

"Yeah, me too."

She smiled. So I smiled too.

"You're handsome," she said, checking me out.

"I look like you."

"You think?"

"Are you kidding?" I couldn't believe she didn't see it. "Hold out your arms."

She did as instructed. They were average at best.

"Well?" she asked.

"I didn't get your arms. Mine are freakishly long." I held them out for her to see.

"Maybe you were a bird in a past life."

"I'm afraid of heights, so not likely." *OK not her arms, but maybe her sense of humor?*

We reached the end of my street. The park was just beyond. It was as good a place to walk in circles as any, so I led her across the street.

"So what do you want to know about me?" she asked.

When I'd set out to find her, I wanted to know everything. But now that I was standing next to her, I felt bad that I'd dragged her all the way here. My pressing questions were answered with a handshake. She was a real person. She got pregnant when she was my age. She wasn't in a position to raise a child. She did what she thought was best for me. What more did I need to know?

"Do I have, like, any siblings?" I asked, unsure what I wanted the answer to be. Because yeah, it would be cool to have a brother or sister, but also a bummer to think about how I'd missed growing up with them.

"No." She looked a little sad about that, so I changed the subject.

"Sorry if I fucked things up for you," I said, in case she wound up failing calculus.

"Actually, you kind of fixed them."

"How's that?"

"Connecting with you forced me to confront some difficult things," she said. "End one relationship that wasn't working, but heal some others."

"Maybe I'm like your guardian angel."

"Would explain the wingspan," she deadpanned. *Yup. Definitely got her sense of humor.*

"So what do you want to know about *me*?" I asked. "It's only fair." She pressed her lips together. For a second I thought she might cry, but she fought it off, thank God.

"You seem happy," she finally said.

"Is that a question?"

"I guess."

"Like I said in my letter, I have a good life."

"I didn't want to read your letter at first," she confessed. "In case . . . y'know."

"I was pissed off?"

"I know that sounds selfish."

"I was struggling a little," I confessed. I decided not to elaborate. She didn't fly all the way across the country to solve my problems. And I didn't need her to.

"You like your parents?" she asked.

"They're cool. You chose well."

"Phew," she said, mock-wiping her brow. "Only child?"

"Yup."

"That's a lot of pressure."

"Tell me about it." *Man, this woman is dialed in.* "What about you?" I asked.

"I have a brother."

"You get along?"

"Better now."

I didn't want to overstep, but since she came all this way, I had to ask . . .

"Can I ask about my dad?" I thought maybe the question was off limits, so her answer surprised me.

"You want to meet him?"

"Is that possible?"

"Yes." She extended her very average-length arm and pointed. "He's right there."

CHAPTER 57
JANE

I spotted our rental car parked in the shade of a giant oak tree as we crossed the street, so when Adam asked if he could meet his father, I seized the moment.

"C'mon," I said, beckoning him toward where Rowan was waiting. "I'll introduce you."

As he walked beside me, I took in the towering frame of the young man I had brought into this world seventeen years ago. He was tall and athletic like his father, and walked with a similar bounce in his step. The nervousness I'd felt when I rang his doorbell had melted away, making room for a surge of pride. I couldn't take credit for what he'd become—that was all Gloria and Marvin. He was of me, but not mine. Perhaps the pride I felt was meant for me, for daring to defy my parents and do what was in my heart.

I walked up to the silver Maxima and knocked on the driver's side window, which was cracked open to let in some air. Rowan bolted upright like I scared him half to death.

"Shit, sorry!" he said as he opened the door. "Did you call me? I was sleeping."

His eyes widened when he saw I was not alone.

"Sorry to startle you," I said. "But there's someone I'd like you to meet."

He got out of the car and readjusted his trousers.

"Rowan, this is Adam."

"Hello, Adam." He extended a hand, and Adam shook it.

They stood there staring at each other for a few seconds. Adam was the exact same height as his father, with the same square jaw and sweep of chestnut hair.

"Nice to meet you," Adam finally said.

"Yeah, same."

Seeing the two of them standing shoulder to shoulder was surreal. I felt every emotion all at once—sadness, gratitude, regret, awe. *If I had made different choices, would these two men be my family? How different might all our lives be if I'd had the courage to tell Rowan the truth?*

"So you guys are still together?" Adam asked. And I was too caught up in my *Sliding Doors* moment to speak.

"We . . . uh . . . ," I stammered.

"We stayed in touch," Rowan said. And Adam nodded, like he knew not to ask us to elaborate.

"You were really nice to come all this way," he said, then looked down at the ground so we wouldn't see the sheen in his eyes.

"Can I give you a hug?" I opened my arms, and he stepped into them. It was awkward. We were strangers. He felt it too. He wanted someone else in this moment . . . *his real mother.*

And with that realization, I got an unexpected gift. Because I learned—*really* learned—that giving birth can be a beautiful beginning, but it's not motherhood. Yes, I hoped to have a baby of my own. But if I couldn't, the experience I longed for was still within reach.

Adam released me from the hug and took a step back. I glanced at Rowan. He was standing soldier still, hands clasped in front of his fly. I couldn't begin to imagine what was going through his mind. Was he proud to have fathered such a brave and sensitive human? Angry I hadn't given him any say about what happened to him? Or just relieved that the meet and greet hadn't been a disaster?

"I guess I'm going to go home now," Adam said, and I understood that the visit was over.

"You know how to reach me if you need to," I offered.

"Same goes for me," Rowan said, and Adam nodded.

"Can I ask you a question?"

He was looking at me. "Of course."

"Why did you come?" And I said the first thing that popped into my mind.

"You wrote a good letter."

The corner of his mouth ticked up, like he was pleased with himself. Of course the real answer was more complicated than that. But I couldn't tell him about my father's letters. How the not knowing if I had another sibling had gnawed at me. How I understood that sometimes you need to untangle all the twisted branches of your family tree to feel rooted.

"Maybe I'll see you again someday," Adam said, then waved and walked away. Rowan and I watched in silence as our son crossed the street, then disappeared around the corner.

"You OK?" Rowan finally asked.

"I think so. Are you?"

"I think so."

"He's got a good sense of humor," I said.

"Must have gotten it from me."

"Obviously." There was so much we'd never know, but there was one thing I was curious about. "Spread your arms."

I demonstrated. He copied me. Nothing spectacular.

"Yeah, I don't know where he got those."

CHAPTER 58
JANE

We put the radio on as we drove to the hotel, both of us pretending to listen to the music so we didn't have to talk. The last twelve hours had been heartbreaking. But also wonderful. I didn't know if I should apologize for what I'd just put Rowan through or celebrate that I hadn't collapsed into a blubbering mess.

Rowan and I checked into our separate rooms with a plan to meet up for dinner in an hour. I needed a shower, but I had to make two phone calls first.

"Hey, Kenny," I said when he picked up on the first ring.

"Well?"

"He's a nice kid."

"Did you cry?"

"Only a little. He's got great parents."

"Did Ro get to meet him?"

"Briefly, yeah."

"What was that like?"

"Awkward. But OK."

"Is he doing all right?"

"Who? Rowan?" I asked, because Kenny's best friend was a former fighter pilot and had surely done much harder things.

"Don't be fooled by his tough exterior," Kenny said. "He cries at sad movies. We kind of all make fun of him for it." The image of Rowan bawling into his popcorn in front of a bunch of air force pilots made me smile.

"He seems to be fine."

"Be careful with him, Jane."

I had no idea what he meant by that, but I told him I would.

I asked about Cindy, who was in her thirty-ninth week, and he said she was tired but doing great. He promised to call me the second she went into labor, and I promised to visit as soon as they would have me. We said our goodbyes, and then I called Mom.

"Was it awful?" she asked. "I would have cried buckets!"

I assured her it was perfectly cordial, and while I was happy to meet him, there were no plans to spend Christmases together. "He's got a really nice family and a happy life," I said. "He doesn't need me."

She must have heard the catch in my voice, because she asked, "How does that make you feel?" And I took a moment to let the droplet of regret over letting him go disappear into the ocean of relief over seeing him thrive.

"Like I did the right thing."

"What's going on with you and Rowan?" she asked in a tone that made me imagine her eyebrows ticking up.

"He's been incredibly generous," I said, ignoring her suggestion that something might be "going on." Yes, we'd been thrust together under highly charged circumstances, but the only thing that was "going on" was the space we were giving each other to process what we'd just been through.

"It's so interesting how things work out," Mom said, and I thought back to the day I found those letters. My father's death had derailed my life in ways I never could have imagined. I didn't know if searching for the truth was addictive, or if pulling that first thread is what made my whole life unravel . . . just that the terrain in front of me felt wide open, and that, even though my marriage was over, I wouldn't have to navigate it alone.

"I have to get ready for dinner," I said, glancing at the clock. Rowan had flown across the country for me, I didn't want to keep him waiting.

"See you tomorrow, Jane."

I showered and changed into the dress I'd brought—a white halter-back maxi that flowed when I walked. It was too muggy for jeans or sleeves, and also, after doing something hard, I wanted to wear something more celebratory than a tank top and shorts.

We met in the lobby. Rowan had showered and changed too. His hair was wet, and his white linen button-front was tucked into slim-fitting khakis. As we walked through Harvard Square, I once again navigated the awkwardness by pointing out the sites. "That's the pit where the skaters hang out . . . that's the deli where the Kennedys ate . . ." Rowan had traveled to way more interesting places than Harvard Square but kindly pretended to be riveted.

The Border Cafe was in a brick building decorated to look like an Old West saloon. It was too loud for serious conversation—*thank God*. We'd both had enough *serious* for one day. I didn't plan to drink, but some Harvard students were celebrating their graduation and bought tequila shots for the whole restaurant, and somehow we each wound up with two.

"I guess we earned this," I said.

"To a successful trip," he said, and we clinked.

The conversation flowed a little better after those tequila shots. He told me about his deployments, and I told him about my culinary adventures in Paris and Rome. After a brief tussle over the bill, he let me pay. I followed him through the crowded restaurant toward the exit, and he opened the door for me like a gentleman would.

"That was fun," I said as he joined me on the sidewalk. I wasn't drunk, but that tequila emboldened me to stand a little closer to him. I told myself the attraction I felt was just an echo of the feelings I'd had all those years ago. We were different people now. He'd surely long since moved on.

"It's been a good day," he said.

The square was bustling with summer tourists. We walked side by side, our hands brushing up against one another's now and again. He asked about Samara, if we were still in touch. I told him she was in London for a month to show off her new baby to her in-laws. "Otherwise I would drag you to go say hello."

"I don't imagine she has a very high opinion of me," he said, and I insisted nothing could be further from the truth.

"It had a happy ending," I said, then immediately regretted suggesting this was the end. But of course it was. He was going back to the life he'd built, and I was going back to figure out mine.

"What time do you want to leave tomorrow?" I asked, as we waited to cross the street to our hotel.

"I filed a flight plan for noon," he said. "But I can move it up if you want?"

"No, noon is perfect."

The hotel had a revolving door, and he stood back so I could go first. We rode the elevator together in silence. He was on the ninth floor; I was on the tenth. When the doors opened, I thought he might hug me goodbye, but all I got was a little wave.

"Good night, Jane."

He didn't look back as he walked down the hall. As the elevator doors closed behind him, I got a panicky feeling in my chest. For the past six weeks, I'd been patting myself on the back for how honest I'd been—with Mom, Kenny, Greg, *myself*. Yet here I was, holding back with the person who deserved it most. I knew I'd hurt Rowan when I stopped writing to him—I didn't need Kenny to tell me that. And I'd been avoiding him ever since. Not because I didn't like him. Because I didn't like myself. Maybe he didn't need to hear it, but I still wanted to explain why I'd treated him so poorly. He'd been nothing but honorable. I couldn't take back the hurt I put him through, but I could apologize for it.

I stuck my hand between the elevator doors and forced them back open. Rowan had disappeared, either into a room or around a corner. I darted out into the hall and jogged to the end. I looked right and then left . . . just in time to see the door to his room closing behind him.

I paused to catch my breath. The last time we'd talked about our past, I'd collapsed into a heap of tears. It was a six-hour flight back to Santa Monica. If this conversation went badly, it would feel a lot longer than that. But my instincts were screaming for me to tell him what was in my heart while I had the courage. And if I'd learned anything in the last twenty-four hours, it was to trust my instincts.

I approached his door. My forehead and temples were damp with sweat. I blotted them with the back of my hand, then extended my arm and knocked.

A few seconds passed. I got a little nervous. Did I have the wrong room? I knocked again, harder this time. And Rowan finally opened the door.

"Hi," I said.

His eyes were red, like he'd been crying. It took him a moment to find his voice. "Hi."

"Are you OK?" I asked.

"It's just . . . been a day."

My heart was pounding. Just like the first time we met. "Can I come in?"

He opened the door wide enough for me to enter. Not an invitation, exactly, but I took it. "Thanks."

I stepped past him into his suite. The door closed with a gentle click.

"Rowan," I said, "I treated you really unfairly."

"I'm not mad at you, Jane."

"I wanted to come visit you, let you teach me how to ski, be together like we talked about." The confession tumbled out of me.

"It's OK," he started, but I cut him off.

"No. It's not OK. I just . . ." And in that moment, I understood why I'd run from him. "I didn't believe anyone would stand by me because no one ever had. That was wrong. I should have confided in you."

"Yes. You should have." It stung to hear him say that, but I was grateful for his honesty. "But I understand why you didn't."

"I'm sorry, Rowan," I said as tears rolled down my cheeks. "I don't know why I pulled away. I guess I thought I didn't deserve you."

"What about now?"

The question surprised me. "What do you mean?" I asked, because why on earth would he ask that now?

"I was hurt when you stopped writing back to me. I tried to forget." He shrugged. "But every time I see you, I'm reminded."

"Reminded of what?" I asked dumbly.

"What I felt that very first time I saw you. That never went away, Janie."

My heart stopped. I was in free fall. I flashed back to that stolen dance at Kenny's wedding, how much it hurt to be close to him again but not understanding why. My heart exploded with emotions—grief for young love lost, regret for mistakes made, but also something else . . .

"So you can understand why learning we had a son . . . ," he started, but his voice caught in his throat. "Sorry."

He turned his gaze away from me. As I took in the heartbreak behind his eyes, felt the warmth of his soul, it was so obvious I almost gasped. I was enthralled by this man the very first time we met. And still was.

I took a step toward him and did what I'd wanted to do for eighteen years.

"Please, can we both stop apologizing?" I asked. Then I turned his face toward mine and pressed my lips to his like you kiss the man you love.

June 16, 2001

Dear Ellie,
Thank you for your letter. I understand why you didn't want to tell me about your relationship with my father. If my prying into your life has opened old wounds, I apologize.

I don't blame you for my father's choices. He was a complicated man who lived life to the fullest. But you don't need me to tell you that.

I will be in the Boston area in a few weeks. I have something I would like to give you. I hope it's OK if I stop by?

I wish you every happiness. Just because we were on opposite sides of the fence doesn't mean we didn't suffer the same storm.

Kind regards,
Jane Berenson Wallis

CHAPTER 59
JANE

I don't know how long we kissed. Or if my feet stayed on the ground. Being in Rowan's arms thrilled like something new yet felt as warm and familiar as coming home.

I slid my hands up his shirt and pulled him into me. I was ready to pick up where we'd left off all those years ago, but Rowan stopped me by stepping back.

"What's wrong?" I asked. For a second I was afraid I'd misread the situation, but then he smiled, and I could breathe again.

"I'm not going to make the same mistake I made eighteen years ago," he said.

"I think things are a little different now."

"Still no harm in taking it slow."

"You think I can't handle Mach 10?" I teased.

"I'm more worried about me." He kissed my palm and pressed it to his chest. "This has been a really intense day. I don't want our feelings to get confused."

"You're kicking me out, aren't you?" I asked.

He touched my cheek with the back of his hand. "Meet for breakfast?"

"I have something I need to do in the morning." He raised a playful eyebrow. "I'll explain on the flight home." And unlike with Greg, I felt like I could tell this man everything.

We said our good nights, then I tore myself away. I knew how I felt, but I respected his insistence that we take it slow. We had a lot of feelings to sort through, and the weekend we met our son was probably not the time to do it.

As I got ready for bed, I couldn't help but chuckle when I thought back to what my mom had asked me earlier on the phone: "What's going on with you and Rowan?" Even Kenny suspected there were still feelings there. Had everyone known it but me?

It took a while, but I finally fell asleep. I woke to the sound of the phone ringing. I glanced at the clock; it was seven a.m. I groggily reached for the handset.

"Hello?"

"Hey," Rowan said. "Did I wake you?"

I smiled into my pillow. "You can wake me anytime."

We made plans to meet up in a few hours, then I got up to follow through on the promise I'd made.

Sullivan's bakery, or Sully's as the locals called it, was on the main drag in Malden. I parked in the lot, then got in line. When I got to the counter, I ordered a pumpernickel loaf and a small box of assorted pastries for the flight home—cinnamon roll, blueberry muffin, three kinds of croissants. And a cup of coffee, because it had been a long night, and decaf wouldn't cut it.

I parked outside Ellie's house but rang Marsha's doorbell first. She came to the door in leggings and a sports bra.

"Jane! How are ya?"

"Sorry to barge in on you," I said. "I brought you a pumpernickel loaf."

"Oh, bless your heart."

She opened the door, and I followed her into the kitchen.

"Sorry about my appearance," she said. "I have Pilates later."

"I don't want to keep you."

"I have a minute. Coffee?"

I held up my cup. "Already in process."

She put two slices of bread in the toaster, then asked what brought me back to the neighborhood.

"I have something for Ellie," I said. "A gift," I clarified.

The toast popped, and Marsha served it with jam and margarine, just like old times.

"I know why you came to see her," Marsha said, taking a sip of her coffee.

"She told you?"

"I figured it out. I forgot Ellie's given name was Gabrielle."

"I hope you're not offended that I didn't explain myself," I said.

"It's not my business," she assured me, then took a second to study my face. "I can't believe I didn't see it before. You look like him. Same blue eyes."

I felt a chill across my skin. "You met my father?"

"He came around a few times. At the end, mostly. I was the one who told him she was in the hospital. Y'know . . . after she lost the baby."

My breath caught in my throat as the last chapter of Ellie's sad story finally came to light.

"Anyway, he never came back after that." She shook her head. "Freakin' men." Then looked up apologetically. "No disrespect."

I wrapped my hands around my coffee cup to stop them from shaking. I knew from her second letter that there was no baby. Which left two possibilities—either she'd lied about being pregnant, or the pregnancy did not go to term.

"She always said it was God's will," Marsha said. "He giveth, He taketh away."

I nodded to let the lump in my throat subside. She lost her baby, then her only sister. My heart flooded with compassion. Yes, she'd indulged a relationship she knew was wrong. But it was impossible to resent her for it after learning how much she'd suffered.

"I gotta get gettin' to my class," Marsha said, standing up. I picked up my plate and dropped it into the sink. We walked out together, then hugged goodbye on the porch. "Good luck to you, Jane."

I watched her walk down the path, then made my way toward Ellie's front door.

"Hello, old friend," I said to the pink flamingo as I rang the bell. A gentle breeze tickled the back of my neck, and I was struck by the peculiar way I'd followed in my father's footsteps. I didn't know if there was such a thing as "one true love," but if there was, neither of us got it right, at least as far as our marriages were concerned. Did my dad, like me, not fully trust his heart? Or were we both afraid to turn ourselves over to the great big love we told ourselves we didn't deserve?

I was about to ring the bell again when I heard movement on the other side of the door. A moment later, I was looking into the cornflower blue eyes of the woman who very well may have been the love of my father's life.

"Hello, Jane."

She didn't invite me in, and I didn't ask.

"Hi, Ellie. Thank you for your letter. It was kind of you to give me closure." I knew now why she hadn't been more specific, but I decided not to say so. "I'm sorry to show up uninvited . . . again," I continued, "but I found something I thought you might like to have."

I dipped into my shoulder bag and pulled out a leatherbound book.

"What's this?" she asked, taking it from my outstretched hand.

"The story of two people who tried to be together."

I watched her face as she flipped through the pages of my father's pilot's log. Every trip they'd taken together was in there, with detailed notes about their arrival times, weather conditions, who the copilot was. Yes, he put her name in there—GM, like in the letters. I liked to think there were some good memories there, and that she might like to have it. At the very least, I hoped she'd regard it as a peace offering and would someday forgive me for barging into her life.

She closed the book, then smiled up at me. "I have something for you too. Can you wait here a second?"

I nodded. She disappeared up the stairs, then returned a minute later clutching an envelope.

"He wrote it to me, but I think it was meant for you."

I looked down at the letter. Her address was written in handwriting I recognized.

"He loved me," she said, without a hint of apology. "But in the end, he loved you more."

December 15, 1983

Dear Gabrielle,
I've been trying to find the courage to write to you since
your neighbor told me about the miscarriage. Obviously
neither of us wanted it to end this way. But here we are.

I hope you know my rejection of this baby was not a
rejection of you. I am not a very good father to the kids I
already have. My son went to military school to get away
from me, and my daughter nearly starved herself to death
because of how I made her feel. And you know what a
shit husband I am.

I care about you deeply. I was the best version of
myself with you. You let me be the person I want to be
and do the things I love. And I guess escape my failures
as a parent.

I lied to you, but I didn't mean to. When I said I
was going to leave my wife I thought I meant it. I had
a vision of our carefree life together, you and me against
the world, just like it always was. When you asked me to
be something more, I got scared. I'd already screwed up
two children, I didn't want to do it again. My son and

daughter grew into principled, upstanding people in spite of, not because of me. My daughter's bravery puts me to shame. I don't know if my piss-poor parenting made her stronger . . . more likely I just got lucky. In any case, I'm not so foolish to want to try my luck again.

Thank you for being a big, important part of my life for so long. I wish you every happiness now and always. You'll always be my first love. On some level I always knew I didn't deserve you.

Love,

Richie

CHAPTER 60
ADAM

Days until training camp: 0

I killed my tryout. Caught thirteen out of fourteen during eleven-on-elevens, and that one miss wasn't my fault—Matty underthrew it. (He apologized.) Coach wouldn't officially announce the lineup until the end of camp, but he gave me a secret thumbs-up when no one was looking. I was strong, I was fast, and I was going to make the team.

Nothing really changed after I met my birth mom. I was proud that I'd mustered the courage to write to her, but she didn't tell me anything that I didn't already know. I was an accident. She was ill-equipped to raise a child. She gave me away so I'd have a better life. Now that I'd met her, I couldn't remember why I'd thought I needed to. Did I want a backup mom in case my real mom couldn't handle my gayness? Was I mad at my dad for trying to force me to play tennis? Or was I just a stubborn kid who decided to do something and wouldn't quit until it was done?

To my surprise, nothing really changed after I told my parents I was gay either. Mom still nagged me to clean my room, and Dad still tried to get me back out on the tennis court. There was no crying, no parade, no holding hands singing "Kumbaya." If they'd known all along, they weren't the only ones.

"You should go say hello," Matty said when he caught me checking out the hot male cheerleader leading warm-ups across the way. We had to share the field with all the other sports teams. We got it first, of course, because football rules. But outdoor practice ended at two (weight room next), and other sports teams rotated in after us.

"Don't make me punch you in the face," I said. Just because I came out to my parents didn't mean I would get T-shirts made, but I was starting to flirt with the idea of being who I was with a trusted few.

"I heard he was a gymnast," Matty said, because he'd figured it out all on his own—well, maybe with a little help from Pam Anderson.

"And?"

"Maybe he'll flip head over heels for you," he joked, and I did punch him, but in the arm, not the face. I still adored Matty, but my obsession with him had dulled. Not because he wasn't a great guy. But I was ready to save my attention for someone who could appreciate my special brand of hotness.

Coach Fitz had convinced me to be a multisport athlete and go out for track in the spring. It would be too late for college recruiters—I only had this season to get noticed—but it would keep me in shape for whatever came next. My weight was still dropping, even though I was eating whatever I wanted. And yes, that included cheeseburgers. I knew when to stop; that wasn't a problem anymore. But I still had monthly visits with Sandy to make sure destructive thoughts didn't creep back in.

I'll never understand why I picked a fight with food. Some say there's a genetic component. Maybe someday I'll ask Jane if she or my dad ever struggled with their weight. Can you inherit self-sabotage by Twinkies like you can inherit blue eyes or a bad hip? Or is abusing food a societal invention, like the aqueduct and Costco?

I'll never know the answers to those questions. The best I can do is know me. And man, had I learned a lot about me. As I walked off the field with my helmet in my hand, I felt a rush of gratitude for all my teachers. Not just the people—Coach Fitz, Sandy, Matty, my mom and dad, Jane—but also the pain. Because that's what started it all. And if it came back around, I knew I could turn to the best parents in the world to help me through.

CHAPTER 61
JANE

Rowan's six-passenger Learjet touched down on the runway at Deer Valley Airport in Phoenix just as the sun was dipping behind the mountains.

"Nice landing, Captain," I said through the headset.

"I do my best," Rowan replied with a smile.

We taxied to our parking spot, then all filed out onto the tarmac—Rowan, me, my mother, and Tarzan the dog, who'd spent the short flight from Santa Monica curled up in Mom's lap.

"You OK, Mom?" I asked as Rowan helped her down the steps.

"I could get used to this," she said, and I blushed a little, because things were going well between Rowan and me, but it was still early days.

Rowan raised the staircase; then I helped him tie down the plane, feeding the rope through the tie-down ring, then securing it with a locking hitch like I'd done for my father as a kid.

Rowan peered over my shoulder, then tugged on the rope. "Nice knot."

He reached for my hand and held it all the way to the terminal. Mom pretended not to notice, but I could see the smile leaking out from behind her eyes.

"After you, ladies," Rowan said as he opened the swinging glass door. Mom and Tarzan went first, then me. I waited for Rowan just inside, then slipped under his arm as we crossed through the airy waiting area, letting my thumb hook through his belt loop. Yes, we were taking it slow, but not *that* slow.

"There you are!" Kenny said, standing up to greet us. He was all smiles as he hugged us, holding on to Mom extra long. It occurred to me that it had been a long time since our mother had been in a small plane, and the memories associated with it might not all be so pleasant.

We piled into Kenny's Suburban—Mom in front, and Rowan and me in the back. As I felt the supercharged air between us, I thought back to that very first car ride in Kenny's Bronco, when I gripped my toes in my shoes to keep from sliding into him. It seemed crazy that I still felt nervous-excited when I was near him, and I couldn't help but wonder if it could be like this forever.

Over the past three months, Rowan and I had talked every day. This was our first trip together since Boston, but he'd visited me at my mother's for walks on the beach and home-cooked dinners, and I'd spent a week with him at his Colorado A-frame. We were enjoying insane chemistry, but we were also working to ground our feelings by sharing intimate parts of ourselves. I told him about my struggles with food, my father's betrayal, how Greg and I had drifted apart, how Kenny and I had come back together. He shared his complicated feelings about retiring from military life, his battles with loneliness, his traumatic memories of war, how he used flying as an escape. And every once in a while, we dared to share our dreams for the future, and how we both couldn't imagine it without the other.

Kenny's house was just off the base, in a gated community for officers and their families. As we pulled into the driveway, I couldn't help but notice the perfectly symmetrical arrangement of rocks and flowering cacti that made up his front yard.

"Your yard is very . . . ," I started, but it was Rowan who finished my sentence.

"You."

And we all laughed.

Kenny opened the car door for me, and I followed him up the walk as Rowan collected our bags. The front door was unlocked, and my brother opened it to reveal a foyer piled high with shoes, sports equipment, baby gear, and backpacks.

"Are you sure we're in the right house?" I asked.

"I'm learning to lean into the chaos."

As I peered out the glass doors into the backyard, I spotted Cindy in a glider, holding their three-month-old son. She looked up and waved me outside.

"This is Jasper," she said as I joined her on the patio. She tilted his face toward me, and my heart melted into a puddle.

"Oh, Cindy. He's absolutely gorgeous."

"You want to hold him?"

"Um, yes, please."

I reached down and took my nephew from her outstretched arms. As I breathed in his marshmallow sweetness, a stunning sense of peace passed over me. For the first time in two years, I stopped wondering if I would have a family, because I'd realized I already had an amazing one.

"When's dinner, Mom?" Cindy's son Nigel said as he bounded around the corner. His little brother Harry appeared a second later.

"I got burgers for the grill," Kenny said. "Mom, you want to help me make them?"

As the boys ran off and Kenny and our mom disappeared into the house, Cindy stood. "If you've got Jasper, I'm going to go take a little rest."

"Of course."

"Hi, Rowan," Cindy said, greeting him with a hug as he stepped onto the patio. And then she was gone. And it was just Rowan, me, and baby Jasper.

I lowered myself onto the chaise and patted the seat next to me to will Rowan to join me. He put an arm around my back, and we sat together in silence, our hips touching as the setting sun warmed our skin.

"He looks like Kenny," I said, taking in Jasper's symmetrical face and full lips.

"I take it you mean perfect in every way."

"Like father like son."

Rowan leaned into me and put his nose to my ear. "We shouldn't wait too long," he whispered, and my heart grew even fuller. Yes, we had only been together for a few months, but I'd loved him for nearly two decades.

"I'm ready."

I pressed my face into his neck. I wasn't sure if I believed in "meant to be," but I did know, as far as my future was concerned, the sky was the limit.

Author's Note

Like many teen girls growing up in the 1980s and '90s, I bought into the absurd notion that being skinny was some sort of virtue. This fallacy was corroborated by TV commercials, magazine covers, food packaging that bragged about being "fat free!" No one talked about how people of all shapes and sizes are beautiful, and I was too impressionable to trust my own eyes. So, a few weeks after my fourteenth birthday, as puberty was padding my belly and hips, terrified of becoming something my father couldn't love, I stopped eating.

I don't know the statistics about Gen X women with eating disorders, only that more than half of my female friends had one. The binging and purging and starving ourselves was often accompanied by a perplexing phenomenon called "body dysmorphia." It didn't matter how much I weighed, the person in the mirror staring back at me always looked "fat." At eighty-eight pounds, I wasn't overweight, so was "fat" a surrogate for "unlovable"? And how had the two become intertwined?

I don't know the answers to these questions, only that pressure to conform can be intense, especially in teenagers, and extends to attributes beyond one's physical appearance. Like Janie, the teen girl who agonizes about not being skinny enough, Adam, the teen boy in this novel, frets that the people he loves will be disappointed to find out he is gay. While the fear is real, the notion that there is anything undesirable about not conforming to an imagined ideal is rubbish.

Telling someone's story means re-creating their inner life in all its misconceptions, as well as being honest about the prevailing attitudes of the time, whether or not we agree with them. Voices encouraging us to be who we are were not amplified in the '80s and early 2000s (the time periods in which this novel is set), so I chose not to inject whispers of body positivity or unconditional self-love into my characters' journeys. This should not be seen as a rejection of enlightened ideals, but rather one author's attempt to be historically accurate about the climate of the times, a climate that shaped how a large number of Gen X and millennial teens felt about their bodies and themselves.

Having an eating disorder can be painful and potentially life threatening. If you are seeking help for yourself or a loved one, NEDA, the National Eating Disorders Association (www.nationaleatingdisorders.org), is a good place to start. I encourage anyone who is suffering from issues stemming from a negative self-image to take advantage of the mental health support systems available online or in your community. And please know you are not alone.

ACKNOWLEDGMENTS

Writing is a bit of a paradox. We tell our stories to start a conversation about things we think are meaningful. But in order to write, we have to shut out the world, because we can't explore our intimate thoughts with other people buzzing around. And then there's the perplexing sensation of feeling the most connected to everyone and everything when we're alone at the keyboard, wrestling those thoughts and images into words, not thinking about if anyone will ever read them, because getting them out is what makes us feel alive.

For most authors, writing is a solitary process, but bringing a book to market takes a village. I have so many people to thank for helping me get to the finish line. For this book, it started with the gentle urging of my super-agent Laura Dail, who had a vision for what this book could be long before I did. To Laura and her top-notch team at LDLA, thank you for helping me wrestle my unruly ideas into stories worth sharing.

After writing comes rewriting. I'm beyond grateful to my outlandishly gifted developmental editor, Tiffany Yates Martin, for her impeccable insights, and the divine Melissa Valentine for making this perfect match. I had so much support from Lake Union for this book from visionary editorial director Danielle Marshall, editors Carissa Bluestone and Chantelle Aimée Osman, production manager Jen Bentham, copyeditor Tristen B., and eagle-eyed proofreaders Rachel M. and Angela V. Thank you, Darci and my amazing marketing team, spearheaded by the incredible energy and vision of Tandem Literary's Gretchen Koss.

Books would not exist without readers. First come the beta readers, who I rely on to tell me if the story deserves to be a novel. Thank you, Debra Lewin, who is always so generous with her time and brain, and Miranda Parker Lewin, Avital Ornovitz, Irene Ornovitz, and Tyler Weltman. My author-readers are also my mentors, cheerleaders, confidants, and friends. So grateful for the counsel and support of Alethea Black, Gary Goldstein, Ken Pisani, W. Bruce Cameron, Cathryn Michon, Wendy Walker, Lucinda Berry, and all the amazingly talented authors of Blue Sky Book Chat: Thelma Adams, Barbara Davis, Joy Jordan-Lake, Paulette Kennedy, Christine Nolfi, Marilyn Simon Rothstein, Kerry Schafer, and Patricia Sands.

I would not get to explore my inner life without the loving support of my family. To Uri, Sophie, and Taya, thank you for allowing me to disappear into my imagination, and figuring out dinner when I stay there too long. My brother, Dr. David Walter, has been my rock for my whole life. I would not be able to write about complicated things without his help finding both the courage and the words.

Finally, to everyone who has read through to this final page, thank you for your love of reading and willingness to go on this journey with me. I know you have a gazillion books to choose from, thank you for choosing mine.

DISCUSSION QUESTIONS

(CAUTION: SPOILERS BELOW)

1. In the story, Jane finds evidence that her father may have had a child with a woman who isn't her mother. Did you or anybody you know learn of the existence of additional blood relatives, and how did that make you/them feel?

2. Jane surprises Ellie by showing her the love letters her father kept until the day he died. Do you have any love letters from an old flame? And would you dare reread them now?

3. Jane sees her mother in a new light after she learns what she endured to keep the family together. Have you ever had a revelation about someone close to you that changed the way you felt about them?

4. Jane keeps her pregnancy a secret from Rowan because she doesn't want to burden him. Similarly, Kenny never tells Jane about their father's affair because he knows it would upset her. Have you ever withheld the truth from a loved one to protect their feelings?

5. Both Jane and Adam struggle with emotional eating. Have you or anyone you know struggled to maintain a healthy relationship with food, and if so, what got you/them through?

6. Confiding in his football coach was a pivotal moment for Adam in his quest to take control of his life. Talk about a pivotal moment in your life and who or what helped you turn things around.

7. Adam is afraid to come out as gay because he fears disappointing his parents and friends. Have you ever hidden something about yourself because you were afraid of how people would react?

8. Adam wants to play football, but his parents are pressuring him to play tennis. What did you want to play/do/be when you were young? And did you have support for that dream?

9. Adam and Janie both have friends who help them when they are facing difficult things. Talk about a time when you needed a friend, or helped a friend in need, and how that friendship evolved or changed after that.

10. Both Adam's coach and his therapist encourage him to pursue small, makeable goals. What are your small, makeable goals, and how has sticking to them transformed your life?

About the Author

Photo © 2020 Maria Berelc

Susan Walter is the author of four novels of suspense: *Lie by the Pool, Good as Dead, Over Her Dead Body,* and *Running Cold.* She was born in Cambridge, Massachusetts. After being given every opportunity—and failing—to become a concert violinist, Walter attended Harvard University. She had hoped to be a newscaster, but the local TV station hired her to write and produce promos instead. Seeking sunshine and a change of scenery, she moved to Los Angeles to work in film and television production. Upon realizing writers were having all the fun, Walter transitioned to screenwriting, then directing. She wrote and made her directorial debut with the 2017 film *All I Wish,* starring Sharon Stone.

For more information about the author, visit www.susanwalter-writer.com.